With ... to Carlo.
May the Light gui de you on your way.
J. H. Tepley

THIS BOOK IS FOR YOU IF...

You instinctively know that there is more to this reality than you were told, and you're looking for answers.

You feel that you're different from the rest, and your biggest dream is to create a difference in the world.

You're tired of standing alone.

WHAT PEOPLE ARE SAYING

"From the outset, this book had me hooked, I felt an instant rapport with the characters. The story is breathtaking; picture a thriller, sci-fi, romance, comedy, and a spiritual masterpiece all rolled into one. I was so engrossed that once finished, I was left so frustrated I actually re-read the book to get back to that world."

- J.J. A reader from the UK

"This book captivates your imagination and you develop an almost instant personal relationship with the main characters. The story does not leave you, and you catch yourself thinking about it throughout your day, longing for time alone so you can read on..!"

- J.T. A reader from the USA

"You need to read this book. It uses an adventure story to break down the nature of reality so you can understand it. The teachings can drastically transform your life – they did mine!"

- M.O. A reader from the UK

"Since finishing the book, I re-read it a few times and every time I found new gems that stroke a chord deep within. My favourite quote is, "Find something worth dying for - and spend your life living for it". As in, "Find what you stand for and be willing to sacrifice everything for what you believe in." This book is for everyone on their path to becoming a warrior and finding their inner peace."

- N.B. A reader from Bulgaria

"I recommend this book to anyone that still has the fire within, and the will to get up in the morning and fight! Whatever it is you're fighting for, whatever the cause, this book will encourage you to go further, dig deeper, and feel stronger about it!"

- H.P. A reader from the USA

"This book is designed to rewire your mind. It will do it gently and subtly, and only if you let it. But once you do, you won't look at the world the same way again. This is not an ordinary novel. If you let it, it will show you a different way of looking at the world. It doesn't describe or focus on what most novels do. The best analogy is The Matrix: if you were to describe it to someone living within it, you wouldn't focus on that which it shows you, instead you'd direct your reader to the underlying code. Lightwatch is a book about the code that has always been there, at the edge of your perception."

- I.B. A reader from the UK

"The Lightwatch Chronicles book is reminiscent of The Alchemist by Paulo Coelho, in its linking fantasy and ethereal mystery with the human psyche, finding our path, and our constant struggle to grasp and understand our own emotions... but with its own unique flair. I loved every bit of it."

- V.A. A reader from the USA

"This book will be deeply appreciated by those who are striving for personal excellence. I know very few works of literature that convey so much practical wisdom and do so through such fantastic means of expression, in every sense of the word. Literally every chapter contains some very profound insight that made me think, "Holy ... how cool is that?!""

- I.P. A reader from Russia

"I remember diving into the first chapter of the Lightwatch Chronicles and getting goosebumps everywhere. I just paused for having an ice-cream, started again and bamm – goosebumps. I couldn't help it. And the story only went better and better. Crazy interesting!"

- B.K. A reader from Germany

"It's hard to describe this book because there aren't any mainstream references that do it justice. It's like a piece from another world where the characters take you on an unforgettable journey into the mind. I was captivated by the plot, and it also felt like the book was communicating with me trying to teach me more about myself. A thoroughly enjoyable and enlightening experience I can recommend to everybody."

- J.B. A reader from Denmark

"This book will take you on an incredible journey and if you read between the lines, you'll never look at the World you think you know in the same way ever again. Jane H Tepley, also known as The Ancient One, takes you on a fascinating journey which you will relate to in some shape or form. Storytelling mastery at its finest."

- H.B. A reader from the UK

"I can't stop thinking about this book! It's filled with life-hack gems and you can't help but ask yourself "what do I stand for?" From the beginning to the end you're hooked. I recommend this book to anyone longing for meaning and purpose, this book has many answers, just read between the lines."

- V.T. A reader from the UK

"To create great things and to have a life full of joy and health it's necessary to believe in the unexpewcted power that we have within ourselves the Lightwatch Chronicles will introduce you to a wonderful world where you will remember that you can accomplish anything as long as you believe that. An amazing story of self-mastery endurance, inspiration and wonderful treasures are waiting for you."

- C.C.R. A reader from Mexico

"Awesome story full of thought, wit and the characters you will grow close to. I love how it stimulates the imagination and at the same time makes you look deeper into yourself."

- B.B.H. A reader from the USA

"Congratulations on picking up a copy of the Lightwatch Chronicles. But before you begin I would like to offer the following words of advice. Forget everything that you think you know. If you're feeling lost in this world, this is a story for you, if you long for a deeper meaning, pick up this book. It will become your best companion!"

- C.A. A reader from the USA

"The Lightwatch Chronicles is a thrilling tale that transports you to multiple worlds that literally spring to life off the page. It may be fiction but it contains great wisdom woven into the story that can be applied to real-world situations. Whilst following the main characters on their quest, you will feel like you are learning their lessons with them and will often find yourself looking deep into your own mind and questioning your inner self. I would highly recommend this book to anyone who wants to improve their mind whilst being entertained at the same times. This book would make a great film too!"

- J.T.W A reader from the UK

"Do you like medieval fantasy or sci-fi type adventures? Here you have both mixed up wonderfully in a story based on mythologies very few people know about. I got trapped in the book by the story and the hidden message, and the more I was reading the more I wanted to read. Hopefully the part two will be available soon! I am waiting with all the patience I have to continue on the journey of the Lightwatch."

- J.O. A reader from Québec, Canada

ABOUT THE AUTHOR

J.H. Tepley is a teacher, writer, speaker, and the founder of ARIYA — a self-mastery movement for the warriors in spirit. She trains her students in the path of warriorhood, teaching how to understand yourself on a deeper level and use the power of your mind to influence reality. To see through the smoke and mirrors, so you can find and follow your true Path. To help you unlock your power to serve the world greatly. You can't stand strong if you don't know who you are, and what you stand for. Jay gives you tools and skills that you will need on your quest.

Jay currently lives in London. She holds a master degree in Linguistics and is fluent in four languages, including Japanese. She is an author of mind mastery books, The Master of the Elements and The Mindgates Blueprint, as well as a number of other books on Western Meditation that will be published later this year.

Her journey spans over many years and many countries. Often referred to by her students as 'a teacher or teachers', from a young age, she chose to dedicate her life to her mission, striving to be the Light that helps others see. For over 19 years, Jay has been travelling the world training and researching mind-empowering techniques of the East and the West. Her work led to the creation of the Ariya Training – a unique system for awakening the power within, consisting of meditation, extended perception and awareness exercises, mindfulness, calisthenics, and breathing techniques. Her mind training will lead you to reawakening your true essence, through own mental and spiritual understanding.

By transforming yourself, you're changing the world.

You are more than you think you are.

Join us. Because time is changing.

Website: www.ariyamindtraining.com
Facebook: www.facebook.com/ARIYAcreed
Twitter: www.twitter.com/ARIYAcreed
Instagram: www.instagram.com/ARIYAcreed
www.instagram.com/jhtepley
www.instagram.com/lightwatch.chronicles
Youtube: www.youtube.com/c/ARIYAMindTraining

Books by J. H. Tepley

The Master of the Elements
The Mindgates Blueprint

The Lightwatch Chronicles
Book I: *The Guardians*
[upcoming]
Book II: *The Journey*
Book III: *The Awakening*

THE LIGHTWATCH CHRONICLES

BOOK I

THE GUARDIANS

J. H. TEPLEY

London, 2018

Published by

Filament Publishing Ltd
16 Croydon Road, Beddington, Croydon,
Surrey, CR0 4PA, United Kingdom.
www. filamentpublishing.com Telephone: +44(0)208 688 2598

The Lightwatch Chronicles by Jane H. Tepley
ISBN 978-1-912256-56-3
© 2018 Jane H. Tepley

Photography by Magna Stills
Cover art by Ommega
Art direction J.H. Tepley

Printed in the UK by IngramSpark

THIS BOOK IS DEDICATED TO
ALL WARRIORS IN SPIRIT.

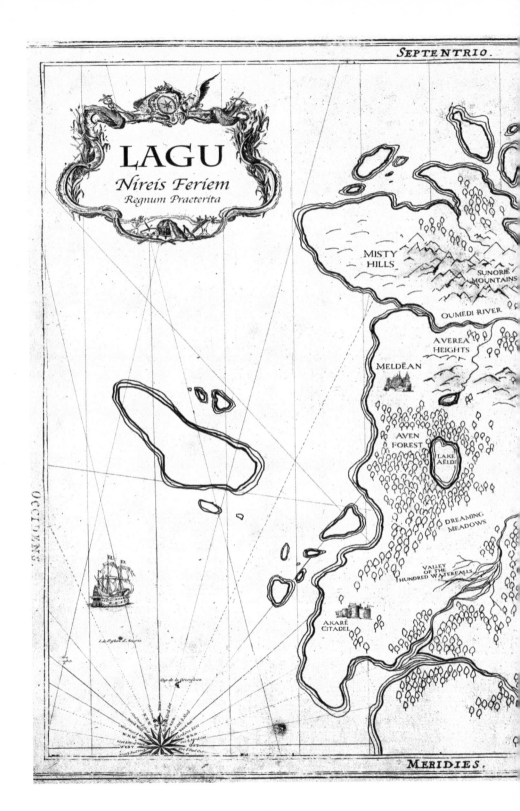

LAGU

Nireis Feriem
Regnum Praeterita

MISTY HILLS

SUNORIE MOUNTAINS

OUMEDI RIVER

AVEREA HEIGHTS

MELDĒAN

AVEN FOREST

LAKE AELDI

DREAMING MEADOWS

VALLEY OF THE HUNDRED WATERFALLS

AKARE CITADEL

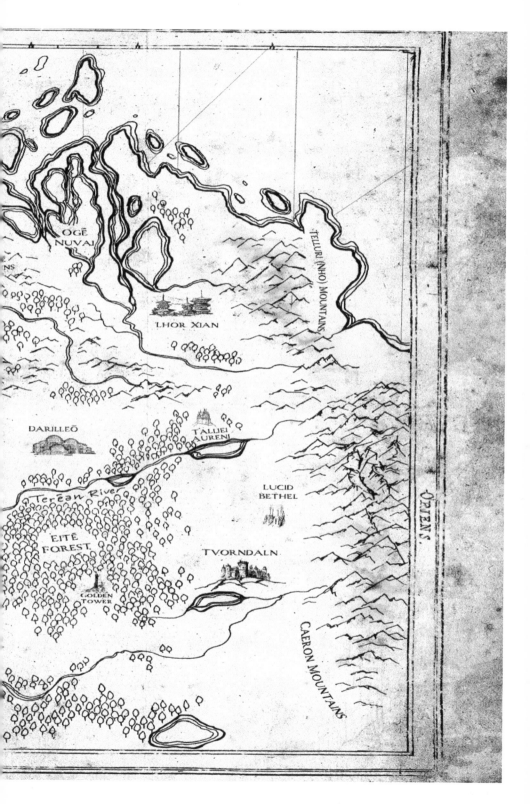

OGĒ NUVAI

TELLURI (NHO) MOUNTAINS

LHOR XIAN

DARILLEŌ

TALLIEI AURENI

LUCID BETHEL

Terēan River

EITĒ FOREST

TVORNDALN

GOLDEN TOWER

OPIENS.

CAERON MOUNTAINS

CONTENTS

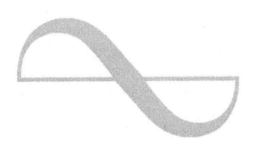

FROM THE AUTHOR

"A time will come when people will forget. Many will lose the memory of all that made them strong, their Light within, integrity, loyalty, and honour. Many will stray from their path, tortured by their own fear and blinded by the Shadow. But we will return, remember this, we will return again to show the way, and to awaken the Sleeping Stars, and once more will the world herald the Tale of the Guardians."

This is not an ordinary book. For almost as long as I can remember, I lived with it, by it, and through it – since this story appeared one day, forcefully demanding to write it down, it has become intertwined with my life in more ways than I can think of.

The book you're holding in your hands is a rebel that stood up against all rules of novel writing. It didn't let me follow the traditional path of gathering ideas and coming up with the story. The legend was already there, whole and complete, and I could do nothing but to write it down just as it was.

I often felt like a detective looking for the clues and connecting the facts. Hours on Google Maps and further hours spent studying the map of Lagu, learning the meaning of ancient words, solving mysteries and discovering new details was at times so fascinating that going to sleep seemed like an absurd chore. This story is a glimmer of a legend that counts thousands of years; so old that it had been all but forgotten. It was first spoken over the sun-scorched sand of faraway lands, amongst the worshippers of fire. Now it has chosen to return in a new form, holding the answers you might have been blindly seeking, perhaps all your life. It calls to those who are ready to hear the message. And if you're ready, after having read this book you'll never be the same.

This story can teach you how to use the power that you have always felt within. It is for you who have dedicated your life to bettering yourself, fighting against all odds. For you, who believe in miracles even though the whole world tells you otherwise. For you, who strives to be the Light that helps others see. Throughout this story are scattered the secret keys. I dare you to find them in the real world.

This book is a gateway. Step into the legend. The adventure awaits and the time has come.

PROLOGUE

"And as their courage began to fade, they grew more and more fearful of the Shadow...for they believed that nothing could stop it spreading and that their world was doomed to succumb to it, just as their faint hearts already did.

But there were Stars amongst them who knew the truth and whose spirit was free from fear. The Ariya warriors kept their watch, unseen and unknown, and even a handful of them were enough to hold the Shadow at bay. They faced it all — the dark poison of doubt, the cold of loneliness, and the pain of loss. Many had fallen in that battle; but those who remained, mournful of their comrades kept fighting even harder for they knew that the time was changing and a new dawn should be upon them before long."

All comes from One that is Light, and unto One it shall return. Only the sleeping consciousness knows nothing of its nature, and its true power. Those who have awakened the Light within are Stars – the silent warriors who turn their mind into their weapon against the Shadow. They take the hardest Path, so others can know peace.

While roving through the labyrinth of lives and rebirths, it happens that some lose the memory of their Higher calling; yet even the Sleeping Stars never stop searching for it. Still, there are those who keep the inner flame alive and choose to dedicate their lives to following their mission – they are known as Ariyas, the noble spirits bound by the inner Code of integrity and truth. The greatest amongst them are the Guardians – the legendary seven Great Stars who protect the Gates of Time and Space, their quest as old as the existence itself.

Many songs and myths were coined about the Guardians throughout the millennia, not all of them remembered. Our world has all but lost its own, but the changing time shall reawaken the faded memories, and bring the flame back from the ashes.

This story is about four young Ariyas, a warrior team of Minor Stars, bound together by the power of the Crystal. The complex energy structure was created during their training on Siltarion by the High Adepts, with all the knowledge and magic they had. Many years took a special series of mental drills, which gradually changed the Stars energetically and mentally until one day it became part of their essence. The arcane masterwork looked like a lozenge-shaped gemstone when called upon, so they nicknamed it 'Crystal'. The name stuck.

A while ago, the Quarta saw their homeland destroyed in a war with the Shadow. After that, all they had known were the feverish dreams, the pain of loss, and the coldness of foreign lands.

After the Fall, it was the Crystal that had saved their lives. It helped the Stars breathe the air of different worlds, and heal their wounds. Most importantly, it allowed them to travel, if only they kept all four splinters together. And travel they did – when the enemies are on one's trail, staying in one place for too long would be a mistake that could too easily prove lethal.

Were they lucky to survive? They could not tell. Life was tough, but it went on, and they tried to make the most of it. They were too young, and too well trained, to give up. All in all, "adventures are good", as Tei often said.

The Quarta wasn't short of them since the Fall. For that, they partly had themselves to blame. Not all their decisions were well thought through. Oftentimes, the Quarta were too brassy and too adventurous for their own good. A strange uncanny luck seemed to have followed the Stars, though, as welcome as it was undeserved. It offered the only sound reason why the four were still alive, through all the fights, the dangers, and the youthful nonsense.

But it all changed a few months ago.

The Ariya Code

- Live in accordance with your Highest Purpose

- Follow the Path of the right thoughts, the right speech, and the right actions

- Cultivate mindfulness and compassion in everything you do

- Make every day your training ground

- Stay silent about your mission; let the results of your work speak for themselves

- Perceive what cannot be seen by the eye

- Treat your comrades as family

- Use your power to the benefit of others

Chapter I

Tseri-Mai Verai
The Trapped Stars

It had been raining since the very morning. Rain trickled down the window, splashed on the road and danced on the umbrellas of the passersby. Heavy clouds, ruffled and rushed by the cold wind, sealed the horizon.

"They have rotten springs here," stated Nesteri who stood by the window, giving the soaking city down below an absent stare. His ashen hair appeared even more greyish now.

The dwelling in Meguro was exhilaratingly close to the sky. When looking outside, Nesteri felt like a bird might feel, spreading its wings and gliding through the wind, high and higher, the city sparkling beneath. It made him think of Dragh – his pet raven and a true friend, the faithful companion of his younger years. Nesteri missed him.

Hagal nodded silently, without taking his eyes off a book, his slender fingers fiddling with a bookmark. The immaculate white shirt peeking from underneath his emerald dressing gown made him look typically aristocratic. Even in these unfamiliar clothes.

The main room of their rented flat was bright and simple – and almost tidy – if not for the desk in the corner, buried under the superfluity of scattered papers.

"Yeah," answered Tei, the only one with short dark hair, his deep blue eyes harbouring a faint glow of disquiet. His shirt was red, and half unbuttoned, with messily rolled up sleeves. The Star was pensively strumming a guitar. "Worry not, soon there will be more fun for you out there."

"Fun, you say?" Nesteri scowled and turned away from the window. His style was ink and watercolours, a sleek black top with metal buckles paired

25

with distressed charcoal jeans. "I hate parties. You know that. I really wish there was a better way for us to find him."

"So do I," Tei shrugged. "And if you have any bright ideas, genius, do share." He returned to strumming.

Nesteri didn't answer. There were no better ways of finding Farien that he could think of.

There wasn't much of that fight they could remember. The attack was sudden and as fierce and ruthless as the Shadow would have it; the Quarta had escaped death by a hair's breadth. That wasn't new, but the explosion that followed had torn the team apart, scattering them into space. When their consciousness returned, they were only three. Farien was nowhere to be seen.

They knew he must be still alive, and nothing else. "You could communicate through the Crystal," their old teacher once said in passing. Now, more than ever, the Quarta wished they had had a chance to learn how.

Tei would moan occasionally about wishing to be one of Great Stars, so he could travel at will just like them. The winged Guardians of Light, Great Stars were ancient and mighty, and wielded formidable power if the legends could be believed.

But the Quarta weren't Great Stars. They were Minor Stars, and there were only three, and they were stuck. This planet had taught them what being trapped really means.

Yet the Farien's fate was most worrying of all. Wherever he was, he was on his own. Too easy a target, if the demonoids tracked him down. And that they would, was only a matter of time.

How does one find someone in a world he knows little about? In a world one doesn't belong to? Many long evenings and a turbulent storm of ideas yielded just one answer. Music.

"Music travels as fast as thought does," Nesteri said. "It could be our messenger."

"We would risk too much, drawing attention to ourselves like that," Hagal objected cautiously.

"Better to risk than to be prisoners here," Tei cut him off. "Sounds like a simple enough plan. It may work. Let's give it a go."

Although in no singing mood, their warrior discipline showed them the way. It was easy indeed. Almost too easy. The last disciple of the famous bard Demaré, Tei certainly knew how to compose. And, by Light, could he sing! Nesteri added to it with his mastery over words, covertly yet deliberately spellbinding, and a duo was born. Hagal who shrank from anything public had managed to find a way to stay near but detached. Writing, his favourite pastime, became his shield. He did compose some of the lyrics and volunteered – somewhat a bit too eagerly – for the ungrateful task of handling correspondence.

"Hagal, you'd do anything not to be heard singing, would you?" Tei chuckled.

Hagal casually ignored Tei's jest. He was sketching a layaremth in his notebook – a gold winged horse, his family crest – and pretended not to hear.

Hardly surprisingly, they were a success. The Quarta's music stirred the souls. The magic of their tunes was storms and stardust, not of this world. The downloads numbers soared, and the videos with the mysterious handsome singers swept across the cyberspace like a forest fire.

A nomination for the Best New Band came within a few short months. Unexpected and flattering, it was swathed in a dark veil of danger. Those who shine too brightly attract all sorts of eyes. They flip up an easy target. The Quarta knew that.

But there was no other choice.

The neon colossus of the city sprawled around the ocean bay like a mythical hydra with its multiple heads. Tokyo was unlike anything the Quarta had ever seen before. It throbbed with a dazzling, forceful and alien vibe that contrasted sharply with the gentle and soothing feel of the land itself.

And yet again, the Stars were lucky. They weren't the only strangers there. The quirky tapestry of types, the cosmic masquerade on the streets had readily embraced them as a sea swallows a drop. Nobody cared, nobody noticed. It was almost as good as being invisible.

Other than that, the city was far from kind. The Stars' extended perception was nothing short of a curse here. They could sense, see and feel the subtle energy currents that plagued the place, toxic and suffocating like a heavy smoke. It oozed from everywhere – the tangled snakes of electric lines overhead, the cobwebs of wires in walls, the cold darts from the countless devices. It made it so hard to rest, sleep or meditate. The menacing network of underground trains was the worst, with their dark tunnels and ominously buzzing jumble of signs and cables. The Quarta was forced to learn to drive. Cars, although not ideal, were better.

The Stars did what they could. They had sealed their flat with energy screens; although deteriorated quickly, those did help somewhat. But even the screens were powerless against another pestilence – small electronic objects, omnipresent here. Hagal tentatively made peace with laptops, but plainly refused to use smartphones.

"They burn my fingers and give me a headache," he said.

"True, but they can be handy at times," Tei's attitude was less barbed, especially since he had discovered that the little devices could record and play music.

Nesteri, on the contrary, was quite intrigued. The idea of an endless virtual library appealed to him. Yes, it was limited to the knowledge of this planet, but still. The Star had quickly learnt about the power of blogs and social media, and it was mainly his effort that helped the Quarta spread the word. His resistance to the unknown radiation seemed to be greater, but long hours in front of a laptop were taxing even for him.

Ding! Startled from his thoughts, Nesteri walked to the table and picked up his phone. Tei gave him a questioning glance. "Just an event reminder," Nesteri clicked to switch off the screen. "I'm pretty sure the demonoids could be on our trail by now," he dropped a casual remark to no one in particular.

"I wouldn't be surprised," Tei answered. He put his guitar aside. "While you're fiddling with that thing, look up the floor plan and exits for us, just in case."

"Aye, captain."

Tei slowly got up and stretched. "Right, it's time to make a move." The clock on the wall was giving him an unambiguous hint. "Let's see what we've got here." A plastic cover rustled in his hands. Inside the cover was a rented black tie suit, almost the right size, although Tei expected that the sleeves would be too short again.

"Huh, it actually doesn't look too bad!" Tei's voice soon came from the hallway.

"What?" Nesteri came closer to witness the preening scene. He threw Tei a sidelong glance. "Tei, you're enjoying this, aren't you…?"

"Well," Tei smirked, somewhat awkwardly. "I do think we pull it off, even if I say it myself."

Nesteri grimaced. "You know what we're packing ourselves into, right?"

"I bloody well do. But come on, it's still an *adventure* of sorts," Tei said, fumbling with his tie. "This thing that goes around the neck looks a bit weird."

"Where did you put the car key?"

"Over there, on the desk."

"Found it." Nesteri came back, jingling the keys in his hand.

Tei ran his fingers through his hair. "And anyway," he added, straightening his bow tie, "since we're stuck here, we may just as well try and enjoy *some of it*." He looked over at Nesteri. "What do you say? Nothing. Exactly. You know I'm right."

By the time the Stars arrived in Yokohama, the skies had cleared; the afternoon sun broke through the clouds. A carpeted path stretched before them, vividly red in the last of the daylight. On both sides, the usual swelter of press photographers was bristling with their cameras and ladders. Dense facial hair covered some of their faces; for the Quarta, an unusual view.

The three looked breathtakingly sharp in their black and white, as they walked along towards the entrance. Three long shadows run after them on the ground, thin and deep. On Siltarion, the Quarta's looks were nothing special. This world seemed to hold a very different opinion, though. Tei smirked at the thought.

A group of fans surrounded the Stars, jostling and chirping excitedly, asking for photos together and autographs.

"Those stupid flashes," complained Hagal in a low voice, "make me flinch. They seem like tiny energy attacks."

"Argh," Tei frowned. "I wish you didn't say that. Now I too feel that way. Damn." He forced another smile to the cameras, before disappearing with his friends inside the building.

The agonisingly boring award ceremony descended into an agonisingly boring afterparty of fake smiles and unending toasts. Nesteri volunteered to drive home, a perfect excuse not to drink. Tei and Hagal had a trickier job secretly watering their drinks down, and leaving them about the place. The Quarta couldn't afford to lose their presence of mind. Not now. Not in a place like that.

The slow torment of hours was dragging and waning away, yet of Farien there was no trace. If he were in the room, or anywhere near, the Stars' extended perception would let them know. They would sense his presence, as he would sense theirs. But space around remained deftly still. Farien did not come.

Meanwhile, the party raged on, shaking to the rhythm of convulsing lights and the deafening cacophony of music. It was getting late.

Nesteri suddenly felt a soft ball of paper pushed into his hand – Tei passed by, throwing him a short intense glance. Nesteri made his excuses and quickly vanished, leaving the company to their drinks and jokes. Having found a spot that was brighter somewhat, he unfolded the napkin. Its creased surface revealed a short line in the familiar Siltarionese script, in Tei's resolute handwriting:

"Maeth averin. Tie-ni roendē." [1]

Their walk to the car park led through the silent maze of night streets. Tei casually opened the box he was holding, and pulled out a dainty block of cut crystal. Its facets and their band's name in gold glistened in the murky glow of streetlights.

---

[1] "Let's go back. Meet you outside."

"Well, that was sort of fun," Tei looked at Nesteri who was busy with his phone. "What are you doing?"

"Updating our pages with some snaps I took. A little thing, but it helps to spread the word, I've noticed. People share photos and such, then more people join. That's how it works."

Tei looked over his shoulder. "What an eyesore. I've never seen so many pictures of myself in my life."

"You gave me an idea. I can print them out for you and decorate the walls."

"Get off."

"Photos are great. They are like…like catching the butterflies of time. You know? Any moment you want, you can order it to stay forever. I like that."

A sudden vision from childhood flashed before Hagal's eyes, the smell of grass, the coolness of the creek, and the butterflies, dozens of them, sparkling like gemstones, fluttering past. His eyes, opened wide in wonder, and the whisper of the breeze, and the warmth of the earth, and the world around that was just meadows and skies, skies and meadows, and flowers, and summer, which seemed to be never ending. The butterflies of time…

"How can you put up with that thing burning your fingers? It's sort of irritating," Tei said.

Nesteri shuddered. "Yeah, I guess. I just told myself to ignore that."

"For Light's sake, this is getting tiring," Tei suddenly changed the subject. He put the block of crystal back in its box. "Too long! It's taking *too long*. Where is he?! With all that noise we've made, I hoped he would answer at last."

"So did I. I looked for him everywhere at the party, but no."

"What the heck is going on with him? I wish he'd move his lazy arse and look for us as well."

"I bet he probably is."

"That would worry me even more," Tei frowned. "After all this time, it would mean that we're rubbish at this, all of us."

Tei and Hagal stopped outside, waiting for Nesteri to bring the car down.

As soon as they got in, Tei tore his bow tie off and threw it in the glove compartment. He had clearly pined to do for a while. Hagal and Nesteri did the same. "This neck ribbon is *ridiculous*!" Tei scowled undoing the top buttons on his shirt. "It looks like something girls would wear…"

The night drive home was quiet on the empty road. The full moon brightened the sky. Nesteri glanced in the rear view mirror. In the cold shine, Hagal's face appeared drawn and mournful.

"Hagal, what's up? You're too quiet, even by your standards."

Hagal wrinkled his forehead. "I've never been known for excessive verbosity, as far as I'm aware," he rubbed his face. "And what to talk about? I've had enough. Being on this planet is a drain. I'm worried about Farien–"

"–aren't we all."

"…and I wouldn't mind getting some sleep, too. I'm not a night owl like you are."

"Or a night raven, rather," Tei joked nodding at Nesteri's left wrist. A small silver raven, a distant memory of Dragh, twinkled on his leather strap bracelet.

"Night is when the stars come out…or go out," Nesteri quipped.

Tei chuckled at his words, recalling many a merry night out, back in his Academy days.

"Well, without me. I'm going straight home," a shadow of a smile touched Hagal's lips.

"I sure hope we'll be out of here soon," cut in Tei, "and that this mess is a one-off."

The road lights flickered and blinked unexpectedly, like an old sea lantern in a stormy wind. One more blink and they were gone. The highway plunged into darkness. The moon shone lonely above, a single eye. Strange tension trembled in the air.

"What the heck…" Tei broke his sentence midway.

"Oh hello," remarked Nesteri almost nonchalantly. "Well, that didn't take long."

"Not them, for the love of…" Hagal rolled his eyes. "This was the last thing we needed tonight."

A blast of dazzling red light hit the road in front of them a moment later. Nesteri threw his arm up, covering his eyes, and slammed on the brakes. The tires screeched. The car skidded on the slippery road, whirled and landed on the other lane.

Tei, who despised seat belts, was thrust forward and despite his trained senses made a predictably close encounter with the windscreen; he rubbed his forehead and swore unintelligibly under his breath something about high speeds and lame drivers.

"Next time, *you* drive!" snapped Nesteri. He re-started the engine and pulled to the side. Trying to keep on driving now would not only be pointless; it would be dangerous.

The Quarta got out and divided, moving as far as possible from the car. The night surrounded them with chill and whispers; the smell of rain still lingered in the air. The quiet was deceptive. The Stars could clearly sense an energy barrier, a safeguard measure of their enemies. The dark screens sealed the battlefield tight, so no one else could get in, no one could take in the rear.

The ground shook with the sudden thunder of explosion. A lashing gush of heat breathed out the acrid smell of burning, as stones and cinders shoot into the air. A torn hole gaped in the road like a fresh wound, widening slowly, its melted edges collapsing inwards.

The smoke soon cleared, and the pale silver of moonlight revealed two figures in the dark uniform, too familiar not to recognise.

Rangy red-haired Phatiel and his companion Nedros, squint-eyed and tabby like a stray dog, appeared side by side for a split of a moment, and then divided, ready to attack. The demonoids had been on the Quarta's tracks for long enough to get their patience strained. A couple of years had passed, yielding no results but the contemptuous looks and ridicule from their cohorts. The four irritating youngsters had so far always managed to outsmart them, disappearing and reappearing again in unpredictable places. It was getting too much.

"You missed – again – you dizzy-eyed jerk!" hissed Phatiel to Nedros in Dark Speech.

"Shut your gob. You're no better," Nedros hissed back. "I bet I'll finish them off before you do, loser."

Tei attacked first. Tongues of amaranthine flames flashed through the cold night air – only a moment too late. Avoiding the blow, Nedros fired back; dark purple snakes of lighting whooshed past, a near hit, singing Tei's hair.

Iridescent flames clashed and swirled, slicing through the gloom of the night, shining in every raindrop, reflecting on the wet road, enshrouding all in a halo of glow, bewitching and deadly. Those who made combat part of their life should know enough about loss not to be swayed by it, but fighting without Farien felt odd. Now they were three against two; but what they gained in number they lacked in experience.

Phatiel was fighting Hagal and Nesteri with such a look as if he was having fun; the Dark Star was good and he knew it. The wound on Hagal's right leg proved it blatantly well. With every passing moment, the situation was getting worse.

It was taking perniciously long. Hagal was slowing down, Tei noticed. 'I need to come up with something, quick!' Tei thought feverishly while exchanging blows with Nedros in a wordless fury.

'The Triangle attack,' he remembered suddenly his teacher's words, 'if one of you is unable to fight, use the Triangle.'

Another blow and Nedros fell to the ground screaming, his convulsing hands trying to reach instinctively for the horrid burn on the left of his face. Phatiel glanced at him, surprised. That moment of distraction was a godsend. Tei gestured the sign of triangle to his team.

They instantly positioned themselves. A threefold strong energy jolt smashed onto the demonoids like a blinding wave, blasting them out of this dimension, back to where they came from. The portal collapsed behind them, the sealing shields burst and disintegrated. The battlefield plunged into silence.

Tei smiled dryly, wiping the dust off his sleeves and trousers. "Caught out by such an old trick! Amateurs."

"These clothes were surely not made for combat," Nesteri muttered disapprovingly, trying to find his cuffs on the ground. "Hagal, you alright?"

"I'll live." Hagal tore off the ragged bottom of his trousers.

"I'll sort you out as soon as we're back," Nesteri said watching Hagal making his improvised bandage.

"That would be appreciated, thanks."

Nesteri walked around, checking carefully and incinerating any traces of blood, before getting back in the car.

"We're good to go," he said slamming his door shut. The Star checked the side mirror, which was miraculously not broken. "A kingdom for a shower and sleep."

CHAPTER II

SEYANE SEYA

HOPE AGAINST HOPE

"Pssst! Psst!"

At the sound of the voice, Nesteri reluctantly lifted his eyes from the manuscript.

"Psst! Nerri, I know you're not sleeping!"

Nesteri sighed, rolled up the scroll he was reading, got up and opened the door. "What?"

Farien greeted him with a cheeky grin. His lilac eyes were full of mischief. "Tei may need our help. He may desperately need it."

"Let me guess."

"Yep. It's past curfew and he still hasn't come back. We have to rescue him. We are his unsung heroes. Or rather, we soon will be." Farien sniggered.

"Sure." Nesteri snorted. He put his boots on and walked out of his room, quietly closing the door behind him. "Onwards, to our immortal glory!" He whispered.

"Shh!" Farien whispered back, holding back laugher.

They sneaked down the tower's spiralling staircase, crossed the dark courtyard, and hid behind a large memorial stone by the Academy's front gate. From there, they could clearly see the light in the porter's window.

"We can't use the same trick again," Nesteri whispered. "He won't buy it."

"What then?"

"Let me think. We have to fetch him out somehow."

"Tei is outside the gate right now, I can sense him."

"I know he is." Nesteri drummed his fingers on the stone. "Alright," he said in a low voice. "Here's the plan. Give me your headband."

"What for?"

"So he doesn't know it's me! Hurry up."

"Okay, okay…" Farien undid his headband and handed it over to Nesteri.

"Listen here," Nesteri said unfolding the band and wrapping it around to cover his face. "I'll knock on the door. When the old bore opens, I'll grab his journal and run. I bet he'll run after me. You pinch the keys and let Tei in. Yeah?"

"Nerri, you're genius!"

Nesteri smirked. "Working on it."

Farien was about to say something, but suddenly the earth shook and the sky turned into flame. And the horror of the Fall was upon them again, the fights and the fires; and the blackened Academy's ruins resounded with the cries of the dying. "Nesteri, help me…!" Farien yelled as a horde of demonoids seized him. "Help me!!" Nesteri leapt forward, but there was only darkness.

He woke up with a start, heart beating heavily in his chest. 'It was a dream,' Nesteri said to himself trying to calm down. 'Just a bad dream.' He rubbed his face. The vision was unsettlingly real.

It was pouring down with rain the day after and the following day, too.

Tei and Nesteri had decided to brave the weather; Hagal's wound forced him to stay at home.

He was now leaning over his notebook, sketching. Line by line, once familiar landscapes, places and mythical animals came to life under his pencil, pulling his mind away from frustration and the nagging pain.

Painting and writing were Hagal's true passion. Had he had a say, it would have been the path he would have chosen for himself. His family's wish and position demanded of him to become a warrior, though, and Hagal dutifully obeyed. It was clear he would never equal Tei. Yet Hagal always strived to be the best he could, even now, even despite there was nobody to feel proud of him anymore. He believed that a firm resolve was akin an oath to oneself – once made, it should be followed steadily and wholeheartedly. The warrior discipline had taught him many things, and it was one of them.

After a while he paused and gazed blankly into space, playing with the pencil as though it was a dart. Outside the window, the rain-streaked sky was offering nothing but the shades of gloom. The persistence of weather was somewhat impressive.

'This horrible rain,' Hagal thought. He'd rather it didn't portray his mood quite that well. 'It seems as never ending as our stay here.'

Farien's silence was becoming ominous. 'He must be alive, or his part of the Crystal would come back to ours...why not a least give us a sign?' Days were passing by, bringing no answers. 'Let's pray we'll find him before demonoids do.'

It had always confounded Hagal why the Dark Stars couldn't just leave them alone. You fight someone who got in your way, someone who had wronged you or yours. Why bother chasing strangers? 'All that energy they spent on trying to hunt us down...why? There must be some reason. Our teacher might have known...'

Their teacher did know.

The Quarta's more than a fair share of fights and danger was not because of what they did; it was because of who they were. Light Stars had a way of influencing the world around by the virtue of their energy alone, their very presence weakened the Shadow – and it had always been ruthless to those to dared to stand up against it. The Quarta and other Ariya warriors were silent guardians, the spokes that stopped the wheels of darkness from crushing this realm. Their hardships were the price for their power.

Just like in any other place the Quarta stayed before, strange things had been happening in the city since they arrived. In mystifying ways, serenity and good fortune had entered the lives of those who lived nearby as if a blessing spell. The Quarta would be quite surprised if only they knew.

The pale leathery coldness of the sofa was all comfort their dwelling had to offer. Hagal sat down, his hands joined loosely together, and closed his eyes. He needed rest, and meditation was his most trusted escape. Shortly, a slender lozenge of throbbing light – his fragment of the Crystal – flashed between his hands. Quivering glares filled the room, shrouding Hagal with a scintillating glow. He looked as if asleep; his thoughts drifted to distant times and places.

Woven from the golden dust of memory, sprung back in his mind the luminous gardens by his family home on Siltarion. He would go there often, with his parents and sisters, or alone with a book in his hand, to listen to the murmur of streams and the joyful ringing of birdsong. Only a few miles away lay Venth Marean, the capital – a graceful city of white stone, engirdled by the rock and crystal mountains. Hagal remembered his first trip there – excited and wide-eyed, overwhelmed with the new colours, sounds, and scents, he was clinging to his mother's hand, a timid four-years-old. The gemstones in her necklace were green and aquamarine, just like the sky above…

Hagal knew he would never see it again.

The staggering tower of a bookshop reigning over the nine floors was a perfect place to get lost. Finding anyone in that maze without extended perception would be a true wonder. Anyone but not Tei. He would get predictably stuck in the music section on the third floor, Nesteri deducted. His guess was right.

Having sensed Nesteri's presence, Tei raised his head and pulled his headphones off. "What?"

"Look," Nesteri said, handing his phone over.

"Although no groups have claimed responsibility as yet, last night's explosion is believed to be a terrorist attack. No casualties have been reported. An investigation continues," the article read.

Tei raised his eyebrows. "Creative."

"Weird, isn't it? We're lucky they didn't have cameras there," Nesteri smirked.

"True. Having the locals chasing us would be the last thing we need." Tei handed the phone back.

"What were you listening to?"

"It's called 'Reflections'. The singer has a nice voice," said Tei showing the album cover.

"She looks like Hagal's older sister."

"Hah, you're right, she does a bit. Funny." Tei looked pensive. "Let's get some drinks before we go."

In spite of the rain, the queue downstairs was long as usual. A smiley girl in a dark green apron over her uniform soon turned up with a menu.

"I know what I'm ordering already," said Nesteri. "Tei, you should really try a—"

"No way, I'm not drinking that odd green frothy stuff!"

"But it's actually quite—"

"No. You have it. I'm ordering a juice."

"Fine," Nesteri shrugged. "But still, you should give it a go one day."

The Stars walked upstairs by a narrow staircase and sat by the huge glass wall. A busy crossing outside glistened in the streetlights. Dusk was falling; the shadows, subtle at first, but deepening with each passing moment, were swathing the city.

"The strangest place we've ever been to," Nesteri said melancholically, watching the scattered beads of umbrellas down below. He held the cup in his hand for a few moments, then took the lid off. Tiny green bubbles covered its surface.

Tei gave him a sidelong look but said nothing. The forbidden memories, unwanted, flooded into his mind again, memories of another rain and another planet, of running together with *her*, holding hands, drenched to the core and laughing...

He played with the straw in his juice, trying to make it look casual, forcing the vision away before Nesteri might notice.

"That article earlier," Nesteri continued his thought, "the locals just make things up to comfort themselves, it seems. They're overcome with fear. I've been noticing it for a while now. They don't tend to stand up against the Shadow...they just let it spread."

"Maybe they don't know how," Tei answered sipping his juice. "We haven't met anyone so far who would be trained in our kind of combat."

"True. Hard to imagine they don't have Ariya warriors, though."

"Would be odd if they didn't. Maybe they keep it secret here."

"I guess you're right. I've seen only fighters."

"Fighters?"

"Those who use their bodies and weapons, not the energies of their mind."

"Ah, yes, gotcha."

"I'd be curious to meet some Ariyas here. Maybe we could learn something from them."

"You think?"

"There's always an opportunity to learn if you look for it." Nesteri got up, put his empty cup in the recycling bin and buttoned his jacket. "I like this word," he suddenly remarked.

"What word?"

"Mo-e-ru. It sounds nice." Nesteri pointed at the label by the bin, which said 'burning'.

"Never thought of it. Your mind works in the weirdest ways."

"Paying attention is a good habit."

The Stars walked out of the bookshop. Tei opened his umbrella to the busy patter of droplets. The JR station sign across the road shimmered green through the rain.

'So annoying, this weather,' Nesteri mused idly, while waiting for the lights to change. 'I wish I could command the rain to stop like our teacher did…reality is energy, he used to say, all of it. I should've listened properly back then. Still, what if I have a go?"

Out of sheer curiosity, Nesteri concentrated and sent a mental impulse, as if he were to fight, imagining the sky clearing out. After a moment, he opened his eyes and expectantly looked around. The dark water curtain remained unperturbed. Nothing happened.

'I guess it doesn't work that way… Never mind.'

Accompanied by squelch and splatter, the Stars walked across the road, their umbrellas and clothes gilded by the chaotic dance of neons. The crowd was passing by, nameless, wet, and silent.

As soon as they entered the station, the rain stopped.

It was almost midday, long past their usual exercise time. Nesteri, with his hair up, was on his own, perfecting a series of movements, repeating them time and time again. According to Hagal, who kept the record of days, three years had passed since the Fall of Siltarion, but Nesteri didn't feel that their fighting skills got much better since. They never finished their training, broken midway by the war. 'I wish I knew what it was we missed out on...'

A knock on the door snapped him out of his meditative state.

"What's up, Tei?"

"Stop straining yourself, you maniac."

"What do you want?"

"Come, I need your input with a new song."

Nesteri scowled. "Alright. Be with you in a bit."

He went through his sequence one more time, before finally joining Hagal and Tei in the sitting room. The Star wore local style clothes, black and light grey; the collar raised in his usual manner. His hair was still dripping wet after a shower, but he didn't care.

The room was bathed in the early afternoon sunshine. Tei sat by the table, onslaught by the might of paper and crumple scattered around. "Here, some ideas from Hagal," he said, handing over a page torn from a notebook. "See what you think."

Nesteri took the lyrics and read through. "Nice...but I'd change this part," he threw Hagal a glance across the room.

"What's that?" Hagal looked over his laptop.

"Our song will rekindle
Embers in the night skies
Long before we'll get killed
For the fire in our eyes..."

Nesteri read out. "It sounds kind of ominous. I don't like the idea of getting killed."

"Sure," Hagal agreed lightly, returning to his writing. "Do what you want."

"Mind if I go grab a tea across the road?" asked Nesteri when they finished.

"Yes I do mind," Tei frowned. "Especially since the damn demonoids are on our tail."

"Come on, it's only round the corner."

"Stop annoying me."

"I'll be fine. It'll take them some time to get back."

"Uhm…"

Having received Tei's tentative consent, Nesteri slung a jacket over his shoulders and sneaked out, before Tei could change his mind.

The Star walked out of the door and threw the hood over his face. Not everyone knew about their band, but his golden-green eyes often attracted more attention than he wished for.

His risky escapade was not a sensible idea, he knew. But the reward, the precious time alone, was worth it. Being around others all the time was wearisome. Nesteri was used to the fact that others couldn't see into his way of thinking. He learnt to keep his musings to himself. Talking to someone who didn't understand felt lonelier than when he was on his own.

It was as if an invisible glass wall surrounded him, a spell of solitude. With time, Nesteri made peace with the thought that he had always been a stranger everywhere he went. Even his own family had treated him as if he was a guest who inconvenienced them at the wrong moment. They were polite but cold. Since his childhood years, his loyal raven Dragh was the only living soul Nesteri felt close to.

To his relief, the café was almost empty.

"One matcha latte please, no sugar."

The curious local mixture of green herbal powder and milk tasted surprisingly good.

Nesteri went upstairs, to his favourite long wooden table by the window, and sat there holding his cup with both hands. He focused his energy to change the composition of the tea. It was safer for him that way. The Quarta had to do it with all food and drink here.

For a few moments, Nesteri remained still, gazing through the window with an absent stare. Finally, he pulled a pen out of his pocket and grabbed a napkin. Drawing patterns of circles and lines helped him organise his thoughts.

Farien had been silent for so long that Nesteri started suspecting that he might have ended up in a different part of the globe. But where? How long could he survive on his own? What happens if…? Nesteri forbade himself to worry about it. Worry was a waste of energy. Worse even, it meant not being present in the moment – for the warrior, a costly mistake. *'Stay present with what is, accept it as it is, act as if you were waiting for it,'* their teacher would say. Nesteri forbade himself to worry; yet… paralysing cold crept into his mind more and more often as days slipped by.

'Before we get killed for the fire in our eyes…' the ominous Hagal's line suddenly popped up, invading his thoughts. Nesteri shook his head. There was something disturbing about those words.

He finished his tea and was about to get up when his eyes wandered down to the napkin he was doodling on earlier. Nesteri blinked in disbelief. 'I don't remember sketching any of these…'

The piece of paper was strewn with symbols and sigils. One of them looked like a key. Another one was the sever-rayed emblem of the Septenary…surrounded with random words in Siltarionese runes. There was also his Academy crest and his family's coat of arms. The rest he could not recognise. Nesteri stared at them, puzzled. 'Weird. How come I don't remember?' His finger pensively traced one of the Septenary's symbols.

He could swear it lit up at his touch. A bright blue shimmer flickered and waned. 'What the heck..!' The Star rubbed his face. 'I'm seeing things. That's it, I really need more sleep.' Nesteri pushed the napkin into his pocket and hastily left the café.

His way home was carpeted with fallen cherry petals.

Two more weeks passed.

The fourth month of the year was almost over; a warm breeze carried the scents of spring. Bathed in the afternoon sunshine, skyscrapers gleamed with all their might of steel and glass.

"You know, the only thing I like about here," said Tei, "are those shiny towers. They look to me a bit like Marean's crystal mountains, only smaller."

Hagal pulled a face. Nothing in this city could even remotely compare to the lost homeland for him.

"Wait," Nesteri said suddenly. He spotted a vending machine. "I'll be right back."

He soon returned, with a grin on his face and a paper cup of matcha latte in his hand.

"Feeding your addiction again?" Tei chuckled. "Nesteri, you'll turn green."

"That's how *you* usually look in the morning," replied Nesteri with a quip. "People will think we're brothers."

"Get off, I haven't been drunk since the Fall, not once."

Nesteri focused for a moment, transferring his energy into the cup. "A sip, anyone?"

"Cheers, but I'm not joining in your weirdness."

"I'm good, too," Hagal said.

Nesteri shrugged. "More for me." He nodded at the small park across the road as the Quarta waited for the lights to change. "Shall we go check it out?"

"Look, look, it's them!" an excited girl's voice suddenly came from behind.

"No way!" someone else answered.

"I'm telling you, it's them!!"

A group of girls surrounded the Quarta, some jumping close, the rest frantically taking photos. "Autographs! Can we ask for autographs?" the girls chirped all at once, as they swirled around with their phones and notebooks. Attention spread like a fever, drawing more and more passers-by in.

Tei's face became tense. "Guys, this is no good," he said watching the gathering grow bigger. "We need to get out. Split. I'll see you in the park." He ducked and swiftly disappeared into the crowd.

"Hagal, go left, I'll go right," Nesteri said throwing the hood over his face. His matcha cup was gone already, snatched by a pair of eager hands. Somebody caught him by the wrist but the Star swiftly freed himself. "Now!"

Both vanished as quickly as shadows, leaving only puzzlement behind.

"Shinobi...?" a confounded girl's voice said.

A tranquil bliss of green by the riverside, the park opened up before the Stars with its alleys and sidewalks, and the golden lace the sunrays filtering through the leaves. It seemed out of place amongst the stifling maze of brick and concrete.

"Well done, team," Tei said when they were back together. He looked around. A small fountain behind him tinkled with cold splashing glitter. The azalea blossoms trembled in the wind. The park was empty. "Let's wait here for a bit." He plopped down on the bench. Nesteri and Hagal joined him.

The breeze sighed rolling through the alley. Nesteri looked up at the lapping leaves, his face suddenly empty and distant.

"What's up?" Tei asked.

"Nothing, just thinking," Nesteri replied.

"What with?"

"Shut up."

"Come on, don't be shy."

"You really want to know?"

"Yeah."

"Fine. I've noticed something," Nesteri said after pause. "This planet… It's not like any other place I know."

"What do you mean?"

"Hard to describe. May sound a bit odd."

"Most things you say sound odd, carry on."

"It happens when you meditate. You can see not just one, but many levels of reality, as if a ray splits into many colours. You know? A bit like a labyrinth, or a hall of mirrors. This planet feels like a key to all of them, a portal to something greater. You know what I mean?"

Tei shook his head. "Nope, not really. I've never noticed anything like that. Hagal, you?"

"I don't recall seeing any other realities. But I wouldn't dismiss Nesteri's observations out of hand. Truth to be told, I try to not look around too much. I find this place disagreeable, both the energy and the architecture."

Tei sniggered. "Hagal, you never miss your chance for a good rant, do you?"

"Just saying," Hagal crossed his arms. "Being here wears me down. It's like a prison of some kind, and I can't wait to get out."

"Yeah, I hear you. But you'll never find another place like Siltarion, you realise that? You're not the only one who lost your family there. We all did. Staying trapped in the past and getting bitter about it leads to no good." Tei put his hand on Hagal's shoulder and added, "The past never comes back. Ever. Let's try and look into the future, and make the most of being alive."

"Thanks, Tei. You're right. I'm sorry," Hagal pensively looked at the fountain. "I know all that. It's just – if we really had to get stuck somewhere for ages – I wish it wasn't here."

"I'm with you. Pull yourself together. Shouldn't be long now."

"By the way, have you seen that last draft I wrote?"

"You mean 'The Key to Mirages'? Yeah, not bad. I'd shorten it a bit."

"Do as you please."

Tei thought for a second. "Actually, I may have a tune for it already."

"I hope it's not the one you were singing in the shower earlier," Hagal's glance was an inimitable mixture of feigned concern and laughter.

Nesteri chuckled. "Writing music certainly takes him quicker than it does to shower!"

"That's how I roll," responded Tei with a smirk.

Nesteri suddenly jerked his head right, so sharply as if something was there, something he tried to see. He soon looked back, his eyes surprised and cautious.

"Did you catch that? At the corner of your eye, just then."

"Catch what?" asked Tei quickly.

"Too late, it's gone. I wonder sometimes where your mind is."

"Look, I'd sense someone's presence. There was no one there! Probably a squirrel or some such."

"I'm pretty sure it wasn't," Nesteri looked across the parkland with a frown. "I think someone had been watching us."

"Who?"

"I don't know. I couldn't see who or what it was. Just a few sparkles."

"Weird," Tei followed the direction of Nesteri's gaze. "Honestly, I didn't sense anything." He looked again. "I wouldn't worry yourself with that. It clearly wasn't demonoid. They don't waste time hanging around in bushes... Hah, unless they were scared of catching the stupid bug from you."

"Well Tei, you're a living proof that there's nothing to fear. You had it from birth."

"You just can't handle it that I outshine you in every way."

"You bet. I couldn't even dream of that *rare intelligence* of yours."

A shadow of some dark memory suddenly crossed Tei's face. He knew exactly what Nesteri meant, the hidden mockery in his words rang clear. Tei pressed his lips together and unwittingly glanced away. "I'll let you off this time."

CHAPTER III

E-SOWILŌEN ARETO

THE COUNCIL ON SOWILŌ

The rising sun cast trembling opulence of gleam on the dark waters of the sleeping ocean.

A new day came with fleeting gifts of dew and the sweet freshness of the breeze. Snowcapped mountains gleamed from afar, their foot still shrouded in shadows. The last pale stars were vanishing away.

A Great Star sat in silence on the beach. Her wings were wrapped around lightly over her warrior attire, platinum and dark-green; long hair of midnight silver flowing in the wind. The Star of Time Past watched the waves, which rolled serenely on the sandy shore, white stallions with their foamy manes. She never grew bored of that view.

Finally, she sighed and rose. The morning calm burst into tinkling crystals; birds lapsed into a surprised and watchful hush, dazed by the power of the song. A fading echo was still ringing in the air when new tones joined, called forth by the heart-stirring magic of her voice. The music whirled and lashed into the sky with tongues of rainbow flame, the air turning into liquid fire.

The conflagration stretched up its flapping wings, writhing and soaring as it shone, and now it flashed with blazingly white light, clear as a diamond, impossible to see with mortal eyes. The music surged and swept around, crashing like a wave.

Then suddenly, it stopped. The flamed subsided, and the last lonely note drowned slowly in the whisper of the ocean.

"Tertia pars combusta est[2]," said in that silence a male voice, deep, sensual, and commanding. "Antares, look what's happened to the beach!"

---

[2] "One third [of the earth] was burnt up", Apocalypsis (*Lat.*)

Antares opened her eyes to give the unexpected guest a scornful stare. A swarthy winged figure stood there with a cheeky grin, his huge arms crossed on his chest. Crimson and leather, his long coat had seen better days. Thick jet-black hair, shiny as a polished rock, fell down to the Star's shoulders. Green flames were dancing in his gaze.

"Kano. Great timing. You've ruined my another verbal lattice, dear sir."

"As always at your service, my lady," Kano sneered. He glanced down at the melted coat of sand under their feet. "Restoring that would be a joy."

Without waiting for an answer, Kano snapped his fingers. The beach returned to what it was. "Peractum est.[3] "

"I would assume you didn't trouble yourself to come here just for that?" Antares's voice rang with feigned reserve, in contrast with laughter in her ambery eyes.

"Nay, a mightier task was laid on me this time, I'm the harbinger of the news, the messenger of gods—"

"Kano, for Light's sake, what gods...?"

"I dunno. Some gods, whatever," Kano answered with a grin. "My dear lady, Sirit is calling a Council," he added, as if hesitantly, after a pause. His face was serious now.

Antares' eyes widened slightly for a moment and then became very narrow.

"I did suspect she would. I had a premonition earlier."

"Scio[4] ," said Kano. "I took it as a chance to see you. It's been a while since I could delight in your presence." He threw Antares another cheeky glance from under his lowered eyelashes.

"The joy your presence brings I'll never hope to match, my Star," Antares parried. "Well met. It feels so much like a quiet before the storm."

The Shadow, Antares thought. She could sense it stirring, readying for a strike, billowing restlessly for a long time now. *Sirit is calling a Council*. She never does it unless the danger is too close.

"I will be joining shortly."

"I'll wait for you there. Vale et Lux tecum![5] "

---

[3] Done. (*Lat.*)

[4] I know. (*Lat.*)

[5] Until then and may Light shine upon you. (*Lat.*)

"Lux tecum, Astra mea," Antares replied.

Kano smiled lightly and disappeared.

The Star of Time remained standing pensively, looking at the rippled vastness of the ocean before her. Behind, a narrow path led to a manor of columns and spires, dark wood and pale stone, towering amongst the flowery meadows.

A moment later, she was gone. Only a few sparkles slowly faded in the air.

They gathered on Sowilō, the domain of Sirit, the Star of the Future and the Guardian of the East.

All Stars of Septenary were already there; all except for Vanand.

"I did imply she should arrive *immediately*...I might have just as well said nought," Regulus, the Star of Time Present said, her eyes as grey as mist. Her robes were ochre, white and gold; the metal cuffs on both wrists engraved with secret signs. Long glossy hair in the colour of waxed chestnuts flowed over her shoulders.

The Council was to take place in Sowilō's eastern part, just as it had done for thousands of years. The colossal stone forum of pyrite was framed with the pillars of blue jade; eternal fire burnt on the tripod in its middle, and shimmering motes of gold swam in the air around it. The seven-rayed star on the ground sent out faint blades of shine, ephemeral and iridescent like the northern lights.

Seven stone thrones stood tall on each of the points of the star. Sirit presided in the East, with Regulus to her right and Kano to her left, followed by the empty Vanand's seat. Antares was facing her in the West, joined by Famaris and Aratron on her both sides.

The glow of six filled the forum, brightening up the shadows before dawn – when amongst themselves, the Stars eschewed the Light-suppressing bracelets. The subtle rings of energy helped to conceal their wings and to disguise and veil their real power, so others could be safe; yet the invisible aids were vexing, so vexing, and suffocating to wear. The Stars were happy to be free from them.

The Star of Eternity Vanand had finally arrived and gave a sign for the Council to begin.

Sirit was the first to speak. As she rose from her seat, the morning sun limned her hair and wings with a fiery glow. She wore long ceremonial robes, red and gold, and belted with a chain with keys.

"Aimayo-e, Septeneris Verai," Sirit greeted them in Aē, the language of Great Stars. "It is not often that I call you all here, to the most hidden of places. We need to work out a strategy most urgently and in the greatest secrecy. *Time is changing.* Some stirring news has reached me, with Vanand's help. Before long, our unity will be put to test; and hard will be that test indeed. The Shadow plans an attack on the Gates of the Past, so they could muddle and distort the memory of all worlds. Without memory, strength and integrity are lost. It's hard to fight not knowing who you are and what you stand for. The enemy seek to make the Ariya warriors blind, weak and unable to withstand their power. If their minds could be swayed, the enemy believe they could be darkened and turned into voiceless servants of the Shadow."

Antares said nothing, only slightly narrowed her eyes. Sirit continued:

"The strategy has taken them a great deal of toil…they are not ready yet. We have time. The Shadow's main line of attack will be Antares' source luminary, Alpha Scorpii. They hope that if the Guardian is destroyed, the Gates of Time would be thrown open."

"How about we stop them?" said Famaris, the Star of Space. He wore his usual shades of green and aquamarine; the gentle waves of flaxen hair were tamed with a chased brass circlet.

"They have accounted for that we may try," Sirit replied. "The Shadow's forces have been gathering in secret enormous amounts of dark energy to strike with. There's still a narrow chance of us repelling the attack, but only to be facing a new one shortly after. That strategy would drain our resources and weaken our armies. It's just the trap our enemies expect us to fall into."

"What's the best variant of the future you suggest?" asked Kano. "Any weak points in their defence?"

"Yes," Sirit's emerald eyes flashed. "Short-sightedness is the main one. The Shadow cannot see ahead far. It's their own demise they are forging; they seem to have no inklings of that. Although that battle may be lost, it shall teach us about where our slips are. We will be stronger for that. Another battle at the Second Half of Time will bring Antares back, with even greater power than before. The Sword and the Crown will brighten up the sky, heralding its return."

"If Antares becomes any more powerful, the Shadow shall be in real trouble," Kano smirked.

"There is no certainty, of course?" asked Regulus.

"Future is never a certainty, only a possibility," Sirit told her.

"What steps do you propose?" Regulus was practical as always.

"Resorting to a caelir."

"You mean one of those subtle power vaults?"

"Precisely. We would do with that enormous power on our side."

"I know what you speak of. We've done it once before."

"Yes. Only this time, I would suggest a planet in the sector G-5X38BR6J – the clearest point of projection of the Big Plough. By choosing to be born there, we will become the blood of its blood, the fire of its fire, and awaken all the energy that it holds within ourselves."

"What planet is that?" Famaris, the Stars of Space, asked.

"The Blue Planet, just on the outskirts of the Milky Way."

"What? Becoming Fixed Stars?" Kano didn't care to hide a shadow of distaste.

"It is but temporary price."

"Without Antares at the Gates of Time, we would be in as much danger as everyone else of losing our memory," Regulus sounded unconvinced. "What if that happens?"

"That's something I thought of already," Sirit replied. "There is a way, and the promise has been made. Each one of us is strong enough to stand their ground. However, if the worst were to happen and our sight were to be darkened by the Shadow, the Mirror Maid, the Guardian of the Firth Time, shall bring our true consciousness back in the Year of the Wandering Star."

"I actually know the Blue Planet somewhat," Famaris interjected again. "It's very…peculiar, to say the least. Its power attracts all sorts of eyes; the Shadow is particularly strong there. What are our chances?"

"One in a five," said Sirit. "The highest probability we have, comparing to all other variants I could see."

"Well, we have retrieved your source star with way less than that," Famaris pensively remarked.

Antares raised her head. A cold determination glistened in her eyes, but her voice sounded as calm as usual when she spoke.

"The Second Half of Time is a long wait," she said. "Someone will have to guard the Gates, and keep them closed, while I'm not here."

"Appoint the one who shall stand in your stead," said Sirit. "You know the best who would be strong enough to shoulder such a weight till your return."

Antares paused for a moment. "You know what I'm going to say. Vega would be the only one I would trust with this mission...if he was here."

"I did expect you'd say that," Sirit replied thoughtfully.

"Is there a way to bring him back?" asked the Star of Heaven. He glanced at Sirit, and then at Antares. Aratron rarely spoke; the music of his voice was too hypnotic. His crystal blue eyes and long hair, white as frost and crowned with a platinum circlet, would look ferocious if not for the kind and serene expression on his face. The passing centuries had not changed him; and yet despite the youthful appearance, in his layered robes, turquoise and argent, he looked ancient and majestic.

"Vega's envoy never returned since he had fallen in that battle centuries ago," Regulus said. "And he's still not here *at present*."

"That's true." Sirit looked up as if counting in her mind and then said, "I see him coming back...a while from now, and as briefly as a flicker of a candle flame. Three minor demonoids will have set up a deadly trap. He'll see his final fight on the Blue Planet before dead silence will embrace his soul once more."

"The Blue Planet again...but wait, nullo intellego!" chimed in the Star of Underworld. "I don't understand. What, in Light's name, was Vega doing there, of all places? And how could someone *like him* be seized by just three minors?"

"It wasn't his decision, so to speak," Sirit told him. "Over a thousand years will have passed since the Gates of Time Past stood closed. Vega will have lost the memory of who he truly was. He couldn't use his power as he didn't know of it."

A strange expression flickered in Antares' eyes.

After a silence, Aratron, the Star of Heaven, spoke again, as if weighing his words:

"We could intervene."

"We could," Sirit answered. "At our own risk, though. Such intervention would create an inconsistency of time, too hard to hide from the unwelcome eyes. The side effect of energy release would be even more evident. There is no way to hide at outburst like that."

"I understand," Antares said. She paused for a moment. "Yet this is still a wiser choice than allowing the Gates to stand unguarded."

"It's not the only price to pay. An operation like that means a complete entanglement, his life and your life, a sun of his sun, a shadow of your shadow—"

"Our lives are intertwined already, Sirit, and you know that," Antares retorted.

"But you know equally well that we could only take him from his time and bring him here, nothing more. We couldn't force him to wake up. He would not even remember you, nor would he be able to join us until his full consciousness returns…and it may take some time. Not even I can tell how long."

"His memory may falter, yet his essence hasn't changed. Vega is one of us. He will remember, I believe in him."

"Shall it so happen that we fail to wake him up in time, the Gates of Past would be left open to the Shadow. The catastrophe would sweep across the worlds, devouring thousands of years and thousands of souls—"

"There's no need in mentioning it, Sirit, I realise it fully. You speak like there's something better you could suggest?"

"Only that you may choose a different Star."

"If I could do, I would."

"The risk is way too high. You sure there's no one else?"

"I'm sure." Antares paused and looked Sirit in the eyes. Her amber gaze was focused and sharp. "I'm not a child. I would not take this most uncertain path, or risk our mission for some petty reasons. Look into my heart and you'll see the truth in my words. We need Vega. Not because of me, but because he is the only one who has the strength this task calls for.

The risk of bringing the right Guard is not as much as the horrendous price we would pay for a hasty choice."

Sirit nodded and sat back in her seat, deep in thought.

"I do think we need a contingency plan, though," Regulus voice was troubled. "Maybe one of us…Famaris or Aratron, you, perhaps?"

Aratron shook his head.

"Too perilous. I would not venture it," Famaris admitted. "That frequency is not familiar to me. Space is my domain, not Time."

Silence fell after his words.

"What now?" asked Kano finally, curiously calm.

"There may be something yet," Famaris spoke again. "Something we have not yet considered." He glanced at Sirit, then at others present. "Let's see what Vanand has to say."

All turned to the Star of Eternity.

Still figure shrouded in a dark sapphire cloak, Vanand moved for the first time since the council had begun. The golden glove on her right hand gleamed as she touched the heavy hood, which always covered her face. No words were spoken – and no words were needed. In Vanand's eyes, pupiless and cobalt blue, the answer was already there.

Chapter IV

Res Cai Lúis, Luini Caenna
What You Seek Is Seeking You

"Not even in a sleep
Can my heart find a rest
On this spring night.
Trapped in my dream,
All I can see are cherry petals falling, falling…"
~ *Oshikōchi-no Mitsune*

"Shall we return, do you reckon? There is something I wanted to finish today," Hagal said with a stretch. He looked up at the sky. The scattered clouds were painted with a gleaming outline.

Tei said nothing, staring blankly at the water droplets, ceaselessly running down the fountain's stand. His mind seemed far away. One glance at him, and Hagal knew. Clear as a bell, Tei was thinking about *her* again.

They never spoke about it. Farien and Nesteri held their own views, and although Hagal did understand their reasons, he couldn't find it in him to condemn Tei as openly and harshly as they did. A secret sympathy was kindling in his heart, though never said in words.

"Daydreaming, heh?"

"I…what? Yeah…no, I mean, not at all. I was just…"

"Someone just admonished me to leave the past behind."

"I know," Tei closed his eyes for a moment. "It's only right. And trust me, I try. Or Light, do I try…!" He dropped his head.

"It's alright, Tei. You're stronger than that."

"Thanks, Hagal." Tei gave him a weary smile. *Was he really stronger?* Tei wasn't sure.

"Shall we…?"

"Yeah, let's go," Tei got up. "Just need to find our Lost-Among-the-Trees," he spoke of Nesteri, who had wandered off some time ago.

"I'll just have a look," he said. "Back later." A long while passed since.

"Maybe he is still on his aimless meander..." Tei started in a singing voice a line from the famous poem.

"....teased by the wind and misled by the moonlight," Hagal picked up matching Tei's tone.

They found him soon enough – Nesteri stood in one the side pathways, deep in thought, his blank and absent stare fixed on something up above.

It was too good an opportunity to just let it go. Tei signalled to Hagal to keep quiet, while he soundlessly sneaked up from behind and poked Nesteri in the back. Taken by surprise, the Star swung sharply to the side, turned and struck the attacker from the right, quick as lightning. Before he knew it himself, Nesteri was holding Tei to the ground, ready to break his neck. His warrior training conditioned him to react quicker than he could think.

"Someone is overreacting," said Tei with an ironic grin, completely unruffled.

"Tei, you jerk," Nesteri said grudgingly, letting his friend go. "Your retarded jokes!"

"Hah, blame yourself!" Tei snorted. "Your zoned out look was damn asking for it. Situational awareness, mate." He got up, dusted off his clothes and looked up, too. The fading sky and the green treetops above offered no excitement. "What were you staring at?"

"What? No, nothing... Just thinking."

Share that dream? Sure. Nesteri knew what would happen. Tei would just sneer and give him one of those jeering looks of his, and understand nothing. There was no point.

The rush hour slumped down upon the city with the stifling mess of streetlights, smoke, and crowds; the agonising cries of car horns pierced through the air.

"How we get back? Bus?" Nesteri looked around unexcitedly.

"Not through this hell," Tei cringed. "No way. Let's walk. It's not that far, come on."

And true, it wasn't far, much closer in a straight line. The roadworks lengthened the Quarta's path somewhat, but even though, the walk seemed a better option. Behind the temporary fence, two workers on a break sat on a makeshift bench. They talked, ash flicking from their cigarettes, their voices drowning in the noise of drills.

Some hundred yards away the noise had eased, consumed by other restless city sounds. A quiet side street was a nice change. Taking that shortcut would reduce their journey to seventeen minutes instead of twenty-two, the satnav on Nesteri's phone said.

Empty and peaceful as it was, the row of derelict factory buildings on both sides looked hardly welcoming in the last of daylight, its blank windows gleaming like blind eyes. The Quarta hurried their step. An ice-cold breeze of wind came with a menacing breath of danger. Hagal shuddered.

"I have a bad feeling," he said in a low voice.

"What?" asked Tei who walked slightly behind.

Hagal glanced around. The street looked quiet and deserted. Across the road, the battered old fence bared its rotten teeth of boards behind the barbed wire.

"Could be the demonoids' screens but I'm not sure. Walking, perhaps, was not the best idea."

"Should be alright. We're almost—"

Before he could say more, an unseen force suddenly knocked Tei to the ground. He realised what it had been, too late. Energy fetters, strong as iron, cut into his skin, bounding him with their paralysing grip. Tei jolted and writhed trying to break free. In vain.

"Damn demonoids!" Nesteri hissed through his teeth. He tried to tear the net, but it seemed to have only tightened its grip.

"Leave me and fight!" ordered Tei to him. "I'll find a way."

This time, the enemies were three. The first two, in their long murky uniform, leathers and metal clasps, the Quarta knew too well. Their belts and armguards carved with cursed symbols seemed to exude the poison of dark energy. Cold hatred glowed in Nedros' only seeing eye, the left part of his face burnt and disfigured.

The third was a wiry stranger in an onyx cloak. A hood covered his face, revealing only his pointy chin and long charcoal hair. A heavy signet ring with a blue gemstone gleamed on the bony pointing finger of his left hand, pale as death.

"I'm Moriel," announced the stranger with a crooked smile, taking his hood down. His derisory gaze swept over the Quarta. "Just so you know who had the pleasure of relieving this world from your burden." Although not old, his face was lined and haggard, engulfed by the grim feeling of superiority. He looked uncannily Siltarionese, except for the eyes, pinch black with bloody rims, typical of a Dark Star. He voice, disturbingly smooth, bore no trace of an accent.

"Off with the courtesies, let's get this trash out of the way," said Phatiel brusquely in Dark Speech. The demonoid nodded in Tei's direction and jeered in his faltering Siltarionese, "Your fight is over, losers."

"Not that quick!" Hagal threw his jacket off.

"Such cutie pie," Moriel sneered negligently. "You bring back all the joys of kindergarten. You're two against three, in case it has escaped your notice somehow. I reckon that the attack by Triangle you'll so dearly miss was one and only trick you had up your lame sleeve. Oh, do correct me if I'm wrong," his lips curved in a fiendish sneer again. "Spare us the trouble, kids. Submit at once, before we made you–"

"Shut the hell up, you demonoid scum," Nesteri's voice was ice. "Even the two of us are enough to kick your arse."

"You're pathetic," Hagal heckled. "You came to fight us, or for a chat?"

"Die!" snapped Phatiel, attacking as he stood. Hagal swung aside and the perse stream of fire missed him, thundering into the wall behind. Shards of glass flashed in the air; bricks, stones, and dust flew blasted to all sides. The fence flopped to the ground, a crumbled pile of cinders.

Phatiel looked around, trying to find Hagal through the dust. That pause was his slip. *Tarry and you are dead.* A moment later light blue flames hit Phatiel's upper arm and shoulder, singing his hair and burning his lower neck. Another half of inch towards his heart that blow would have been lethal. A dark red stain showed on his uniform spreading slowly, as slow as in a bad dream. The demonoid hissed with pain and lashed again, fired up, ever so more ferocious with anger.

Block, parry and evade…evade, block, parry, parry. Nesteri was fighting two at once in an incessant dance of life and death. *Lose your focus and you are dead.* He had no chance of striking back, not once. Nesteri's only shield was speed. The enemies were taking the time to wear him down, he knew.

Slow down and you are dead. Two near misses left his body strewn with injuries and cuts; his torn shirt was spattered with blood. He didn't even notice. Evade, parry, block, evade.

The wreathing net of purple flames forming overhead was just the opportunity Nesteri needed. Quick as an arrow, he leapt towards Nedros taking the Dark Star by surprise, then tumbled and rolled off to the side. The energy net clung to the demonoid, pinioning him. *Stop and you are dead.* Next moment, Nedros swayed at Nesteri's blow and fell down to the ground like one bereft of life. Dust clouded his fall.

"Minus one."

As soon as that, an ice-cold blast from Moriel came leaving Nesteri's right arm paralysed. "Sly bastard!" the demonoid spluttered with rage. "Just you wait, I'll make you squeak." His new attack was a scorching hell, burning and stinging like a thousand of wasps. Moriel threw his left hand forward, forcefully drawing Nesteri's energy away, sucking it into himself.

Nesteri's left hand clenched into a fist so hard the knuckles whitened, but he remained silent.

Moriel's mouth twisted into a wry smile. He knew he could have killed the enemy right away, but there would be no fun in making it so simple. 'Not yet, not yet…soon.' He looked around for Phatiel.

Wounded and close to having lost, Phatiel was a sorry sight. It was a question of a few more moments.

"Disgraceful." Moriel cringed in disgust. "And you two call yourself warriors? You've turned being useless into an art. Idiots! There, I'll show you how it should be done."

The Dark Star raised his hand.

"Hagal, look behind!!" shouted Nesteri, but all too late.

Moriel's attack hit Hagal at the back and blasted through him with the agonising yell of pain. Dragged by the force of blow, his body hurled and smashed against a pile of debris from the wall. Grit and dust were settling down slowly.

"You didn't have to interfere," cringed Phatiel spitting out blood. "I was doing just fine."

Moriel only snorted.

"Hagal!" Faltering from pain, Nesteri ran over to his friend. He didn't have to look to know there was no hope. Hagal's light sandy hair was glued with blood, his eyes froze half-open, cold and blank. The blow had ripped to pieces his gored middle body, charring it with a spell of black. What's left of his shoulders and his arms was one dreadful lacerated wound.

"Hagal…"

Nesteri lifted his head sharply, searching for Tei. Bound with his shackles, Tei lied motionless and limp, pale as the leaves withered in the northern gale, his lifeless face laced with the rivulets of blood. The gleam of white revealed the shattered bone.

"Tei…"

Moriel and Phatiel watched, brazenly amused.

"Alrighty then, time to end this game before it gets too dull," Moriel said throwing Phatiel a sidelong look. "Shall I do it, or you?"

Phatiel spoke no word. His lips were tightly pressed together. The Dark Star stood gripping his right arm; blood running down his neck and through his fingers.

The ghost of a sardonic smile twisted a corner of Moriel's lips. "I see you have funeral arrangements to make. Very well. I'll do it."

Nesteri glowered at his enemies. Slowly, ignoring the tormenting burn of wounds, he rose to his feet and straightened up. A trickle of ruby drops spattered on the ground. The Star clenched his teeth.

He realised his right arm served his again: Moriel's earlier spell was wearing off. 'That's handy,' thought Nesteri with a distorted grimace for a smirk. He knew his journey had come to its end; the clouds on the other side were calling for him with the voices of his friends. He was to join them soon. Taking at least one other demonoid to the grave would make it a respectable score. Nesteri raised his hand.

His body disobeyed, against his will. As a stifling wave of vertigo washed over him, the Star swayed suddenly and dropped to one knee.

"There won't be much problem with that one," Moriel observed nonchalantly.

A strange expression flashed through Phatiel's face. Haunting his mind appeared again a burning memory, distant yet raw as a wound. A memory he could not banish no matter how he tried. The vision of a different fight, long ago…yet so uncannily close. Defeated, disarmed and thrown down on his knees, he stood before the enemies just like Nesteri now. Phatiel wished for death, he called for it, in vain. The Dark Stars took his soul instead. The world had crumbled into the abyss of pain, a torture that had never stopped…until his consciousness was no more. Strong gusts tangled his hair – dark auburn back then, not yet red, and the howling wind echoed with the cry of endless sorrow…

Phatiel gazed at the battlefield and for a fleeting moment an unexpected light, as if a pang of compassion flickered in his eyes. The Dark Star looked away.

Forcing together all his will, Nesteri made himself get up again. An acrid shadow of regret passed through his mind, a life that could have been. As through the mist, he saw Moriel's hand rising slowly for the final blow, the lips of the demonoid moving with some words he could not hear.

'So this is what death is like,' he thought now strangely calm, before the deaf darkness swallowed all around.

CHAPTER V

SEPTENERIS VERI

A STAR OF THE SEPTENARY

"When I reach with my inner sight far, far away, to yonder realms beyond the veil
of days, I can see the mist shrouding mountains at twilight. The mist fills up the subtle
flowerheads, dives down into the crystalline streams, and wraps around the feathers of
sleeping birds…the golden dust of trembling starlight is pouring down softly, teasing the
hidden contours out of the dark and awakening the strings of night…
It is there where the souls of dreams dwell."
~Demaré, Chronicles of a Nonexistent World

Hagal woke to the scents of early summer.

He slowly opened his eyes. The room was bright and still, its arched ceiling soaring above like the dome of a shrine. Bewildered, the Star sat up in bed and looked around.

The walls around were aglow with the magnificence of paintings. There were the landscapes and the seas, and the foreign skies, and the creatures like he'd never seen, so vivid that they seemed alive. Hagal couldn't help but marvel for a moment at the incredible skill of the unknown master.

The afternoon sun was caressing a corner of the open window, reflecting in the twinkling lozenges of glass.

'Where am I?' With a sudden shudder, Hagal realised that he hadn't got a clue. He absent-mindedly traced with his gaze the dainty carvings on his bed trying to gather thoughts. The memory of what had happened last was slowly seeping back.

'They killed me…!' Hagal's eyes opened wide as he remembered it all, the fight, the scorching blast, and the writhing agony of death. Startled, he took a deep breath, his heart pounding with a shock. Suppressing angst, he frantically checked his arms, his chest, his body looking for wounds, yet there were none. The folds of his dressing gown slid off his shoulders to show the perfectly unscathed skin. Not even a bruise. 'Insane...' Hagal shook his head in disbelief.

'Have I been captured?' he wondered as he looked around again. 'No ties or chains, though. And it's rather careless of them to leave the window open...' He listened as if someone might be there, but the only voices were those of birds.

Hagal soundlessly got out of bed and slipped towards the window, the azure carpet soft beneath his bare feet. 'This is by far too cosy for a prison,' he mused in passing, now utterly puzzled.

Outside, he was greeted by a vista of windswept treetops, distant mountains, and green fields and meadows chased with the restless silver of streams. The aquamarine sky of his childhood stirred up his soul, filling him with deep longing.

Familiar frequencies suddenly touched his senses, as if his friends were here too. 'Tei? Nesteri? Perhaps my wishful thinking...would be too good to be true.' It was clear though that he wasn't on his own. 'I wonder how big this citadel is...and how many guards are out there. I'd better find my way out before they come for me.'

Hagal turned towards the door. Only now did he notice a low velvet bench with a neat pile of clothes on his left. He caught his breath. The too familiar bluish-grey uniform, he recognised it straight away. It was all there – the white undershirt, the trousers and the fitted jacket with a clasped collar, just like in his academy days. 'I never thought I'd ever hold it in my hands again...' Forgetting for a moment where he was, Hagal gazed at the Quarta symbol gleaming on the left shoulder of the jacket; those were for teachers to tell the teams apart. Hagal blinked away unwanted tears. 'Light, where am I??'

His lace-up ankle boots were waiting there as well, so incomparably more comfortable than anything he had had to endure on the Blue Planet. While dressing up, Hagal suddenly caught himself lost in memories, daydreaming, as if succumbing slowly to the serene magic of the place. He shook his head mentally scolding himself. *He mustn't get distracted.*

The arched wooden door looked solid. Hagal slunk close and listened for a while. The outside seemed clear, and yet he hesitated. Finally, he gently put his hand on the cold brass of the handle. 'I bet it's locked.' To his surprise, it wasn't; under his push, the door silently gave in.

A large hallway opened before him, bright with golden sunlight. It flooded in through the glass dome and the resplendence of a latticed window by the staircase at the farther end. Hagal saw five other doors, flanked with giant winged sculptures in long robes. They all were of breathtaking beauty, and all armed; although some of their weapons he had never seen. The movement and the grace frozen in stone were called to limn ancient deities, or maybe legendary Great Stars, Hagal was not sure. Hefty green crystals mounted in brass were shimmering above, a glow faint in the daylight glory.

He had a feeling someone else was there, although no presence he could see. Hagal walked warily towards the stairs when a slight waft of air behind him made him freeze. One of the doors slowly opened a crack. Hagal jerked around, taking instantly a fighting stance, but suddenly he smiled and put his hands down. The frequency he sensed was loud and clear, although impossible.

'Tei?!'

Now the door opened fully. Tei, in his uniform trousers and dishevelled from sleep, appeared before Hagal. He was without a shirt, showing off his chiselled muscles.

"Tei! Light save us...you...you're alive?!"

"Yep," said Tei with a yawn, "I think so." He grinned and patted himself as though to make sure. "Unless this is an afterlife of sorts."

He cautiously glanced around and gestured Hagal in, then quickly closed the door behind them. "It's safer to talk here than outside."

"Tei! But how?! I can't believe it's you! I can't...just can't understand it," Hagal spluttered. "I swear I saw you dead...I saw how Moriel–"

"Spit out that name," Tei scowled. "May it be cursed by thousands of winds."

"I'm lost," Hagal shook his head, feeling confused and more emotional than he cared to admit. "As lucky like Doregi's children, they would say! I can't believe it...Tei, I'm..." he opened his arms, the friends hugged briefly, "so happy you're alive."

"It's good to see your silly face, too. Being alive feels great," Tei smiled but soon turned serious. "By the way...no wounds, you've noticed that?

69

Something I just can't get my head around. The last thing I remember was the blast that went straight through. I should be very much a bloody mess right now, by any standard."

"Bizarre," Hagal assented. "Most bizarre. Seems like a miracle. If I didn't believe in Light, I would start now. I only wish I knew what's going on—"

"—and what the heck this place is."

"Quite!"

"I wonder if the other two are here. I sense as if Nesteri may, at least."

"I'm pretty sure I can pick up his frequency, too."

Tei was now fully dressed, his short hair looking neater somewhat. The Quarta symbol on his shoulder bore a ruby outline.

The friends exchanged glances.

"Let's try and find him before whoever owns this palace finds *us*," said Tei in an undertone.

The first door on the left led to a mirror room of an unknown purpose. Its walls, although devoid of lamps or windows, were glowing with unusual brightness. Hagal and Tei cautiously walked in. As soon as that, their own countless copies jumped at them, hundreds of eyes and faces. A moving phantasmagoria of reflections copied their every movement, staring at them from the ceiling, walls and floor. Surprised and startled, the Stars retreated at once.

"What the heck was that?!" Tei shook his head.

"No idea whatsoever," answered Hagal in a similarly low voice, "Perhaps a training room of a kind…or a torture chamber? I shall be so relieved when we're finally out of here."

"If we're prisoners, which I'd think we are, the guards here are useless idiots," Tei smirked. "Look, they forgot even to tie us up! Amateurs."

"I haven't seen anyone so far, bizarrely enough," Hagal admitted. "I did expect my door to be locked and guarded, and someone to watch over the hall. They must be all downstairs or outside. I can't sense anyone."

"Neither can I. This place is darn odd."

"It is indeed."

Next door revealed a narrow staircase with stone steps spiralling up. The turret was strewn with a filigree of windows, their brass latches tarnished with age. In the late afternoon sun, thick pieces of cut crystal in the window frames flared with rainbows.

"We'll check this last," Tei decided.

The Stars passed Hagal's bedroom and walked to the fifth door. The lush emerald carpet drowned the sounds of steps.

Mysteriously left unlocked like the rest, the door opened to a grand library. Arching towards the ceiling carved shelves guarded a treasury of ancient books, tablets and manuscripts in nameless languages. Auric and ephemeral, pale shafts of light flowed in through the slit windows above.

"Whoa, Hagal, this looks like your house!" whispered Tei.

"The library at mine was nothing close to this," Hagal whispered back. *If it's a prison I don't want to run away,* a cheeky thought flicked through his mind.

They walked in slowly, awed, wading past the shelves through the stripes of sunshine and shade and the sunshine again, their faces and shoulders bathed in a milky glow. Hagal's amethyst eyes sparkled, wide open as if he was a boy once more. The place felt like home.

In the middle, a curious pattern sprawled on the floor – circles and lines, great and smaller, all connected, inscribed with unknown symbols and words. One more step and a strange shiver travelled down the Stars' spines, harsh and jarring, as if some unseen force barred their way. Hagal and Tei backed off without a word.

The desk by the window at the back sparked with the wonder of mysterious artefacts. A long scroll with ornate writing and fantastical animals in gold took up the most of it, surrounded by books and candles, a golden hourglass, engraved brass spheres of unknown promise and clear crystals with blue mist restlessly swirling inside.

Burning with curiosity, Hagal leant over the manuscript wishing dearly he could read the foreign language.

"Funny," Tei's voice came suddenly from behind.

"What?"

"Just realised something. Ever since the Blue Planet, trying to locate Nesteri has been our darn regular pastime. Remember that time in the park?"

"Uhm, I do," Hagal nodded without taking his eyes off the manuscript, "and before that, at the concert. Oh, and in that shopping mall. And that café around the corner..."

"Guess what, he did finally get me to try that weird green stuff he kept drinking. Light, I thought it would be awful! But it didn't actually taste as bad as it looked," Tei smiled at the memory. "When I—" he suddenly broke his sentence midway and lapsed into an astounded silence. Intrigued, Hagal raised his gaze.

A painting was there on the right, alive and mesmerising with it the choice of colours, and at the first glance, Hagal recognised the style he had seen earlier in his room.

Against the turquoise skies, a windswept mountain peak towered solemnly amongst the wisps of clouds. There on the rocky edge perched a majestic beast. Its scales were gleaming, dark as the starless sky, its four sharp-clawed paws left torn scars on the ground. Imbued with magnificence and strength, the dragon spread its wings, ready to fly...and for a split of a moment, the Stars thought they could hear the whistle of the frosty wind.

Nesteri's feverish dreams were drenched in pain and haunted by the Shadow.

The hell of the fight swallowed him again, seething with heat and fire, the blasts of attacks and the stench of burning blood. Tei fought there beside him, but too far, too distant to cover, and death was too close. 'Look behind!' Nesteri wanted to shout but his lips didn't move and his mouth stayed dry and silent.

Too late. Darkness swelled and lashed out like an angry knot of snakes, darting through Tei's chest, and the broken cry shook the sky.

Hagal's dead face loomed before Nesteri now, a pale mask, his body slowly falling to the ground, soundlessly like a dry leaf, every moment lasting a lifetime. Nesteri leapt towards him, yet Moriel's flames came first, bursting through Hagal, and in an instant he was gone, turned into ash and cinders.

His face alone remained, seared and black and crumbling, until it was nothing but a murder of crows flying off. *Too late...* An attack hit Nesteri, burning, writhing its way to his core, scorching his bones. The agony of pain ripped him apart, and the darkness spun dizzily as death reached for him.

A boy was standing in the morning mist, alone and with a raven on his arm. The meadow before dawn was grey and quiet, and shrouded in secrets. *"You are too late,"* a male voice said in the hush. *"The stars are gone and you still haven't found the key."*

"Too late, too late," cawed the raven flapping its wings.

"What key?" the boy asked. Nesteri looked at him. The boy's face was his own. "Pray tell me."

A key appeared in front of him, shining gold through the mists, chased with the traces and a filigree of runes. It looked so beautiful, the most wonderful thing Nesteri had ever seen, and he timidly stretched his hand towards it, mesmerised, almost holding the key now, but the raven snatched it away and shot up into the sky.

"No, stop!! Come back!!" Nesteri screamed trying to run after it, but the bird was already gone.

"Too late," said the voice.

"Please, please, come back..."

He felt cold, so cold, a little boy running through the meadows, hopelessly, the ice of tears clouding his gaze. "Come...back..."

"Not until you're ready," said the voice.

'It's a dream, it's only a dream,' Nesteri suddenly knew and yet he was trapped in it, strangely numb, unable to wake up.

He writhed on his bed, his eyes closed but restless. Tei and Hagal quietly walked in.

"Nesteri!" Tei called.

Nesteri didn't hear. "Too late, too late," his lips repeated mindlessly.

From the tall window on the right, the soft breeze wafted in.

"Nesteri!" Tei touched his shoulder.

Nesteri shuddered. His gaze was haunted and blank.

"Nesteri, you alright?"

I feel pain. I feel no pain. I'm dead. I'm not dead. His mind was so empty right now. "I don't know," Nesteri uttered finally in an insipid voice. He looked at Tei as if trying to remember who he was. "We have been killed. You, Tei. And you, Hagal. I know it's just a dream."

"No, no, it's not!" Hagal smiled at him. "Impossible as it is, we are undeniably alive."

"I must be alive, I'm hungry," Tei grinned.

Nesteri looked at them again, consciousness gradually returning to his eyes. He slowly sat up in bed and looked around. "Where are we?"

"Would that I knew," said Hagal. "A castle or a palace of some kind. Too lavish for a prison—"

"Yet it still may be," cut in Tei.

Nesteri looked at his arms and chest and frowned in disbelief. "How come that I have no wounds?"

"Well, welcome to the club," Tei grinned again. "Same here."

"How come?"

"No idea."

"Seeing you in those uniforms makes me feel like I'm back at the Academy again," Nesteri uttered with a tone of surprise. "Where did you get them from?!"

"These were the only clothes we could find," Tei said. "You better organise yourself too and let's run while we can. We've wasted too much time already."

"Aye, captain."

"In the face of danger," Tei said copying their teacher's manner, "a Star should remain vigilant, alert and ready."

"Aye, captain!" Hagal and Nesteri responded as one.

"That's better," a smug smile emerged on Tei's face.

"Whoever sends us all this crazy luck, we're very much indebted," remarked Nesteri when dressed.

"I know, right?" Tei smirked. "I hold my ear it stays that way. We'll need some luck to sneak out of here now."

"Talking about it...do you think Farien may be here as well? I can't sense his presence."

"Me neither," Tei frowned. "It may be that there's only three of us again. Hagal, your thoughts?"

Hagal shook his head. "I don't think Farien is here. No."

"Rats," muttered Tei. "Trying to find him on the Blue Planet was tough enough, and Light only knows where we are here right now. For Andekimi's sake! I hope he'll be alright..."

Nesteri suddenly went quiet, his face cautious and tense. "Did you hear that?" he whispered.

"What?" asked Tei in a low voice.

"The music."

Now they all could hear it – the breeze tinkled with soft notes, coming from somewhere outside.

The Stars looked at each other.

"So we are obviously *not* alone here," whispered Hagal. "The frequency doesn't feel hostile, though."

"A demonoid playing a harp would be quite a view!" Tei smirked.

"Would you risk your life to see it?" Nesteri teased him.

"Get off."

"So what's the plan?"

"For some reason, I can't tell how many are out there. But they are not Dark Stars, I'm pretty sure. Let me have a look."

Tei slunk to the window, quietly opened it wider and looked out. He saw a tiled roof below, braved here and there by blossoming vines, and an open terrace of white stone with a long fountain in the middle. Beyond the balustrade stretched flowery meadows laced with the twinkle of creeks. A distant forest darkened on the left, before the gleaming expanse of an ocean, rimmed with the snowy mountains far north-west. Sweet fragrances, elusive and palliative, filled the air.

Tei pulled his head back in and closed the window. "I couldn't see anyone," he said in an undertone. "I really don't feel like another fight right now." He added after a pause.

"With you on that," Nesteri nodded.

They lingered for a few moments, hesitating, listening to the tune as it wove its magic around them.

"I'm pretty sure they must be Light Stars," Nesteri uttered finally. "I can go first, and if they try to kill me you'll have enough time to escape."

"No way, it's my job to go first," Tei declared brusquely.

"I think keeping together would actually give us better chances to survive," remarked Hagal, reasonable as always.

"Darn, Hagal, do you really have to talk so much sense all the time?" Tei pulled a face then looked at his team, serious again. He ran his fingers through his hair. "Alright, decided. Let's go, we can't be hiding here forever."

The music led them down the white stone staircase, and through a pillared hall to the entrance door. It opened to a terrace framed with a marble colonnade. The gentle breeze shook vine leaves on the pillars. A sparkling sash of water cut into the middle of the steps, descending to a wide balcony beyond. The balustrade's supports were shaped as tridents of the Andekimi's sceptre, surprisingly and startlingly familiar. The curious sapphire leaves of some strange plants were stretching towards the sun.

The Quarta noticed none of that, though. Frozen with wonder, they fixed their gaze in front of them, not daring to go forward.

There on the marble railing sat a Great Star, her slender fingers pensively touching the strings of a lute. Her belted dress was gold and emerald and white; gentleness and a gleam of hidden sorrow were in her ambery eyes. Long hair flowed down the Star's shoulders, a shimmering waterfall of twilight silver. Even now, in the bright afternoon glow, her face seemed to be touched with the softness of moonlight. She looked at them in silence, calmly and attentively. The Quarta held their breath, their hearts racing. The Great Star was too beautiful for words.

"Aimayo-e," she greeted them. Her voice was sweet and hypnotic; the mesmerised Minor Stars trembled as its drenching and disarming power went straight to their core. The magic of her presence was intoxicating like wine.

"Your Holy Grace!" Led by a heartfelt impulse, all three went down on one knee at once.

They recognised Her. Before them stood the legendary Guardian of the Gates of Time Past – one of the Great Stars of the Septenary.

The Quarta knew of her from some incredible half-mythical stories, told and retold amongst the Minor Stars for centuries. Guardians of Light of the highest order, the Septenary watched over the seven Gates of Time and Space, protecting the very foundations of this world from the deadly breath of the Shadow. Ancient like the world itself, their power and wisdom were legendary, and their consciousness was said to remain unbroken since the dawn of days. Their names were called upon in the times of danger, and their deeds became sagas and stories told by the fire. No one had ever seen a Star of Septenary, though, thus many held that those legends were nothing but old wives' tales. *So they were true?* The Quarta could barely believe their eyes.

"We are ready for your command," said Tei on behalf of his team, his head bowed.

"My command?" the Great Star put her lute aside and came closer to the Quarta, still frozen motionless. "I think getting up would be a good start," she said in perfect Siltarionese.

The Minor Stars rose, looking at Antares with awe and godly fear. *It was all too surreal to be true.*

The Great Star tilted her head slightly. "I see you recognise me."

"Yes…" Nesteri breathed out. He looked at Antares with undisguised wonder, drinking her in, like a kid who had miraculously found his way inside his favourite book. "We have the honour to address Mevaneth of the Septenary, the Holy Guardian of the Gates of Time Past."

"Almost correct," Antares smiled with her eyes. "But the name. Let's leave the folklore titles where they belong. Disguises are good for enemies, not friends. You may call me Antares."

"I'm privileged to know, Holy Guardian!" Nesteri tried hard not to blush. 'Antares,' he repeated in his mind. There was something about the sound of that name that made him tremble. "Nesteri Astarrien, at your service."

Tei and Hagal followed his wake.

"Away with formalities," declared Antares. "Someone here is supposedly hungry. We shall be wise not to keep him waiting."

Now it was Tei's turn to hide an embarrassed smile. 'Was I talking that loudly upstairs?' he wondered.

"I wouldn't say no to a breakfast since we're at it," he flashed a cheeky grin. "Or any meal that's fitting. I am not sure what time it is."

"Late afternoon," replied Antares. "Almost five o'clock."

The round table in the corner was overshadowed by the blossoming lavishness of vines. The Stars sat on the wooden chairs carved with chestnut and moonflower.

"It's beautiful here!" Nesteri said, finally starting to notice the world around him.

"You must be full of questions, warriors," said the Great Star pouring an unknown drink from a blue translucent jug into the matching cups. A delicious scent spilt in the air. "Ask away."

The Quarta looked at each other. After some awkward silence, it was Tei who spoke first.

"Holy Star Antares," he began, frantically searching his memory for whatever polite forms of speech he knew. "Would you be so kind as to enlighten us about where we are...uhm...presently?"

Hearing Tei struggling through that sentence made Hagal bite his fist lightly, hiding the expression half way between a cringe and a smile.

"This is Meldēan...the Meldēan Hall. And we are on Lagu," the Great Star answered. "The place I call home, my domain. I have arranged it to my liking."

"You have done what?" Tei nearly dropped his cup. "My word, so it is true?! The legends said that the Septenary Stars could wield reality. Is it true?!"

"It's not as big a wonder as you think. Look – everything around," Antares waved her hand, "is but energy in its different forms. Light, split into a multitude of rays. It's what I am, too, and so are you. The power of thought and will moulds energy into shapes. All that you see as 'reality' is merely a dream of your mind."

The Quarta listened, trying their best to follow and to remember, which in their current state was strenuous somewhat. Hagal wished wholeheartedly he had his notebook with him.

Nesteri, meanwhile, sat mesmerised and quiet, his thrilled gaze fixed on the Great Star, the world becoming a blur. He always stubbornly believed in the existence of the Septenary, despite the taunting of his peers, despite Farien's snide remarks, despite Tei calling him a helpless dreamer.

But even the most wonderful tales were now as bleak as shadows, for to describe the mesmerising beauty of the Great Star was beyond the power of words. Her very presence was imbued with magic, ancient, inebriating, and disarming, healing the soul from sorrow and lightening all pain. Antares seemed so close, and yet so alien to everything he had ever known. Reflections of yore lived in her luminous eyes, and forgotten legends, and faraway lands shimmering with the distant glory of the days bygone. 'If this is an afterlife, it was worth dying for,' a smirk twitched a corner of Nesteri's lips.

"Holy Star," he asked, "are we all dead, then?"

"You're very much alive," Antares smiled.

"But I remember—"

"You don't remember, you assume. Another instant and you would be dead, that's true. The operation was timed rather well, though, even if I say so myself."

"Why the last moment?" ceremonial politeness was never Tei's forte.

"I had to wait to keep the Wave as low as possible," Antares explained.

"The Wave?"

"The impact of my interference on the temporal continuum."

The sound of those words took Nesteri back to his Academy days. "But..." his mind was racing, trying to make sense of it all, "if you please, what possibly would make you go to that trouble? Why did you save us? Why?"

"*Because time is changing*," Antares replied. "You are a rock against which the Shadow must crash and recede. It has been foretold."

Her answer made no sense to him, but Nesteri didn't dare to ask again. He took another sip of the mysterious drink. 'Funny, I don't seem to feel hungry anymore. What even is this?' he wondered.

"Holy Star, I do apologise if you shall find my curiosity excessive," Hagal's command of the courtly language was notably effortless. "But I would like to know how long we have been here, if I may."

"Counting the time on Lagu, one night and almost a day now. No time has passed on the Blue Planet."

"How is that possible?"

Antares cupped her drink in her hands. "The time on Lagu and the planet you came from are not synchronous," she said. "No matter how long you may stay here for, when you return, it will be the same moment you were gone."

"How could that..." Hagal looked up closing his left eye, taking in what he had just heard. Suddenly he frowned, blinked with both eyes, and then regarded Antares questioningly again. He clearly needed some more details.

"Holy Star..." Hagal's voice was now almost sweet, unusually for him. He was dying of curiosity, one could easily to tell. "I would be grateful for an explanation why that is, if you would be so kind."

Antares gave him an enigmatic smile. "You may find out later."

"Later? Could that perchance mean...?" Nesteri held his breath. His attempt to sound nonchalant was clearly failing. "Could we...?"

"Be my guests for as long as you like," Antares said. "I hope you will find it pleasant enough here."

Nesteri felt like pinching himself under the table. "You're too kind. We're honoured and much obliged." The once familiar way of speaking felt odd on his tongue after such a long while.

"Light, yes!! That would be epic!" Tei exclaimed simply.

"We hope it is not too much trouble, of course," Hagal added hastily as if to make up for Tei's impertinence.

"You'd be most welcome," an unexpectedly pensive note flickered in Antares' voice. "It shall be quite an interesting time. I haven't dealt with Minor Stars for centuries."

The Quarta exchanged astounded glances, not believing their luck, unwittingly rising up their right hands with their thumbs and middle fingers joined. The old Siltarionese gesture of joy for more than fitting – awaiting them was the adventure of a lifetime!

CHAPTER VI

LOIVERI FARIENIS EMMENTĒ
FARIEN'S FATE

"The bow is shattered; the arrows are all gone.
This moment is your spirit's whetstone—
Forget the fearful heart, do not delay,
Shoot right away."
~ Bukkō Kokushi

When his consciousness returned, the first thing that Farien felt was the merciless sting of cold and the sharp stones stabbing him in the back.

He opened his eyes, pale amethyst just like Hagal's, typical of Siltarionese Stars. Tossed in disorder, his light chestnut hair was a glaring contrast with the murky brown desert around.

'It's so quiet here…where am I?'

His throat was dry, he realised, so dry. As he tried to get up, pain lanced through him, shooting from the right hip; Farien clenched his teeth. He held his breath to remain silent and slowly forced himself up. A cloud of dust flitted from his hair and clothes. Farien coughed.

A barren plain of reddish brown stretched for miles around, merging at the horizon with a torn ribbon of mountains. Pallid stars twinkled in the washed out sky.

Being alone felt strangely uneasy. Farien couldn't shrug off a surreal impression that the unknown planet was watching him, staring at him in a haughty and insolent way. Frozen silence reigned around, so wary as if the slightest noise could make it burst and rain down with the tinkling of broken glass.

'Where is everyone…?'

Farien searched his memory for the clues, but the scattered images swirled and faded away like sparks in the wind.

They were attacked by the Dark Stars…yes, that was it, he remembered it now, the fight, the blinding blast and the darkness that followed. What was it, an explosion? Farien rubbed his forehead. The blast wave must have thrown him here. There was no other answer he could think of.

The place was arid and hostile, just one of those dead planets where life had perhaps never flourished or had long ceased to exist. No plants, no animals, no birds.

Birds. Farien couldn't explain why he loved them so much. He had always admired the silent perfection of all winged creatures – the smooth, almost lazy glide of dohcair, or the light, timid flutter of bevith, glittering like living emeralds. Even moornē, clumsy and slow on land, in water was fast and gracious, the frightened minnows of the eritl scurrying before it like droplets of silver. A world so beautiful once, lost forever.

Farien was one of the only few that had survived the Fall of Siltarion. Perhaps only to carry sorrow in his heart for ever since, the pain that time seemed powerless to heal. Three years had passed but the memory was as fresh as today; not even thirty years would make it fade, Farien thought. The horrifyingly long night…the assault, brute and sudden, a complete surprise; too many had been killed before they even had a chance to know. Those who remained gave all they had. They fought against hope, doomed yet unbroken till the end, but there were not enough defenders… not enough and they needed a miracle. And a miracle didn't happen.

The Shadow was taking over, shrouding the whole planet with a cold mantle of death, when the last obstacle barred its way. The High Masters stood united against the enemy, arresting the attack force to force. They would not submit, and they would not become Dark Stars. Their magic was ancient and potent, and horrendous was the power that they had unleashed.

It seemed as if space itself warped and writhed at the power of their blow. The enemies' ranks scattered and perished in an instant, but hope faded as soon as it gleamed. More legions appeared to take the place of those who were gone, ever more hellish. The High Masters had delayed but could not stop the advance of the Shadow.

The Quarta didn't see the flurry and the agony of the last moments. The monstrous energy wave had thrown their team and a few others far into space, scattering them and thus saving their lives.

If Demaré were alive, he would likely compose some touching and enchanting ballad...yet of what use would it be if there's no one to sing and no one to remember? Farien's lips twisted into a sad smile. Except for Tei, perhaps, who knew by heart an unbelievable myriad of songs and tales. Being the last apprentice of the great bard was the biggest honour he could ever dream of, Tei often said...

'Tei!' that thought snapped Farien back to reality. 'Where are the guys? It's kind of weird but I can't sense them around...I have to find them, they may need my help.' He tried to move and pain darted through him again. Farien hissed. 'Alright, the damn hip comes first.'

He brought out the Crystal to heal himself – a dim glimmer hardly brightened up his hands. 'With all due reverence, this sucks,'' Farien knotted his brow watching the faint sparkles inside the Crystal. 'I've never seen the energy level being this low. How long will it take to restore, I wonder? I'll have to watch my shadow for now.'

Although still thirsty and drained, he could now move easily again, which instantly made all things better. The Star got on his feet, perhaps too sprightly, and as soon as that a sudden spasm of cough shook his body. 'Damned sand!' Farien cleared his throat. 'Hate this place already.'

Sand was a curse. Sharp, rasping, prickly particles, everywhere. Every move stirred up clouds of choking dust, which clung to his hair and clothes, squeaked between his fingers and flew into his eyes. It was as if the Red Planet intentionally tormented him.

"May it be cursed by thousands of winds!" he swore under his breath. "What a hellhole. Gotta get out of here–"

"And where exactly would you go, daaarling?" a sudden voice made him jump. Farien jerked his head to look behind him.

A young woman sat leisurely on the sand close by. Her far from modest dress, dazzlingly blue against her olive skin, revealed a body that would make any man's heart race. Slowly and seductively, she tossed the glossy ebony of hair behind her shoulders, amusement twinkling in her eyes. *Her black eyes with red rims.* In a second, Farien understood.

"Damn you, you demonoid scum!" he shouted venomously. "Get out and I may spare your sodding life!"

"How scary," the Dark Star said, each word dripping with ridicule. "Was that supposed to be a threat? You're too weak to fight. You're on your own. I could kill you right now – just for the fun of it." The demonoid sneered.

"What stops you then, damn witch?!"

"I haven't decided yet," she answered with a broad smile. "I may do. Ah, no, it would be such a waste of that pretty face. Then maybe not. Or maybe still?" Her eyes pierced Farien again, hypnotisingly licentious. "And by the way, my name is Menorita, daaarling," she added, clearly having a good time.

"I don't care about your damn name."

"Oh, but you should, you should. It's worth knowing your mistress' name."

"You're no mistress, witch."

"Light Stars are so cute. I shall keep you, I've decided."

"Shut up, you sack of slime," said Farien with icy fury, raising his hand to attack.

"Don't you even care what happened to your friends?" Menorita teased him. Seeing his hesitation, she added, "I can tell you where they are...and how they all betrayed you."

"Shut the hell up. Ariya Warriors do not betray their friends."

"That's what you think–"

Farien attacked, not giving the demonoid a chance to finish. Bright ambery flames flashed from his hands cutting through the air. Their scorching breath had almost reached the Dark Star, but in an instant it scattered and faded – Menorita deflected his blow without even moving from her place. Nonchalantly, she fired back a thin stream of magenta fire that forced Farien jump to the side.

'I know where this is going,' the sudden realisation made him inwardly flinch. 'I should have let her kill me.' Although he knew the earlier mockery of an attack would not do it.

"What a hot temper, I like it! I wonder if you're that fiery in bed, too," she said in a deep voice, her eyes half closed. She waved her hand and suddenly in Farien's mind appeared a vision of Tei, Hagal and Nesteri in sunny woodland, as real and vivid as if he stood there by their side. "Look. Look well. They have forgotten all about you."

"Shut up. You're pathetic if you think I'll believe any of your crap."

The vision wouldn't disappear, though, remaining so clear that Farien could almost touch the trees.

"Well tell me then, where are they, why not by your side?"

"None of your damn business, witch. Get lost!" Farien finally managed to force the vision away. The sands of the Red Planet surrounded him again.

"You *know* that I'm right, *daaarling*. If they were somewhere near you could sense their presence, couldn't you? Admit it that you can't. They've left you, that's the truth."

"You know nothing about loyalty and honour, demonoid scum. Not for a moment would I doubt my friends. They will come back, wherever they are. Without me, they can't even leave here. Fight or sod off!"

"You are alone. You know it just as well as I do."

Farien hated hearing those words and yet deep down they rang disturbingly true…his senses told him that much. He had to remain strong, regardless. He could not let the demonoid know his doubts. "I don't believe you for a moment," he said in an icy tone.

"Oh yes, you do," Menerita's smile was poison. "You just don't want to admit it."

She sent another vision, bright and clear, of all three walking by a riverside, laughing. "They found a way to travel without you. They don't care about you anymore."

"Nonsense! They would never leave me!" Farien struggled to erase the memory of what he had just seen; this time it was harder.

"For the cursed arts, stop being so delusional, you're not a kid. Can't you see they've left you here to die?"

"Bullshit!" Farien threw at her fiercely.

"You will have to accept reality, whether it pleases you or not," Menorita sensually run her finger down the cleavage of her dress, her gaze wandering and lustful.

Farien felt something stirring up inside him, against his will. 'She's hot,' the sudden thought flicked through his mind, 'I wish I…' he froze, terrified, suddenly aware of what's happening to him. 'Damn demonoids' tricks! I cannot, must not look at her. I will not let her take my mind over!'

His mouth twisted with anger. "If you don't have the guts to kill me, get out! Be off with you, back to the abyss of worms where you're from."

The Dark Star ignored his outburst. "Calm down, sweetie. Although Light has abandoned you, the Shadow will be always there. Surrender, come into its arms. Drink in the sweet oblivion–"

"Damn you, get lost!"

"You have nothing to fight for anymore. Just follow your desires, delve into your darkest dreams…I know how much you want it, how much lust for it. Look, your hands shake. Come, I'll show you pleasure beyond all you've ever known. Surrender…"

"Enough!" Farien straightened up and raised his hand to attack, when a suffocating blast of darkness suddenly enveloped him, swaying on his feet. The Star closed his eyes shut and clenched his fists, so hard that his knuckles turned white.

"I will not…let you…defeat me," he whispered.

The dark waves swelled pulling him in, throttling and pushing from every side, teasing, tormenting, tearing his consciousness apart. How long it lasted for, he didn't know. The gaping chasm that opened before him had no end.

'That's it, I've done for,' thoughts swirled through Farien's head like autumn leaves whisked by the wind. He tried to stay calm, but fear crept in, unwanted, mixed with a strange dark fire, and he shuddered. 'There's no way I can win on my own, with hardly any energy to fight…guys, why did you do this to me? Why?!' a paralysing, overwhelming sense of loneliness swept over him. From the dark swirling haze, his friends' faces floated up at him, and Farien felt his heart die inside. 'I bloody need you now. Where are you, guys? Where are you?! What if…' he gasped, 'what if Menorita was right?" for the first time, Farien called the Dark Star by her name. The venom of despair was flowing through his veins.

'No! I'm a warrior,' a quiet voice whispered within. 'I'll show that witch what Siltarionese Stars are made of.'

'*You can't change anything. Surrender.*' The waves were teasing him with thousands of eyes, black like the eyes of the Dark Star. It felt as if life was being drawn from him drop by golden drop. The world was only pain and sorrow and the whisper of the waves.

'I must fight...'

'*Your fight is over. You're on your own, alone. The Shadow must prevail. There's no hope...*'

With every moment it was harder to breathe.

"There's no hope..." Farien mindlessly repeated after a pause, his eyes closed.

Yet he was fighting still, with all the energy he had. The black hell stung and burnt, and hissed, laughed and whispered with myriads of voices... luring and tempting with the abysses of eyes, all staring at him, calling and demanding. The dark fire coming from his loins was spreading through his body, slowly taking over, crushing his defences, wrenching and intoxicating, making him crave what Menorita promised with all he was. He wanted her, right now, right now...a hot wave of desire made him tremble.

"Take me...I'm yours," his dry lips whispered, struggling for breath.

'*Surrender!*' cried the Shadow.

'Surrender...' Farien repeated in his mind. 'There's no hope. They've all abandoned me,' a breath of cold went through him, darker than death. 'Light, no, I can't surrender...I cannot...'

The black waves wreathed and hit harder, crashing upon him, as tall as towers. And they *were* towers, first darkening the sky, but in a heartbeat tumbling down in giant blocks of stone, their polished walls collapsing in a nightmare rain of death, inevitable, slow and silent.

"No!!!" The shrieking cry shot up scattering into countless echoes. Farien stood motionless, his face as white as a chalk, the cold sheen of sweat covered his forehead.

Then suddenly deaf silence sealed it all. Ceased the roar and the hissing of the waves; time itself seemed to have stood still. Soundlessly, the black towers quivered and cracked, and crumbled apart, perishing, fading away like the morning mist chased by the wind.

Farien slowly opened his eyes. His breath was rasping in his throat. The world around was a dizzy haze. When his vision gradually returned, he saw the Dark Star still sitting nearby.

"For the cursed arts, you are damn *good*!" astonishment in her voice rang genuine. "I never thought you could come out of that, nobody ever did."

Farien regarded Menorita with an aloof stare. He didn't have the energy even to hate her now. He felt nothing. The struggle with the Shadow had taken all his strength.

"Please…" he wheezed. "Go. Just go. Let me be…"

The Dark Star laughed triumphantly. She rose to her feet and slipped towards him with the grace of a hunting panther.

Farien stepped back. There was nowhere to run. Menorita's eyes were now so close, so close, luring and teasing. Dancing in them was the reflection of the abyss, all that remains after the last hope is dead; despair and exaltation. The black waves…

Her hands burned like fire. Slowly and sensually, Menorita touched his neck and slid her fingers down his spine. Farien shuddered as pain and pleasure lashed through him, both at once. He knew what she would do, but had no force left in him to resist. He was defenceless, ensnared in Menorita's arms.

"Surrender to me. Now," she whispered lustily. Farien felt her breath on his face.

And then, as Menorita's lips touched his, the world around vanished, devoured by a raging whirl of darkness. The Shadow energy burst into Farien's body, ripping through with an agony he'd never known, pulling him in deeper and deeper, blurring his memories, shattering his will.

He didn't even notice when an unwanted tear ran down his cheek – the sorrow of fading Light.

CHAPTER VII

LAGUIS TUNEI
GUESTS ON LAGU

"Eritis sicut Deus, scientes bonum et malum." [6]
~*Genesis, 3:5*

The nightfall breeze was soft and warm, and heady from the sweetness of nocturnal flowers. Leaves and cicadas voices crooned a misty lullaby to the world shrouded in the veils of twilight. A flock of luminous night butterflies fluttered past, soon merging into the starry sky.

Nesteri stood by the open window in his bedroom. He still felt stirred and strangely light-headed after all that happened, and not even his usual self-control could make him fall asleep.

He hated to admit it, but he was envious. Hagal and Tei's words about what they saw around sounded like tales of mystery and wonder; they made him wish he could explore the house, too. Especially the library.

The fact that it was next door down the corridor was only making the temptation worse.

'What if I sneak in quickly just to have a look? Nobody would find out,' he mused. He drummed his fingers on the window frame, hesitating.

'Have you forgotten about all your dignity and your family name, young fellow?' his father's frosty voice rang suddenly in his mind. 'Astarriens do not prowl around at night like thieves!'

Nesteri sighed. He surely had not forgotten. Of all things, he would never forget that.

---

[6] "You will be like God, knowing good and evil." *(Lat)*

'Fine, whatever,' he answered in his thoughts, dispirited. He stood there for another while gazing into the distance, then finally sighed and flopped onto his bed.

As soon as his head touched the pillow, though, the memory of the last night came storming back, washing away whatever little inklings towards sleep he had. The hellish nightmare trembled there behind his closed eyelids.

Startled, Nesteri opened his eyes. The room was dark and still; the vaulted ceiling shimmered vaguely in the scant moonlight. He lay there for a long time motionless but sleepless, imagining himself entering the library and browsing through the shelves, looking at the books, looking at the books, looking at the books.

'Why is it,' he thought, 'that Tei and Hagal got away with it, but I can't? I would touch nothing, only have a look. Is that really wrong?'

Although it might be granted to him, he would not dare to seek permission in front of everyone. It would be lame. And childish. And needy. Unfitting for a warrior in any case. Nesteri cringed at the very thought. His pride would never let him sink that low.

'What if we can't stay here for too long? Who knows, we may have to head back or travel somewhere shortly. We always do. Tonight could be my one and only chance. I would be an idiot to let it go!'

'How utterly ill-mannered,' his father's icy voice intruded his thoughts again.

'But Hagal and Tei–"

'Tei is no paragon for you.'

Nesteri rubbed his face. That dialogue sounded too much like what he used to hear so many years ago. And just like then, the stubborn wave of rebellion stirred up in him.

'At the Academy, we're equal,' he said defiantly in his thoughts. He sat up on the bed, wide awake. The ghosts of the past were fading slowly.

'They both have seen it, and Antares didn't say a word. It would be only fair if I could have a sneak peek, too…it would be only fair,' his conscience thus placated, Nesteri dressed and slipped out into the hall's shadows. He praised in thoughts his Siltarionese vision that let him see clearly in the dark.

The carved library door was now in front of him, the last chance to change his mind. He listened with his extended senses – there was no one inside. Nesteri hesitated for a moment, then smiled a naughty smile as he allowed the excitement of the forbidden to take over.

The brass handle gave in without a sound. Nesteri entered, his heart slightly racing, and carefully closed the door.

The library was bound with gloom and silence. Old paper, wood and leather scents reigned here, musky and enchanting as a love spell. Far at the back, behind the towering bookcases, a golden light was softly flickering, forgotten. Nesteri moved towards the beaconing glow with slinking steps, slowly and curiously walking through the maze of shelves and pillars – the taciturn sentinels which seemed to watch him pass.

The light got closer, bringing out Nesteri's shadow deep and clear; it danced against the book spines like a splash of ink. He turned the corner at the end of the aisle and suddenly froze, cold and breathless, his heart skipping a beat. He wasn't alone.

Surrounded with old volumes, sitting before him was Antares, donned in a long shimmering robe of emerald green. Mysterious energy shapes floated in the air around her, casting warm glares on the gold circlet in her hair. The Great Star held a long crystal in her hand. Her otherworldly, mesmerising beauty was even more bewitching in the quivering play of light and shadow.

"Hello, Nesteri," she said when their eyes met.

The Star stood rooted to the spot, his knees suddenly weak. 'What now? What do I do?' he thought feverishly, his heart beating so hard as if it was about to burst out of his chest. Nesteri grabbed the corner of the bookcase. In a split second, he vividly imagined how much worse it's all going to be when Tei and Hagal found out.

"I'm...I was just...I'm so terribly sorry!" Nesteri uttered finally, chaotically trying to gather thoughts. He never blushed so much in his entire life. "I beg your forgiveness, Holy Guardian! Please do accept my most sincere apologies. It wasn't...I mean, I didn't mean to...Oh Light, what now...?"

Antares smiled.

"Do not worry yourself about that," she said. "I knew that you would come."

"You...knew?"

"Of course I did." Antares conjured a big chair opposite. "You have been ruminating over sneaking in quite loudly, you know…Here, have a seat. No need in being so reserved and formal."

Nesteri slumped into the chair and rubbed his temples. He could not make himself look Antares in the face.

"Our teacher would be so disappointed with me," Nesteri's voice was thick with embarrassment as he spoke. "To put it mildly."

"Why?"

"Because we're warriors. We have been trained to sense if someone's nearby, be they enemies or friends. I should have known that you were here…and never have walked in. What a disgrace," Nesteri lowered his head even more.

"Brighten up," Antares smiled again. "My frequency is very far from anything you've known before. There was no way you could have sensed it. It will come in time."

"You're too kind."

"Just telling you what is. There's nothing to be shameful about, and your teacher would surely know that well."

"Thank you," Nesteri said after a pause. He raised his green eyes for the first time. "I've never felt before like I owed anyone anything. I don't know how to put in words, but…you saved our lives. My debt of gratitude is more than I can ever hope to repay."

An unexplainable expression flickered in Antares' gaze at those words. "Don't mention it. We're fighting on the same side."

For a while Nesteri remained quiet, studying the glowing structures that swam in the air around.

"Holy Star…may I ask what you are doing?"

"Creating guiding energy blueprints," said Antares. Seeing a blank expression on Nesteri's face, she explained "These are to help beings in different worlds remember their true essence."

"Can anyone forget that?" Nesteri looked surprised.

"Yes," Antares lowered her gaze as if remembering something. "A time will come when many will forget…and so they'll stray from their path and fall prisoners of their own mind. To use your power, you must *feel it*," Nesteri nodded as Antares spoke, "but the mind can only offer thoughts and reason. Those who lose the memory of Light within themselves, will no longer know love but only fear."

"What does it mean?"

"For people, it will mean the pain of loneliness and emptiness. Fear will bind their thoughts and keep them in its shackles. And for Stars…"

"Yes?"

"The loss of memory will render them defenceless. You can't fight if you don't know who you are, and what you stand for. Many, too many, will be turned Dark without even knowing."

"That's too horrid to be true!" Nesteri's eyes opened wide. "We must do something. We can't just let it happen!"

Antares nodded. "Yes. That's why I am creating these blueprints, see? Humble as they are, they shall be of some help."

Nesteri looked again at the ethereal shapes, his eyes lit up with wonder. 'There's even more magic in this world than I have ever thought…'

"Holy Star," he began after a long pause. He could not make himself address the Great Star simply by her name; it would be too familiar, too awkward. "If you don't mind me asking…"

"Oh, the mirror room that both your friends saw earlier?"

"Yes," Nesteri answered, slightly discomfited. "What is it for?"

"It's just a training room, as boring as it sounds. For energy combat and meditation."

Antares called to life another golden structure out of thin air, then unexpectedly made it float towards Nesteri.

"You can imprint this one if you feel inspired. Here, simply focus on it and think what you want to happen. Keep your intention strong."

The walls of the citadel gleamed coral and white in the morning sun, but on the terrace leaves still glistened with dew.

Breakfast was waiting for them, fruits and milk and berries, and the neat nuggets and slices of food they could not name, and medariē, the drink from yesterday, fragrant and thick like lucid honey.

They ate in silence as it was done amongst the Siltarionese. The ocean breeze was fresh and ringing with birdsong.

'Farien would love this,' Tei thought, taking a sip from his cup. 'Why is he not here with us?' A dark sting of anxiety pierced him through. 'Where is he...?' Tei resolved to ask Antares straight after the breakfast.

Yet it did not happen the way he planned. The Great Star, who touched nothing except medariē for the whole time, rose from her seat as soon as they had finished, spoke of some urgent duties, and was gone.

"I will return as soon as I am able. Do have a look around, if it pleases you."

Left on their own, the Quarta exchanged questioning glances. There was nothing else to do but to run down the steps, cross the wide balcony of white stone, and entrust themselves to the silent wisdom of the path to see where it might take them.

The meadows welcomed the Stars with the rustle of the grass, the birds' chirping, and a cold trickle of the creeks. Above the colourful splendour of flowers fluttered and trembled auriferous butterflies. Hagal had to admit it to himself that he was falling for the beauty of Lagu. 'It feels as if after all these years, I'm finally back home,' he thought. 'I wish I was allowed to stay here.'

A glistening mirror of the ocean opened to their right, but they cut across fields to a nearby forest, darkening soothingly beyond the silver of streams.

They entered, charmed, under its whispering dome, emerald and chrysophrase and jade; the slanted sun rays gilded the moss on the ancient trees. Giant ferns softly brushed their filigree leaves against the Star's shoulders as they passed. Dunnocks and goldfinches voices rang sweetly in the hush.

It was only for a moment, but the Stars could swear they saw a pair of unusual horses that flicked through the thicket, snow-white and horned, their manes shining gold. The vision vanished without a sound, leaving them wondering if it was real.

Hagal and Nesteri walked side by side, talking about the causal structure, traversable wormholes, warping and other paradoxes that Nesteri liked thinking about. Hagal tried to figure out how it was possible for them to return into the same moment when they travelled back.

"So you suggest there could be a temporal thread or a tunnel connecting both Lagu and the Blue Planet, and that we would return through that tunnel?" Hagal asked musingly.

"Well, it's all just theories and conjectures," Nesteri said. "We have to ask Antares if we want to know for sure."

Tei walked slightly behind, silent. He always hated Temporal Theory at the Academy, and in all honesty, time conundrums did not interest him much. *The only time that really matters is right now,* he often liked to say.

Yet he was clearly swaying from the principles he preached. Before he knew it, Tei's mind drifted from the present moment, far and away, back to the days of his fateful stay on Morionwē... and Tayiu. Tei jumped over a huge root arching from the ground, mossy and gnarled with age. Her smile, her skin, the fragrance of her hair – he missed it all so much that at times it drove him crazy. 'My bliss and curse,' he called her in his thoughts. The hardest trial he had ever gone through. Since Morionwē, life had never been the same. If ever there were any cosmic rites of passage into adulthood, it certainly felt like one of them.

Yes, he did what his warrior honour and duty demanded of him. He remained loyal to his team, regardless of the price he had to pay. And yet... it wasn't good enough, he felt. Tei knew he had faltered and betrayed their trust. There was no denying he had lost his self-control, and with that – much of his team's respect. *Weakness and self-indulgence,* he read in their eyes – an unspoken indictment that made his heart sink.

Hagal was beating his own record of impeccable manners, pretending that he never noticed anything, but Farien and Nesteri were way more direct and didn't care to play their scathing remarks down. He could not blame them.

In memory of their late teacher, it was agreed that Tei was to remain the captain, formally at least, but at the bottom of his heart, he didn't feel he was worthy of that role anymore.

"Look, a clearing!" Nesteri exclaimed suddenly, pointing to their right. There at a distance, trees receded hugging with their roots a small glade that opened to the ocean. Its southern end dropped steeply to meet the restless glitter of the waves below. The gusts of wind came cool and fresh, disquieting the grass.

"Enough walking for me," Hagal declared as he leant back against a tree, his bright hair flying in the breeze. Tei agreed with a silent nod and stretched on the ground, throwing his hands behind his head. Nesteri sat beside him.

"I still can't get my head around all of this," Tei admitted, watching the gulls' errands high amongst the clouds. "It feels like I'm asleep and dreaming…and any moment now I could wake up, and I'm back again on the Blue Planet. You know what I mean?" He paused. "And by the way, we must go back. Farien needs us. And yes, I do remember what Antares said about us returning to the very moment of…brrr, hope at least the place won't have to be the same – but it just feels wrong to be here, idle, while he's looking for us."

"I do agree with you," Hagal said. "But how do we return? As far as I can see, we're stuck here just as we were trapped on the Blue Planet. We're at Antares' mercy, so to speak."

"Ask Her to send us back?"

"And what if She says 'no'? Imagine how humiliating that would be."

Tei cringed. "But is there any other way?"

"Remember, there appeared to be a reason," Nesteri chimed in, "why She saved our lives and brought us here. Surely not just to show us around. Hit me if I'm wrong, but we may have to earn our right to leave."

"Earn our right…" Tei plucked a blade of grass and put it in his mouth. "It does my head in, all this carry-on. Great Stars are weird as heck, can't understand their thinking for the life of me."

"She's not simply a Great Star," Hagal pointed out. "But one of Sacred…"

"That doesn't help at all, as far as I'm concerned," Tei said gruffly.

"She is incredible," a strangely dreamy expression flashed in Nesteri's eyes. 'More like a goddess,' he added in his thoughts.

"Nesteri…?!" Hagal's voice rang with disbelief.

"Oh yeah?" Nesteri grinned. "Tell me you didn't think the same. Not for a moment. I saw *how* you were talking to Her earlier."

"Well…" Hagal smiled an abashed smile and looked away.

"Beware, you two," said Tei in the tone of an Oracle. "If legends are true, Great Stars can be very dangerous." He moved the blade of grass between his lips.

"Look who's talking," Nesteri threw him a sidelong glance.

Tei sighed and sat up crossing his arms atop his knees. "I'd give the world to understand what's really going on."

"Hah, welcome to the club," Nesteri said. "She did tell us, and yet annoyingly I can't make any sense of it."

"Did She really? I can't remember. What was it She said?"

"She said that time was changing. And the Shadow must crash and subside…" Hagal repeated pensively Antares' words.

"That for sure, but how can we help? We can't even sort our own mess out."

"We have been summoned here, so Tei can save the Universe, single-handedly," Nesteri quipped.

"Oh, shut up."

"Why, don't be shy–"

"I see my dearest sister is playing an absent host?" a joking stranger's voice rang startlingly clear.

A Great Star showed before them in his warrior uniform, leather and teal, an azure cloak thrown carelessly over his shoulder. A circlet of green gold gleamed in his wavy hair. His eyes were greyish-blue like northern skies, and shone with an unknown, serene and crystallised state of mind, which the Quarta had never seen before, except in Antares. The wisdom of aeons and cheeky laughter mixed in his gaze.

Tei and Nesteri sprang up and froze side by side with their heads bowed; a second later, Hagal joined them, too. They recognised the Holy Star of Space.

Famaris' eyebrows went up; but then he nodded as if having had remembered something. "Well, hello-hello."

"Holy Star Rāymenn! It is an honour to be graced by your presence," said Tei.

Famaris lips twitched into an amused smile. "Stand at ease. I'm not your commander, after all." After a short pause, he added, "By the way, I do know who you are, no introduction needed. And as for *my* name…The two 'n' at the end are blatantly excessive. Call me Famaris."

"Drinks and merriment for all!" announced the Star of Space. He materialised four crystal chalices with dark honeyed liquor sparkling inside them.

"So, how is life on Lagu treating you so far, wanderers?" he asked handing over the chalices with a smile.

"Err…it's been really good," said Tei, struggling somewhat to keep his composure under Famaris' piercing gaze. It felt like if the Great Star was looking straight into his soul.

"Couldn't be that good if you want to run away already," Famaris teased him.

"We don't! We didn't. It's just…we have to rescue our friend." *How the heck did find out what we spoke about?*

"I know. But to change his fate would take way more than you are right now."

The Quarta gave him a puzzled look.

"Don't ask me, you'll learn soon enough. New paths will open just as soon as you are ready. The Present will not grant you what you want, but the Future may. Just trust the wisdom of time."

Embarrassing as it was, the Quarta had to admit they couldn't understand a word of what he said.

"In other words – don't worry," added Famaris in a tone of explanation. "This rain will too bring rainbows. In time." He took a sip from his chalice and glanced at Hagal. "Ask away."

"My apologies," said Hagal slightly discomfited. "It was no more than a vague reflection, and I would hesitate to voice it…"

"Just go ahead. You know what you are like, that question would then haunt you for a long while."

Hagal gasped with surprise. "Yes, you're right. It does happen to me," he looked at Famaris in disbelief. "You read my thoughts?"

"I could of course, but no," Famaris said. "I only notice those you let float out and about."

"Would you care to explain?"

"Sure," Famaris said lightly. "Your thoughts are energy, and as you let them out of your mind, they float around like so many bubbles. You've been trained in energy combat, though, surely you know about screening thoughts?" He paused. "Ah, sorry, you didn't stay for long enough, I see."

"That's right," Nesteri's tone bore a hint of bitterness, "we didn't. I always wished we could have learnt more."

"Well, it looks like your wish is shortly to be granted. Antares certainly has the patience to teach…" Famaris smiled. "So Hagal, what about your enigmas?"

"I was just putting facts and theories together," Hagal responded. "Some random musings of mine, likely to be boring. I was wondering whether the polytheistic concept–"

"Hagal, use normal words," Tei cringed.

"Very well. My thought was whether the idea of multiple gods could possibly be inspired by Great Stars, to some extent at least. I can imagine someone from the past encountering a Guardian and then weaving that memory into songs, which later became myths and parables…a wild guess, perhaps."

"Not quite that wild," Famaris said with a serene and thoughtful look in his luminous eyes. "There are many reasons and we are only one of them. Although…it is also true that some worlds no longer hold the memory of us, yet they may still remember what we stand for. The people there would give us different names, sometimes correct, sometimes misleading, whatever it is that makes sense to them. And yes, following that train of thought they would portray me often as a god of wealth, the Star of Future as a goddess of wisdom, or Regulus as a goddess of justice…and so it goes on."

"Regulus?" Hagal didn't recognise the name.

"The Guardian Star of Time Present."

"And what about… Holy Star Antares?" curiosity got the better of Nesteri.

"Really, haven't you worked it out yet?" Famaris answered with a cheeky smile, finishing his drink.

He rubbed his wrists and suddenly got up, picking up his cloak. The empty goblets vanished.

"Time is calling for me," the Great Star said. "And you, too, will soon be on your way. Just one last thing," his blue-grey eyes swept the Quarta. "Not everything you leave behind truly is a loss. By letting go of what you used to be, you open doors to what you may become." Famaris' smile was strangely pensive as he spoke. "Hugs and kisses for Antares. Narië!" He added and was gone.

The Quarta remained sitting as they were, trying to gather thoughts.

"Light, they are odd," uttered Tei finally. Famaris' parting words had stirred a stinging restlessness in him. Tei got up, combing his hair back – a habit from the times when his hair was still long. "Back in a bit. See you at the house."

"Where are you going to?" Nesteri threw him a surprised glance.

"I don't know. I just need to be alone."

CHAPTER VIII

NENUI SENOTURĪS
THE MYSTERIES OF DESTINY

The land was traced with a glittering lattice of rivulets and creeks, rolling their cold waters from Averea Heights. Hagal and Nesteri found Antares sitting on a fallen tree amongst the moors. A huge white tiger sprawled at her feet, stretching its neck lazily towards her hand. The stripes and twirls on its fur glowed green.

As the Minor Stars approached, the tiger tensed its back and barred its teeth, and just a heartbeat later it leapt out forward, crossing the distance in a few gracious jumps. Now it stood growling right in front of them – a low, full of suspicion rumble – its tail lashing viciously from side to side. Its yellow eyes glowed with menace. The two Stars drew back a step.

"Quiet!" Antares ordered to the tiger. "O-ie aneis tunei. Renemii," she added in an unknown language.

The tiger looked back at Antares, hesitating.

"*Renemii*," Antares repeated firmly. "Come here."

Still wary, the tiger carefully sniffed both Hagal and Nesteri, then spun and returned reluctantly to plump down at Antares' feet. Its cautious gaze was fixed on the Minor Stars.

"This is Istcé," Antares ruffled the tiger's fur. "Excuse his behaviour, he can be overzealous at times. Istcé is not used to seeing strangers on Lagu. Do have a seat," she gestured at the tree trunk.

Istcé growled again as the Minor Stars moved close. Hagal threw him a sidelong glance.

"Shh, quiet," Antares told Istcé softly, hugging his big furry head. "They'll keep us company for a while, be nice."

"If I'm permitted to ask, Holy Star," said Hagal, "what did you say to him just then?"

"I said that you were my guests and friends. Istcé understands simple words."

"Thank you!" exclaimed Hagal and Nesteri almost in unison, flattered. It is not every day that one was called a friend by a Star of the Septenary.

"I see you've lost Tei?"

"He felt the urge to take a solitary walk," Nesteri answered coldly, as if accentuating every word. It was clear that the rift from the times of Morionwē was still lingering beneath the surface.

"The Holy Star of Space sends His greetings," said Hagal somewhat hastily, in an attempt to change the subject. "I think He was looking for you."

"Oh, Famaris? I know he was around," Antares' smile was soft and warm like rays of sunset. "He was not looking for me, though – that he would never need to do. He was just curious to meet you."

"Why would He never look for you?" Hagal asked, intrigued.

"Because we share a deep energy connection, all of us. We can communicate with thoughts and always know where the rest are."

Nesteri narrowed his eyes. He thought of Farien. 'I wish we too had that skill. It would make life way easier.'

"I understand now," said Hagal. "I first thought it might be because you are siblings. It happens between sibling sometimes."

"Siblings? Ah, let me guess, Famaris called me sister?"

"He did indeed."

Antares smiled. Her silvery hair glinted in the sun. "It's just the manner he speaks. Although in a certain sense, we Stars are all brothers and sisters – the Light that flows through us connects us all. It is in fact what renders us immortal. The body is nothing but a distant image, a vague reflection of the real Self. Whenever the material part is lost, the Light will simply find a new form to manifest through."

"This makes a perfect sense for the Great Stars…but *we* are mortal still," Hagal protested. "I've seen enough to learn that well. More than enough."

"It's an illusion," Antares shook her head. "A dream of your mind."

"But–"

"You are not what you think you are. You maybe think *you* are your body, your emotions, your thoughts? The identity you've created for yourself?"

"Well…that and a soul."

"Those things are but reflections. Your real essence is Light, and even as you go from one life to the next, it always remains true. It is your mind that cuts that continuity into fragments. Your memories are there but locked away, and will remain so for as long as your awareness is asleep. With the Minor Stars, it happens often... hence you don't remember who you used to be."

"Used to be..." Nesteri repeated to himself softly, shocked by what was revealed to him. He looked at Antares, somewhat stirred, his eyes wide open as he realised. "So that means...that a Star can not be killed?"

"Not killed, no. But darkened they can be."

As she spoke, a fleeting shade of sorrow veiled Antares' face, a hint of the words left unsaid.

"...the way he looks. Having short hair is—"

"—stupid and humiliating. Yes, I know," finished Nesteri for her.

They were back at the house terrace, cups of medariē in their hands; the afternoon glow flicked and filtered through the leaves.

Nesteri threw Hagal a questioning glance. Hagal nodded, and Nesteri continued: "It happened when we stayed on Morionwē. That Star we met there... To this day, I don't know what it was she did, but Tei acted as if his brain had melted. He went flat out crazy for her, just possessed. I've never seen him like that, ever." Nesteri paused and pressed his lips together as if remembering something. "She was from the Fixed Stars...she couldn't travel with us – thank all gods for that – and Tei couldn't stay there, either, because of the Crystal."

"He's never been the same since," Hagal interjected thoughtfully. "He is merely a shadow of his old self."

"True," picked up Nesteri. "He *has* changed a lot. He's no longer the captain we once used to have."

"And speaking of the Star..." Antares said suddenly.

Indeed, Tei appeared on the outer edge of the balcony with a bunch of whitish flowers in his hand and a smug grin on his face.

"Hey, check this out," he boasted as he ran up the terrace steps.

"Siētri?! In Light's name…" Hagal lips quivered. "Siētri flowers? How can it be? They grow on Lagu?! Tell me where."

"Pretty much all around," Tei said casually. "Mostly over that way," he waved his hand in the direction of Averea Heights. "This is for you, Holy Star," he added offering his posy with a courteous bow, playfully but flawlessly performed.

"How very kind." Antares looked surprised.

Then miraculously, at the touch of her slender hands, siētri's tightly closed petals started to unfurl as if the night had assumed her reign before its time. A faint pearly glow from the flowers brightened Antares' face. The Quarta looked, surprised and silent. They have never seen siētri blossoming in daylight.

The Great Star put the flowers in a crystal vase that appeared right there, and regarded them with a pensive glare. A vision of Tei collecting them in the meadows floated through her mind. Someone else would have likely double-guessed himself when being in a world he did not know. He might hesitate whether it was at all appropriate and perhaps shy away. Tei did not seem to care. He did what made sense to him, not fearing how it might be received.

"You are…different. Truly you are, Siltarionese warriors," Antares said after a pause, lifting her gaze. "You do what you deem right, no matter what the circumstances. You really yield to no one, do you?"

"Not unless they are fine-looking," Tei answered with a broad smile, the midnight sapphires of his eyes harbouring an audacious sparkle.

Hagal and Nesteri exchanged astonished glances, then looked at Tei as if they had seen him for the first time in years. It certainly felt that way. Lightness and confidence were in his every move. It was as if the magic of the Great Star had washed away all darkness, doubt and grief that long since had become part of him. It was as if his past self had come back. 'But how could that be possible? The past never returns…' Nesteri thought.

"On Lagu, it does," Antares said. "This realm is of the Past; things that are elsewhere destined to wane, find their safe haven here."

Nesteri closed his eyes shut for a moment and took a slow deep breath. Being taken off guard like a child – yet again – was awkward. "That reminds me," he said after a pause, making sure to sound calm, "what the Star of Space mentioned in passing."

"Thoughts screening, I presume?" guessed Hagal who was going to ask the same.

"Precisely," Nesteri nodded. "Holy Star, I hope it won't be too impertinent to ask, but I would keenly learn that skill. If you would be so kind to explain."

"Very well," Antares replied. "I'll teach you how to do it." She paused and looked at Hagal and Nesteri. "Now, both of you. I bid you to forsake the courtly speech. There is no need for it here. You are amongst friends, Lord Trethienn and Lord Astarrien. And stop annoying Tei," she added with an elvish smile.

Her words called hues of blush on both Stars' faces, then chuckles and abashed grins.

Lord Trethienn...nobody had ever called Hagal that. He suddenly realised that as the last in line, the title would indeed be his now. Father's face, with his wise eyes caught in the net of laughing wrinkles, swam up at him from the sea of memory. A strange pang of guilt came with the thought. Hagal shuddered.

"The art of silence," said Antares, "is the warrior's shield. Many paths lead up to it; you shall learn them in time. Mantra is the simplest of all; thinking without thoughts is the one most effective. These will prevent your contemplations from leaking out and being evident to those around you."

"Is there a way to break through someone's screening shield?" curiosity flashed in Nesteri's gaze. He felt as if he was at the Academy again.

"What you can do is down to the level of your strength and training. But there are easier ways of finding out what you want, and more subtle, like the Plerophoric Field."

"Like what the field?" asked Tei. "What is 'pleroholic'?"

"Plerophoric," Hagal corrected him. "It sounds like a cosmic library of a kind."

"It's a good way of describing it," Antares nodded. "The Plerophoric Field is energy that contains the information about everything – all that has or might have been, as well as all that will be and may be. All events, possibilities and dimensions are there as frequencies and codes. Using the power of the Field could make one omniscient if ever there was such a thing."

"Why would there not be?" asked Nesteri. "Are there any data limits?" he added jokingly in the jargon of Blue Planet that made Tei wince.

"Well, yes," a brief smile touched Antares' lips. "The limits of your mind. Few weapons are as powerful and destructive as knowledge can be. The path of knowledge is a warrior's path. Its burden can erode and paralyse the consciousness that is not quite ready."

"So how does one get ready, then?" Nesteri asked again.

"Through meditation. The mindgate at the crown of your head is what connects you to all that is."

"The mindgate?"

"It's what your teacher called the points of power."

"He only told us of three."

"Mindgates are many; the more you consciously open, the stronger you become."

"So…just meditate on the Crown Gate?"

"No. One must not cross that threshold unprepared. It's like a Sword of Light – formidable but deadly for those who can't control it. To bear the weight of knowledge, one needs wisdom first. Start from the first step of the ladder."

Antares' eyes swept the Quarta as she smiled. Suddenly, a dark brown leather notebook and a pencil appeared in front of Hagal. "You're welcome."

"I was just…" Hagal looked discomfited. "I did wish it was there, in truth! How did you…? Ah, of course. How silly of me. Well, thank you. I shall treasure it." He opened the notebook and scribbled down a few lines in a hasty manner.

"The Swords of Light," Nesteri uttered. "I know of them from legends." A vision of those ancient battles and the winged Guardians of Light – the stories from his childhood –came back to him.

"So do I," Tei echoed. "But the ballads say that they had been lost, or vanished, or some such story."

"That they have not," Antares told them.

"Light, so they are real?" Nesteri looked surprised. "I assumed it was an allegory of some kind."

110

"The Swords are real, and they unswervingly fulfil their duty, as they have always done."

"That means that the Great Stars still use them?" surmised Hagal.

"The Sacred Great Stars. Just a few of us."

"But then," Nesteri spoke again, "I heard they were not the usual weapons. Not wrought pieces of steel...something else. Something nobody knew about."

Antares smiled. "That sounds about right."

"About right..?"

"Indeed it does. The Swords of Light are in fact condensed space matter." Antares paused, seeing the blank expression on the Quarta's faces. Hagal raised his pale amethyst eyes from the notebook. "In other words...each of them is essentially a world compressed into a minuscule size. Because of this, they all have self-awareness of a kind. You know the law, I trust – the smaller area, the greater force – it does apply here. The resulting pressure increases the strength of energy a thousandfold."

Hagal tried to imagine, roughly at least, the amount of power needed to condense an entire world and the idea terrified him.

"Holy Star," his voice sounded more like a whisper, "if I may ask...why do you tell us that? If you said that it was not for us to know, I would be not surprised at slightest. Why are you being kind enough to answer all our questions?"

Antares listened while pouring more medariē from the jug. A soft breeze ruffled up wisteria leaves.

"Secrets are born from fear," she said. "And between enemies. The Light Stars know no fear. Not all I know I can share with you right away, though; for some of it, the time is not ripe yet. Some knowledge has to wait until your mind is ready."

"So, Holy Star, you know where Farien is, right?" Tei finally voiced the question all three had at the tips of their tongues.

"I do know, yes."

"What a relief! Could you please bring him here? Or send us to wherever he is?"

"It is not possible, I regret to say. Neither of those."

"But why?!"

"It's doubtful you'd survive an encounter with him and those under whose orders he serves now."

For a moment, the Quarta didn't seem to understand. Then slowly, their faces changed as a terrible guess sipped in. Tei jerked up from his seat, a cold fire burning in his gaze. "Do tell us what has happened. We need to know, right now."

"Please," added Hagal for him.

"Very well," Antares said. She paused. "There was a reason why you could not find him on the Blue Planet..." She told the Quarta all that happened following the fateful fight that separated them, and Farien's last battle shortly after.

They listened in grave silence; Tei dropped listlessly back down on his chair. Nesteri closed his eyes, resting his forehead on the bridge of his interlocked fingers. Not for a moment did they imagine they would never see Farien again. 'Light, is this true...?' Hagal's stare was dead and empty, and fixed on one point. Since losing his family, his friends were all he had. And now even his friends were being torn away from him.

'Farien, you bastard,' Tei thought with despair. 'How could you leave us?!' *I will not shed tears, must not shed tears, not now,* he told himself, clenching his hands into fists under the table.

They were doomed, they knew. As soon as they leave Lagu, trapped in one place, their end would merely be a matter of time. There was no hope. From this very moment, their life was nothing but waiting for death.

"What do we do?" Nesteri's voice was rough and bleak at the winds of the north. "If there *is* anything we can do..."

"He is not dead," Antares told him. "A darkened Star can be retrieved."

"Then we will do it!" Tei exclaimed. "We only need to get there and–"

"Not now," the Great Star shook her head. "You would gain nothing, only share his fate."

"But why...wouldn't he recognise us, really?" Nesteri said, still struggling to believe.

"No, he would not. If the Dark Stars could remember who they are, there would be no Dark Stars. Wiping away their memories is the Shadow's way to keep their minds enslaved. The Dark Stars have no consciousness of this, but they cannot think freely. The energy of Shadow binds their thoughts."

"And yet, can it happen, once in a while, that they still remember something?"

"Rarely. Very rarely. And even then, that memory is no more than a painful thorn. The spell of Shadow is strong, and hardly ever can anyone break free from it on his own accord."

Nothing more was there to say. And so they sat before the Great Star as they were, all three of them, lifeless and taciturn with grief; but no fear was on their pallid faces, only sorrow.

"Do not despair. Not all is lost, warriors," Antares' voice was warm like a sunset. "And your fight is far from over yet."

Tei gave her a questioning glance.

"The future holds many keys to many doors," she added. "Your life can be a bridge connecting worlds, and lead you to a mission greater than yourselves. You have more power than you realise. If you choose to stay true to your higher purpose, you shall be able to get Farien back."

The Quarta did their best to listen and to follow, but Antares' words made no sense to them. Their minds were numb and blank. Silence was all they craved right now.

"Let's talk again upon my return," the Great Star clearly had read their intention. "Until then," she said and disappeared; only a scatter of sparkles twinkled in the air.

A meadow by the lake rang to the sound of swords – Famaris was busy fencing with his double. The blue metal in his both hands flashed, swished and clanged, deadly and quick like a mountain waterfall; Famaris loved fencing, and he loved it well. The double was losing. Predictably.

"Touché," announced Famaris soon enough and erased the double.

"A nice one," Antares appreciatively clapped her hands. "I just don't understand why do you always make them so inept?"

"The fault is not in them," Famaris snorted. "They are fine. I'm just too good."

And it was true. Famaris was *too good*. Antares could recall many a story that proved his words. She stretched on the grass, her dress and wings so white against the dark of green, her hair a cold spell of silver amongst the flowers. Famaris dematerialised his swords and sat down beside her.

"Thank Light for Ewaz," Antares smiled, gazing into the vastness of the lilac skies above.

"My world is by no means better than Lagu," answered the Star of Space softly. He picked a flower and threaded it into Antares' hair.

"The bracelets though..." Antares rubbed her wrists. "Having to wear them all the time is more tiresome than I've ever imagined."

"Ah yes, awful they can be," agreed Famaris playfully, "but what a perfect excuse to come around more often."

They shared the joy of meeting in warm silence. Those who know the unity of souls need no words. The Great Stars saw Existence as the energy it was – the universal wave of Light that lay beyond all levels and permeated them all. They could feel, sense, and see the interlinked oneness, a pulsing ocean of life coming from one Source, beyond love and beyond wisdom, for it combined them both.

Antares nodded as a thin flute suddenly gleamed argentine in Famaris hands – the Star of Space had read her wish.

"My Star, I missed your music..."

For a long, long time, none of the Quarta moved or said a word.

The shadows deepened slowly. The cloudless sky turned into the shade of old bronze, and the twilit world mirrored its hues, topaz, and ochre, and mead. The fountain by the steps splashed liquid gold.

Tei finally broke the silence. Sorrow glistened between his eyelashes as he spoke.

"I will never forgive myself...that I wasn't right there, by his side."

"Tei, it wasn't *your* fault. It wasn't anyone's fault. We couldn't have known," Hagal said quietly, his voice hollow and bleak.

"We should have kept closer together! Or we should...we should have..." Tei whispered fiercely. "I don't know...well, done something! Anything!

We should have been there when he needed us." Tei's hands clenched into fists as he lowered his head. "We have let him down."

Hagal and Nesteri looked at him in silence. They felt the same way, a slipknot of guilt on their throats, their mouths sour with the dull metal taste of betrayal. Their oath was to stand by each others' side. Always. Yet they failed to live up to it. They failed Farien.

A waterfall of memories rushed through their minds, happy and sad, noteworthy and trivial, details that hardly mattered at the time…but now they came back, clear and sharp, heavy with a deeper meaning. The consciousness of loss was setting in, sprouting its suffocating roots, darkening thoughts with a mournful shroud. The evening breeze sighed in the leaves.

Feeling a treacherous tingling in his eyes, Hagal hid his hands under the table and pressed a meridian point under his right thumb. An old trick from his training helped him keep his cool.

"If only we could go back in time…" Nesteri blurted, gazing mindlessly into space. "What if–"

"Dream on," Tei snapped at him.

"But maybe Antares–"

"Time only flows in one direction, Nesteri," Hagal said wearily. "You should know it from Temporal Theory."

"I do, but Antares said that the time on Lagu is not synchronous to Blue Planet. So maybe–"

"It doesn't go backwards, synchronous or not. We should think what to do *now* and where to go from here," Tei cut him off brusquely. Anger tinged his face. 'Stupid loonie, can't he be normal at least in a moment like this?'

"Sure," Nesteri gave in with a shrug. "I only thought it might be worth asking."

"What indeed is *worth* asking," Hagal put in, "is what we can do to rescue him. Antares said there was a possibility, before she left."

"That's true!" Tei jerked up from his seat, suddenly feverishly alert. "She spoke of a bridge. We have to cross some bridge to get to him, or build a bridge, or some such mind-twister. I wish the Great Stars would stop speaking in bloody riddles…" Tei combed his hair back. "Right then, let's

115

try and find Her, and pray that She's still in the talking mood. She's our only hope. Up, up, you two! Let's go."

Famaris had stopped playing a while ago and was now sitting still, his pensive gaze wandering over the lake and far beyond, to the misty contours of the distant mountains.

Antares sighed and sat up.

"What's the matter?" Famaris leant over to gather her in his arms. He liked the energy flow that was born from this closeness – warm, healing, and slightly inebriating.

"That unrest in the sector L-AT28TX-R…" Antares wrinkled her forehead. "I've just been there."

"Hah, let me guess, let me guess."

"Yes," a sly smile touched Antares lips. "They did not even try putting up a fight, just scattered in disarray. I can understand though. There weren't any commanders there, unusually enough, just Loiverai for some reason… the Minor Stars. The number of the darkened ones is growing these days, have you noticed?"

"No wonder," answered Famaris. "The Turning Point is getting closer."

The Great Stars sat meditatively for a while.

"Oh," said Famaris suddenly, changing the subject. "I just had a thought. You know how different energy planes have each their corresponding levels of the mind? Correct me if I'm wrong, but they are all reflections of the four rays time, aren't they?"

"But of course they are," Antares smiled as Famaris teased her with her favourite subject.

And so the Great Stars spoke of the arcane rules, of the subtle levels and the power of time, of the new techniques they had mastered, and the discoveries they had made; and then Famaris jokingly remarked on a complete wreck of a time machine that Sirit had found somewhere. Predictably, Kano had snatched it straight away and took with him to Atar.

He said he would repair the machine but it just ended up lying around, with Kano being way too busy.

Antares knew all well what kept the Star of the Underworld so busy. There was a good reason why demonoids shivered at the very sound of his name...

"My Star," Famaris' gentle voice brought her back from her thoughts. "How are things?"

Antares pensively looked in front of her. "Slow," she finally admitted. "Very slow. The shackles of the sleeping mind weigh on him, strangely strong. It is as if there was something standing in the way. As if his memory was not simply lost but deliberately damaged."

Famaris narrowed his eyes. "What do you intend?"

"You know me. I will find a way. I'm reasonably good at deciphering hidden clues," a corner of her lips twitched into a smirk. "It's just the time...I pray I have enough left."

"What if you...?"

"Farri, we both know that I can't. I must not kiss him. I would not. There is a faint chance it would bring his consciousness back, but a much greater – that the energy would kill him. Nothing is worth such a risk."

"I bet you're tempted still," Famaris said with a cheeky glint in his eye.

He couldn't see her face but he sensed that Antares smiled.

The Star of Time sighed suddenly and softly freed herself from Famaris' embrace.

"I have to go, Farri," she said. "Lanx needs me, and the warriors on Lagu are looking for me as well."

"I know," Famaris nodded. "Till our paths cross again. May the Light guide you on your way."

"And you," Antares returned the blessing.

Lagu had to wait.

Nuru-sha-Shutu called her, where Lanx' army, surrounded by the legions of Scheat, was slowly decimated and pushed back by the enemy.

'I have never seen Scheat venturing so far into the Western territories,' Antares thought with a frown, as she appeared on the battlefield.

Lanx, one of her Lieutenant Generals, was there in his green and grey; his usually sleek, opaline hair a tangled mess of his shoulders. The inferno of deadly blasts surged and swirled around him. Red ran on the right of his face, where one of the attacks reached it. Lanx' golden eyes flashed as he saw Antares. He thanked her with a mental nod; there was no time for anything else.

The right wing was crumbling, as the demonic force of the dark legions descended upon it, ripping through the ranks with the explosions of hellish fire. It broke through the energy screens, sending fragments of soil and dead bodies into the air, but the retaliation came brute and fast.

"Antares is with us!" a bellowing voice cried suddenly through roar of the melee and many others echoed him. "Antares! Antares is with us! Aē annava!"

Those who were not dead rose to their feet again, joining those standing, and leapt to the attack. Light bolts darted across, tearing their way through the shields, blinding, incinerating flesh. Enemy's formation staggered and flailed, scattering into disorder as two armies clashed.

A dazzling beam of white light flashed in Antares' hands, and become a sword. Flames flowed down its frightening blade. "Tseri Meneltar!" resounded her crystal voice.

Scheat shuddered with hate stronger than he could contain. He stepped forward, his hairless head shrouded in a nimbus of grim reddish glow, black pupilless eyes fixed on the Star of Time. Two giant snakes rose from his shoulders, lashing venomously.

The Great Stars stood against each other, silent, as the dark army locked them in a ring. The tempo of the battle had slowed down as if to wait for the commanders to decide.

"Yield!" Scheat screamed through the roar and blasts. A spy had told him all he needed to know. Alpha Scorpii had been taken over by the Shadow. The power of Antares was no more. Scheat was sure of victory.

But Antares laughed.

"Take her!" he shouted to his soldiers, who were drawing in from all sides.

It was his mistake. A terrifying blast brighter than thousands of suns tore the space incinerating those who stood too close. Death came to them faster than a thought. The wounded howled and staggered back. 'One of the Sacred Stars…she is one of the Sacred…Sacred…' a fearful whisper rolled through the ranks.

"Attack!" Scheat yelled again but this time nobody moved.

"Too scared to fight yourself?" Antares jeered coldly. Her sword swung a shining circle in front of her, reflected in the metal claws on Scheat's uniform.

Rage distorted the Dark Star's face. He jumped forward; his long cloak rose snapping from his shoulders like black wings.

"I know of you," he hissed. "Sacred or not, you'll yield to the might of the Shadow, like everyone else."

Antares laughed at him again. "I yield to no one."

A black sword emerged in Scheat's hand – the Sword of Seth, so dark it seemed to suck in all the light around. A ruby-eyed snakehead with an open mouth coiled over its crossguard. One of the Cursed Stars, Scheat had the right to wield a Sword of Darkness. None of its former owners died a natural death, the legend said, and some were found with two small wounds on their right wrist, darkened with poison.

At the sight of the sword, Scheat's soldiers trembled and froze as if an unknown spell was cast on them. The mortifying breath of stupor travelled across the battlefield like a wave, and gradually all fighting stopped. Both armies pulled away, until divided by a ribbon of scorched land sorrowed by bodies of the fallen.

And now there were only two against each other, Light and Dark, their swords clashing soundlessly at such a speed that arms and swords appeared but a blur. Scheat jumped back as if he waged another blow, to win a moment's respite. He then charged again, thrusting at Antares full in the chest. In a flash, the Star of Time was out of the line of his attack, her sword a deadly swish right by his ear. The blade bit into the scaled flesh on his right shoulder and the snake fell wreathing to the ground. Instead of blood, dark yellow slime fountained from the wound. Scheat pivoted in wordless fury towards Antares, but not quickly enough – her blade raked his face as he turned. The Dark Star let out a furious yell.

Darkness, deeper than a starless night, poured out of his eyes, the wild prehistoric horror that paralysed the mind and took away the will to live and fight. But Scheat's spell of fear was powerless against Antares.

Only for a brief moment could the Minor Stars see their commanders clashing in a dance of death; the true fight was not there, but on the higher levels of perception that only Great Stars could enter. It was not their bodies, but their minds that clashed – a will against a will, Light against Shadow.

Parrying Antares' blows was like fighting lightning. She moved so fast that she seemed to exist in different time. With every blow that missed the target, rage was blinding Scheat, a dark wave that gradually clouded his precision, making his movements more and more chaotic. And yet, he only made a slip once.

But once was enough. Another blast came, even more shattering than the first, as Meneltar's blade pierced through Scheat's right shoulder, tearing off his arm, flesh and bone, and stopping on his ribs. Scheat's light armour gasped open, the wound filling quickly with slime-like blood. The attack went through his entire being, so agonising as if his body had exploded from within, the darkness in him revolting against the energy of Light. Scheat howled and dropped his sword, grabbing the stump with his left hand, blood spurting through his fingers. The streams of light stung him, burning from the inside as if hot metal was flowing through his veins. He slowly went down clawing for his sword, his eyes fixed on Antares, then strengthened up again.

Half conscious from pain, Scheat was forced to withdraw from the subsequent energy levels back to the lower planes, where his army could see their commander again: staggering, with a distorted face, viciously clutching the Black Sword in his left hand.

Antares soon appeared in front of him, and as fast as that Scheat swung suddenly and threw his sword at her face. The Dark Star wished for it to go right through her neck, but Antares jerked aside. The blade swished past, its edge cutting a bloody trace on her left cheekbone. Red spattered on the whiteness of her armour. Meneltar flashed in Antares' hands smashing the sword of Seth aside before the snakehead crossguard could touch her.

The black sword hit the ground, skidded and turned, and landed with a rustle of heavy coils. A giant black mamba with ruby eyes lifted its head slowly, rocking from side to side, in the spot where the sword had just been. But before it could leap forward, Meneltar shot up from Antares' hands, a diamond white eagle with vast wings and razor claws, and dived from above, burying its talons in the scaled body. A moment later, and its beak cut into the flesh just under the snake's head. Scheat shuddered and coughed blood.

The giant snake wreathed and became a sword again, then faded into black wispy vapour. Thin threads of soot trembled and tangled like spider webs, until Scheat absorbed them into himself. Meneltar returned and perched on Antares' shoulder.

The Dark Star's face looked like a skull now, his eyes glowing with demonic fire. The spy had clearly lied to him, putting him purposely into this trap. Scheat would find him, seven hells, we would. And ask him a few questions.

"We shall…meet again," Scheat's voice was coarse and raw, "and soon. No Guardians can stop the advance of the Shadow. You will yield. You *all* will yield to me!" He shrieked and disappeared, taking his nefarious army with him. And in an instance, they were gone like a bad night's dream, leaving only the dead behind. The cold wind sighed over the gored plain.

Antares wiped the blood off her face with the back of her hand. Lanx walked up to her. "My general," he began, bowing his head. "Your help was more than timely. The assault was so unexpected, we simply did not have the opportunity to–"

"I know," Antares responded. The laceration on her cheekbone was now gone, only a narrow dark line still remained. "It looks like someone had sent them here. Someone who wanted to bring Scheat down, the way I see it. Double your Watch. Have them scan the space around for disturbances. The enemy may return, and sooner than we think."

"As you command," Lanx nodded and intended to add something more when a sudden spasm of pain cut his breath. His numerous wounds were taking a toll on him, against the effort of his will.

Antares saw that. She stepped forward and put both hands on Lanx' shoulders. The general flinched imperceptibly but then smiled a faint smile. "Thank you," he muttered somewhat discomfited. The presence of the Guardian was soothing like a salve. Lanx closed his eyes briefly, taking his guard down. A wave of healing energy filled him washing the pain away.

When the general opened his eyes, the damage was all gone, both from his body and his armour, as if he moved back in time. Lanx shook his head and beamed a smile of gratitude. It was not for the first time that Antares helped him in the last couple of thousand years, yet Lanx could never properly get used to it. He felt half a boy again, every time she was around. 'There's no other Star under whose command I'd rather serve,' a thought ran through his mind.

Lanx' army slowly drew close and gathered around. Those who had never seen the Star of the Past before, looked at her with curiosity and wonder.

Antares took Meneltar down from her shoulder, and at her touch the sword returned to its old shape. She held it with both hands and closed Her eyes. A dazzling flash of light shot from the blade, forceful yet gentle as a candle flame. Its power, healing and enlivening, flooded all with an iridescent glow. Time became slow and slower…moments drifted by, dense, thick and sweet like drops of mead. The warriors around strengthened up, inspirited, astonished, feeling strength coming back into their limbs. An amazed mutter travelled through the crowd.

Barely visible through the luminous veil, Antares stood motionless, holding the Sword of Light. But in an instance she was gone, the myriad sparkles swirled and faded as if they had never been; only the wind sighed under the leaden skies.

The stopped by the outer balustrade. The ocean beyond was indigo and aquamarine, laced with the streaks of bronze.

"Left of right?" Nesteri asked wearily. The pointlessness of their search was too blatantly obvious. There was no way to even know if Antares was still on Lagu.

"Right," Tei said at random, just so it looked like he made a decision.

A narrow path led northwest. They walked in silence, hoping for the new vistas to lighten somewhat the weight of grief. Far in the distance, the snowy peaks of the Sunori Mountains gleamed softly in the fading light.

The Oumedi River carried leisurely its waters, a wide brush stroke drawn in copper ink. The air was fresh and full of ocean whisper. Night was falling.

"We'll get him back," Tei's voice rang suddenly in the twilight hush.

Hagal cast Tei a questioning glance.

"Just think what our teacher would say," Tei carried on. "Despondency is a disgrace. We have to pull ourselves together. We are warriors. Farien is alive, Antares said. And as long as he's alive, there is hope. We'll find and free him, no matter what it takes." He paused, then added passionately, "Light and all gods, a Star of the Septenary is our ally! We'll get through this. We'll find a way."

His words were simple yet so true, so soberingly true. Hagal and Nesteri exchanged glances. The heavy veil of sorrow that shrouded their minds until now suddenly lifted as if by some magic spell.

'Our teacher knew why he had chosen him for the captain,' Hagal mused.

"Well said, Tei," a strange fire flashed in Nesteri's eyes. "Thanks for the reminder. I needed to hear that. We were too quick to get blinded by emotions. Childish, how very childish. It's not what we were trained to be. Emotions are useless. They can only lead you astray." He threw his right fist forward and Tei and Hagal joined him, all three touching knuckles. "We'll get through this. Our will and Light are stronger than anything we may have to stand up against."

The last glimpses of sunset died away, the world becoming atrament and rustle, rich herbal fragrances and twinkling of the stars.

"Shall we go back?" Hagal suggested finally. "It may be more sensible to just wait for Antares there."

"True," Tei conceded. "Listen to Hagal, he is always right. She might have returned already, thinking about it."

Their Siltarionese vision served the Quarta well, guiding them back through the dark fields and over the creeks. By the time of the first moon, the Meldēan Hall appeared before them gleaming white, as though etched on the canvas of the night sky.

They run up the terrace steps.

CHAPTER IX

VELII KÉIS

THE PATHS OF CHOICE

Meldēan was empty and full of shadows.

As soon as the Quarta entered, large crystals on the walls gleamed dimly and then brighter, filling the halls with a warm glow. The polished floor strewn with unknown sigils glimmered with reflected light. The sound of steps echoed within the walls.

'The symbols…!' Nesteri's eyes widened. He could swear he saw the sigils lifting off the floor and hovering in the air around him like so many auriferous keys. But when he blinked the vision was gone.

"Nesteri, you look drunk," Tei commented nonchalantly as he glanced at Nesteri's face.

"I feel like I just as well may be," Nesteri muttered. "I'm seeing things…"

"Well, that's nothing new for you," Tei sneered tiredly. "I wouldn't mind finding a drink of sorts, actually. I'm not sure if I'll be able to sleep at all after all that."

The sigils quivered again but this time remained in place.

"Have you seen that?" Nesteri blurted foolishly.

"Seen what?"

"The signs…the symbols on the floor, they moved."

"Someone here definitely needs more sleep," Hagal remarked ironically. He had already walked up the grand staircase.

Nesteri mentally scorned himself. It was one of those moments when he would have been wiser to keep his mouth shut. He looked away. "You're right. Sleep is a good idea, I guess," he said to change the subject.

Back in his room, Nesteri took his uniform off and even made himself lie down, however pointless it was. Hours were passing by, long and empty until he could swear he remembered every line and curve on the vaulted ceiling. Finally, he gave up, dressed again and went down to the hall then out on the terrace. The fresh breeze ruffled his hair.

The world was grey and watchful in this pre-sunrise hour. At the far end of the balustrade, Tei was sitting motionlessly, his hands twined over his left knee. Sensing Nesteri's presence he turned his head.

"I couldn't sleep," Nesteri admitted coming closer.

"I didn't even bother," Tei replied, lifeless and bleak. He narrowed his eyes and lines of worry traced his face. It was as if that one night had aged him years. "I couldn't stop thinking about Farien and what had happened."

Nesteri put his hand on Tei's shoulder. "Hey…remember what you said last night? We are alive, there is still hope. We'll work this out," Nesteri repeated those words as a mantra, as if he was still trying to convince himself as well.

"I remember," Tei's eyes betrayed that he struggled to believe it now. "What if we don't? We left him there to die." His head dropped. "I've failed. Failed for the second time." The thought slashed him like a whip.

"Tei, this time it wasn't your fault."

Tei threw Nesteri a brief glance but did not answer.

"Hey, Hagal," Nesteri said suddenly without turning his head.

"Morning," Hagal responded from behind as he walked up to them. He clearly had not slept a wink. His look was feverish and dishevelled, with a strand of wavy hair falling across his face. He didn't care to notice.

Tei lifted his gaze and studied Hagal for a moment – no jacket, rolled up sleeves, the shirt half undone – and a ghost of a smile touched his lips. "Copying my style?"

"What? Ah, that…you mean, this," Hagal put his notebook down and clumsily started buttoning up his shirt, still completely absent. The mute exhaustion, ache and darkness rushed in on him, as if Tei's mood was contagious. "I need a drink," Hagal said in a husky voice. "Light, I'm tired…" He dropped beside Nesteri on the stone floor.

"If you find any booze, bring me some," Tei said wearily, staring into the distance.

The gloom was slowly devouring itself, yielding to the dull hunger of another daylight. At last the golden streaks of dawn shot from behind the roofs of Meldēan Hall, victorious. The sky lit up with rosy hues, hazy and scintillescent like a giant gemstone.

A moment later the cold shadows on the balcony trembled and brightened – and to their relief, the Quarta saw Antares. Clad in dark green and diamond white, the Great Star stood before them, a circlet twinkling in her hair.

"Holy Guardian!" Tei jumped off the balustrade and straightened up. Nesteri and Hagal jerked upright, startled and instantly alert. All three snapped to attention and froze.

Antares looked at them, her gaze mournful and kind. "Stand at ease," she said. And all of a sudden, it felt as though a strange spell of warmth spread from her to the Quarta, enshrouding them, washing their grief away. They understood now, with clarity that made them tremble, the essence of Antares' power – it was the sweet, inebriating and enchanting power of Love, all-healing, all-embracing, transforming the soul on the deepest level.

"How very fortunate you have returned, Holy Star," Nesteri began. "We need your council–"

"The bridge!" Tei almost exclaimed. He had never been the one for discreet negotiations. "Please tell us all about that bridge. We want to safe Farien, as quickly as we can. We'll carry out your orders. Just tell us what to do and we'll do it."

Hagal remained silent. The awareness of what a mess he was right now dawned on him, painfully clear. The Star cringed and looked down. No more was there to add to what had just been said, anyway.

"Very well," Antares said. "I can show you the paths of choices…if you're ready."

"We are ready," Tei blurted out, not really sure if what he said was true.

Antares nodded. "It will be as you wish. Not here, however. Places keep their memories too well. These walls need not hear what will be spoken."

"As you command, my lady," Tei bowed his head briefly.

"Stubborn you are indeed, Siltarionese Stars," Antares looked at Tei pensively somewhat, narrowing her eyes. "There is no need for titles, I believe I told you that before."

"I'm sorry I forgot," Tei said hastily. "Too much to think about, all at once."

"Look behind you," Antares suggested out of the blue.

The Quarta turned their heads. There on the balustrade, three faceted crystal cups glimmered in the morning light.

"Medariē for the road," Antares smiled lightly.

Nesteri thought he heard a hint of tiredness in her voice.

They headed north, towards the Sunori Mountains, through the sunlit tapestry of brooks and meadows.

The Quarta walked in silence, trying to keep their minds empty of thoughts. The silence let their senses deepen, open up, and drink in all the magic spilt around – the cold tinkling of water over stone, the whispers of the grass, the unknown birds ringing high amongst the clouds.

A little grove welcomed them with a quivering dance of sunshine in the foliage, white-rimmed and filigree. Antares who walked slightly ahead stopped by a fallen tree to wait for the Quarta. A wandering ray of sun brightened her face then slid playfully down, to her neck and shoulders, till it was lost, caught in the shimmer of her hair. 'Light, she's breathtaking,' Nesteri thought despite himself. And suddenly, the world was gone, all fading, melting into white except Antares' face, and a strange shiver took over him. When their eyes met, Nesteri's heart skipped a beat, his throat suddenly dry. He looked away at once, as quickly as one would in panic.

Tei and Hagal sat on the fallen tree before the Great Star and Nesteri on the grass beside them. He was still trying to shake off a lingering feeling of inadequacy as if he had done something wrong...something to be ashamed of. But what? He wasn't sure. Right now, there was no time to think about it.

"Listen then," Antares spoke. "With every choice we make, we open up new realities and close some others. Best strategy is to navigate in such a way that keeps numerous doors open, as many as possible. But what you were doing, you were gradually cutting your choices down, until you had reached your dead end, quite literally. That fight on the Blue Planet was supposed to be your last. I think you can see that for yourselves?"

The Quarta nodded and Antares continued, "It's like the game of chaturanga, or chess. You will find that every time you make a move, the world responds to it in a certain way, and with some experience and dexterity one can predict those responses and play to win. But there are also powers greater than ourselves...and those can overwrite all choices, throwing you right into the Mirror Time. It's something you have now lived through. You call such happenings 'miracles' but there is an order to them as well. The Universe is all patterns within patterns within patterns..." Antares paused. Her luminous eyes studied the Minor Stars. She knew this test was what they needed to be free. It was going to hurt, hurt badly, she also knew. Part of her wished she didn't have to do this.

"You have three choices," unexpected weariness rang in her voice again. "Or perhaps potentialities would be a better word. There is, of course, a possibility of going back to the Blue Planet where your lives would be taken by the demonoids, right there on the spot. You don't consider that, I hope. Another path would be to remain on Lagu for a time, allowing destiny to fulfil itself. If so, you would be able to get Farien back." Tei pressed his lips together at her words. "Lastly, you could create a time loop and return a few years back, to the days of your homeland. You would retain your present consciousness but dimmed. In other words, you would know everything that would happen later, yet with no power to change anything."

Tei shook his head. "Too much, too quick. I'm sorry, Holy Star, but please explain this once again. What time loop?"

"It's time with no future."

"Thank you, I know that. Temporal Theory has never been my thing, it's true, but I remember that much. What I mean is... is us going back to Siltarion really going to be that bad? I'm quite sure we could work out something once we are there," Tei looked at his team. "Am I right, guys?"

"Absolutely!" Hagal's face lit up. "We would be perfectly fine. Better than fine, in truth. I agree with Tei completely." He glanced at Nesteri who was silent, but it didn't matter. "If only we could go back to Siltarion, it would be all I could wish for."

"One thing to keep in mind," Antares said slowly, "is that that choice would only make you go through everything once again – and nothing more. The trap of the repeated time can often be a soul-destroying torture. You're sure it's what you want?"

"Yes...yes, I am," Hagal didn't seem to listen, i̶ ̶...̶ ̶d̶ with hope. "Whatever it takes."

"Very well," Antares said. "But before making your decision final, ask *both your heart and your mind* for counsel."

"So...can we really cross to the other side, right now?" Hagal asked almost in a whisper, transfixed on the portal, his heart beating a heavy drumbeat at his temples. 'Don't, don't...don't jump in, not yet,' he repeated in his thoughts feverishly, his breath stuck in his chest. 'Don't you dare. Stay. Stay here. Let Tei go first.'

"It's open both ways, yes," Antares' voice was soothing silver.

As if to prove her words, a pair of yellowy-blue bevith emerged out of the portal and chirruping flew away. The Quarta watched them disappear into the distance. 'So this is how sietri got onto Lagu...' Hagal thought.

It felt all too surreal to be true, their long-lost homeland just as they remembered it – the meadows dappled with pale morning sunshine, the scudding clouds on the aquamarine sky, the crystal mountains barely visible and the distance...a dream, an impossible dream come true.

The Quarta stood, strangely paralysed, gazing through the portal.

"If you let your past become your future," Antares said, "it's all you'll ever have. In your present time, Siltarion is gone; yet all those years since then you'd lived looking back, with no purpose ahead, only regrets."

Tei sighed. 'She's probably right,' he had to admit to himself. "So even if we do go back, nothing would change at all?" he asked.

"You'd die in your current body. Your consciousness alone would travel, only to become a silent witness to all the events that are fated to unfold. Farien would remain as he is."

Tei frowned and bit his lower lip. Going through everything once again suddenly appeared too painful to consider; and yet the temptation was still there. Going riding and shooting with his older brother would certainly be fun. And that bunch of timewasters, Day, Terenel and Fiorran, and Egelvi, better known as Lordie Lord, would all be waiting there for him with their usual jokes and nonsense, and terrible ideas that only their collective genius could produce.

Tei smiled at the memory, but his smile faded as he thought of the Fall. He wasn't sure he had the strength to witness it again. And then there was the Blue Planet... and Farien. And Morionwē. Many things were there that made him shudder. Moments that he wouldn't want to look back at. After a pause, Tei turned to his team. "You heard it. Care to share your thoughts?"

For the first time since they left Meldēan, Nesteri broke his silence. His eyes flashed with an unusual expression as he spoke.

"I'd give a lot to be back home," he said, "but he turns not back who is bound to a star. There clearly was a reason why our lives have been saved. It doesn't matter whether I can understand that reason, but such a debt cannot be taken lightly. Our honour bids us to replay it, and we can go no sooner than it's done. I'd never let petty emotions sway me from my duty." He paused. "And if you're asking for my personal opinion, Tei, I'll tell you this. I haven't got a clue what staying on Lagu is going to be like. But I'm ready to accept whatever happens on the unknown path, if following it I serve Light. That's me."

He fell quiet again and turned away, pensively staring through the portal. Nesteri thought of his raven Dragh, the only living soul he was close to back in his Siltarion days. 'Tei must miss his friends,' he mused. Friends, heh? An ironic smile twisted Nesteri's lips. There were a few who would offer their company at times, and share a drink and a laugh, and even put up with his 'strange ideas about the world'... for as long as he played it down. They didn't know who he really was underneath the mask, and they didn't care to know. In all truth, those meetings usually left him tired. Books tended to be better companions than people, Nesteri had discovered.

Particularly people like his parents. From his youngest years, it always seemed to him like if they lived somewhere in a distant world which was their own. It was cold and aloof, and spiked with rules he couldn't understand. Nesteri rarely saw his parents talking to each other. As he grew older he couldn't help but question what it was that kept them together. They spoke to him only when they had to, and more often than not it was an admonition of some kind. Something he should be doing or shouldn't have done. Did he love them? He did, he thought, but he did not miss them. He never seemed to miss anyone. Somehow he always felt alone, even in a crowd. 'Maybe there is something wrong with me, after all,' Nesteri wondered, not for the first time.

Tei stood deep in thought, his eyes half-closed, weighing Nesteri's words. Then slowly, almost hesitantly, he turned to Hagal. "Nesteri's talking sense," he said.

But Hagal didn't seem to hear. He froze, mesmerised, with the rest of his willpower fighting a magnetic pull to go back right away, to forget all reasons and all logic and just go. Everything he ever loved was there, so close, so close, and the fields and the skies of his childhood were calling for him. Memories flashed through his mind, the people and places and times he missed so insanely much. Only one step and...

He could be back home, where his family waited for him. He could be there with them, for them, could see their smiles again.

Right now.

He could read Natya, his sweet youngest sister, her favourite bedtime stories. She would always ask if he had written any new...

It's only one step.

There's an unfinished novel on the desk in his room...

One.

Step.

A miracle he didn't even dare to pray for, his dearest wish would come true, now. NOW.

He could do it...

He could...he can, he will!

Go for it, go!!

"Hagal?" Tei's voice suddenly shattered the spell and forced Hagal back into the present moment.

Hagal flinched. A different memory had stormed into his mind, unwanted, uninvited. He tried to push it away but it came back, more vivid. The memory of Morionwē. Tei's story. The hell he must have been through. The pain that had scarred his soul, and robbed him of all he used to be. And yet...Tei did not let them down.

Now it was Hagal, *his* loyalty and honour were put on test. It was *his turn* to show what he was made of.

His hands unwittingly clenched into fists. If he yielded to his longing now, how could he ever call himself a warrior? *"One day, you will face a choice that is greater than yourself,"* his father said to him once. *"Remember this. Never choose what is convenient. Choose what is right. It can be hard, but the truth is hard sometimes."*

Hagal knew he could not respect himself if he forgot his duty. If he ran away like a frightened child. The only choice was there, torturously clear. He would not let his friends and comrades down. He would not become a traitor.

'Damn it all!' Hagal lingered for a few more moments, his eyes crinkling to stave off the unexpected tears. The Star focused on his breathing, struggling to bring his composure back. After what seemed like an eternity, it worked. Hagal breathed out through his clenched teeth.

"I am with you."

He threw a farewell glance at Siltarion, which he was now losing forever, for the second time.

A pale horn of the fourth moon was rising slowly over the rocking obsidian of the sleeping ocean. Far away, a night bird made itself heard, and another answered. A light breeze rustled through the trees.

Antares looked down from the balcony, her hair bright with moonlight shimmer. She thought of the days bygone, and the legends of old, and the long forgotten worlds she once knew. The ocean was sighing softly, its waves anointed with cold shine. The night was drawing to an end.

A soft glow flashed by Antares' side banishing the shadows, as if the morning came before its time – and in a moment, Sirit was standing there. The Great Star was still in her warrior uniform, red and gold; a cloak of dazzling white flowed down from her shoulders. It was clear she had just returned from a mission.

"Sirit, Aē kē tonellyé, Light is your guide! Good seeing you."

"And you," Sirit smiled. "All seems to be well?"

Antares' gaze turned pensive. "I would say so. They are strong. Although it hasn't been long enough for them to get back to their senses fully, I believe."

"We still have time," Sirit answered, for a moment as thoughtful as Antares. "You know I trust your judgement, just as you would trust mine." Sirit changed her look into a long gown, dark like vintage wine.

Antares nodded.

"The sector L-72DXRT-226," Sirit continued, changing the subject. "I heard what happened there."

"Yes," Antares said. "Someone had sent Scheat down to take Nuru-sha-Shutu, it appears. He clearly did not hope to see me."

"We need to check that trail. It may be a just ploy, but it could give us some hidden details." Sirit paused and suddenly a light smile touched her lips. "We've got company."

"We do indeed," a smile flickered in Antares' eyes as well.

Even before the arched front door of the house opened, before the sound of steps could reach their ears, the Great Stars could tell who it was.

Walking towards them down the moonlit stairs was Nesteri. He looked like someone who wished he could turn back but it was too late. What made him come here at this hour at night? Nesteri wasn't sure. He blamed his mind, too full of questions to sleep.

He looked at Sirit with his eyes lit up with wonder. "Holy Star of the Future?" he asked affirmatively, bowing his head and putting his right arm across his chest. "It is an honour."

"Sirit," the Star of Future said to him. "Well met." Even the cold moonshine was powerless to dim the bright gold of her hair.

Nesteri's gaze swept over both Stars of Time. "Let me guess. You knew. You knew even before I came here, right?" For a split second, he felt awkward like a child talking to adults.

"We did, yes," Antares said.

Nesteri sighed and rubbed his forehead. "I guess I'm still not used to the fact that you know everything."

"Not everything," Sirit answered. "Nil ut nimis," she added in a language Nesteri never heard before.

And yet, to his surprise, he understood her words as readily as if they were his native tongue. *Nothing except what's necessary.* How could that be?

What language was that? 'Oh great', Nesteri thought, 'more questions. Even more flipping questions.' Just what he needed most.

The night, meanwhile, was hesitant to leave; she lingered shyly, whispering in the leaves, hiding from the brazen attention of moonlight, sighing behind the balustrade. Full of life nocturnal shadows enclosed the balcony like a velvet wall, now and then glancing timidly with the luminous eyes of sietri.

All three sat on the benches called into existence by Sirit, and Antares made silver chalices appear. 'Mediarië,' Nesteri guessed taking a sip, but he was wrong. The drink was very different, dense, and sweetly scented. And heady, he quickly realised.

The conversation flowed and glittered like a tranquil river; the melody of Antares' words mingled with the crystal clear notes of Sirit, and Nesteri listened to the music of their voices, enchanted. The drink felt warm inside him, slowly filling his body and his mind with quiet bliss. The tension that shackled him at first was gone, all vanished away. Unexplainably, the Great Stars seemed so close now, as close as nobody had ever been. Nesteri glanced at Antares sitting on his right. The magic of her presence seized him for a moment; when he met her gaze his heart stopped, and then fluttered like an ensnared bird. Nesteri pressed his lips together. Falling under that spell would be too easy. He could not, he *never would* allow that to happen.

The two Ceiverai shared the stories of uncharted realms, of higher dimensions and of distant kingdoms; and as they spoke, an inexplicable longing grew in Nesteri, a strange burning for the places and the times he had never seen.

Now he understood so much more – why the Septenary was so rarely seen by the Minor Stars, why Vanand's face was always covered with a hood, and how her power over music was different from the force that Aratron possessed.

Despite his ardent efforts, Nesteri eyelids were gradually getting heavier; the toll of sleepless nights was weighing upon him. The fourth Moon, Eilya, stood high in the zenith.

"Antares, why don't you sing something for our guest?" the Star of Future suggested suddenly.

"I suppose I could," a fleeting smile, half-knowing, half-amused, flashed in Antares' eyes.

Asteen appeared in her hands, a dark chestnut base with softly glistening rows of strings. Antares played a few chords for a test, and a heartbeat later her voice filled the crystal stillness of the pre-dawn hush.

Taken off guard, Nesteri swallowed his breath – never in his life had he heard anything so... mesmerising. The music flowed and trembled weaving its spell over him, through him, becoming one with him. Nesteri listened, hungrily, rapaciously, drinking each sound in as if it were an elixir of life. He realised, despite himself, something moved deep inside his heart, something he didn't even know was there. He felt drunk, and alive, alive like he had never been before.

Sirit was listening too, resting her chin on the roof of her interlocked fingers, her emerald eyes half closed, thoughtful.

Nesteri thought of nothing. He was looking at Antares, hypnotised, unable to take his gaze off her. Strange gentleness brightened up her face...

He woke up to the rumble of talk and laughter coming from downstairs. Nesteri got up and looked through the window. On the balcony stairs down below, he saw Antares with Tei and Hagal sitting next to her.

"It's just how it was. Nesteri would write the lyrics and I hassled with the tune," Tei said. "And then we sang together. Or with... Farien. Or I just sang myself. Even back in the Academy times. I always played music."

"And I played the grateful audience," Hagal chimed in.

"What, can't you sing, Hagal?" Antares teased him.

"But of course I can!" Hagal protested indignantly. "I am a warrior, we have been trained. One cannot master his mind without mastering his voice. It's just... I just prefer to listen."

Nesteri passed through the main hall brightened with the timid morning sunshine. The heavy terrace door stood ajar.

"Hah, I wish!" Tei's voice was coming from the outside. "I sure do. But it takes..." He paused noticing Nesteri. "Oh, look who is coming! Morning."

"Morning, Nesteri!" Hagal and Antares turned their heads as well.

Nesteri entered the terrace and lingered for a moment. The memories of last night were fading now, ephemeral and wispy like curls of smoke. Did all that really happen? Was it a dream? He wasn't sure. The rustle of leaves was too ambiguous an answer.

"Nesteri, what's up?" Tei threw him a puzzled look.

Nesteri realised he stood in silence for a while, forgetting to answer greetings, looking blank. He lowered his head to hide an awkward smile.

"Err, morning, morning. A bit sleepy still," he said joining the rest. "All's good." The Star spotted a big silver plate in the middle with slices of fruits. He picked one.

"Sorry, Hagal," Tei said, returning to the previous subject. "I interrupted you again. So you were saying?"

"Nothing too interesting, as usual," Hagal smiled. "Just random thoughts. I was just saying that in Laeriē, our kingdom on Siltarion, we had an old adage 'bright as hair' when someone was innocent, remember? It would sound funny if someone said that about you, Tei."

"True," Nesteri added. He tried all fruits from the plate and was wondering what to do with his sticky fingers now. "Most Laerians had sandy hair, or pale, or grey…Tei is quite an exception."

"An inglorious one," Tei grinned. "Well, I'm not sure why this is. My granddad, probably…or might be even earlier. I don't know much about it. I'm a stray, really, nothing like the Trethienns…or the Astariens. Nesteri's family is one of the most ancient ones."

"Ancient it may be," responded Nesteri somewhat pensively, "but it's all just ash and whispers. The legend goes that once our power was greater than that of the House of Trethienn and even of the Noriats, but centuries passed since."

"Well, at the Academy, it didn't matter where you came from," Hagal interjected. "Only how well you fought. Myself I was reasonably good in energy combat, but Tei was always better with melee weapons."

"You forgot to add – with singing," Tei sniggered. "Oh shut up, Hagal, you were just as good as me."

After some hesitation, Nesteri finally tore off one of the leaves by the stairs, quickly wiped off his fingers and threw the leaf away, pretending he knew nothing about it. "So what's the plan for today?" he asked.

"It's our last day in Meldēan," Antares said, "spend it however you like. Get some rest."

"Last day?" Tei asked.

"There is much more to see on Lagu than one decrepit house," Antares smiled. "Besides, adventures–"

"Oh," Nesteri put his hand across his face in a mocking manner. "Please don't mention the a-word to Tei, whatever it is, he will get up and run there. Straight away."

"Come on, I'm not *that* bad!" Tei grinned. "So, when are we leaving??"

"I will be back at sunset," Antares said. "We shall leave on the morrow."

'Oē sandori umené ta,' the triangle of Regulus' thought was slowly fading in the air.

'Time is nothing but a vessel.' That thought had an irregular shape and Vanand had balanced it out by adding some spherical elements, 'the point without a beginning and an end exists eternally, creating a counterbalance for the predetermined continuity. Light is a domain of the former and the master of the latter.'

'Yet I am surprised.' The streamlined shape gave the thought a peculiar trajectory. 'Active vibrations of mental impulses rule over chaos by creating new conditions for the theoretical causality and that–'

'–that is nothing but a proof of its flexibility,' Vanand picked up on the thought. 'A perfect form always creates a synergy with the content, and the aim of evolution is the eradication of stereotype. Here change is the condition of stability.'

Next to the Great Stars, a few embers fell softly from the sky, gradually turning into snowflakes covering the ground. Frosty fields glittered in the moonlight for a moment, but then the sun rose, fetching irises and daisies from under the snow. Regulus thoughtfully plucked one of them. In her hand, the flower had become an orange, but as the Star opened her hand, the fruit spread its wings and fluttered away, a bird already. Meanwhile, a nearby forest was fading out of sight, soon to reappear elsewhere. Such was Regulus' world Mannaz.

'This is a common rule,' typically for the general statements, the thought of the Star of the Present took the shape of a cube. 'But the intrinsic power of emotion would surely enhance the mental impulse at its core?'

'Excess disturbs the balance. A manifesting impulse must be controlled and unbiased,' lecturing notes flashed in Vanand's thoughts. 'The oneness of all Creation leads one to a logical conclusion about the superiority of a universal key. This brings one to the logical conclusion that the manifesting impulse should be independent of the influence of emotions, which inherently do not tend towards a universal plane of expression.'

Regulus nodded – she agreed with Vanand.

A storm broke out at night. The squally wind shook the ancient trees, black clouds glowed and bellowed with the fiery cracks of lighting. The rain came down forceful and heavy, ringing against the windows. Its dark wings flapped on the roofs of Meldēan Hall and crushed, surrendering into waterfalls of trickle.

But the new day started its reign calm, as peaceful as is if the storm had never been. The wind subsided, leaving in its wake thousands of glittering diamonds of dew. Birds timidly looked out of their nests.

Antares greeted the dawn in solitude. She was flying towards the Aven forest, brushing her hand against the rainy dampness of leaves. The water droplets flashed with little rainbows in the morning sun.

Far to her right, the solemn peaks of the Sunori Mountains towered over the Oumedi River. Further east lay Lhor Xian with its lost secrets, and Ogē Nuvai, the Vale of Great Lakes, shimmering in its slumber. Beyond that stretched the cold expanse of water, barren and wind-ruffled. It was the mystical North Ocean, where from the Drifting Isles came at night the plangent wailing of teriu, and where on the White Archipelago grew the Magic Trees.

The western border of the Aven forest was a rocky beach, disquieted by the impatience of waves. Antares found a boulder to land on, speckled with moss and little shells. The Great Star sat down. The West Ocean opened before her, brightening slowly. Antares frowned as she thought about Vega and the strange skeins of fate that first had taken him away and now had brought him back.

Long and dark was the battle of Aris; its monstrous bellows had devoured more lives than Antares wanted to remember. It was Famaris who had finally found her on the battlefield, too close to death to fight, and took her out. Win they did, but the price they paid gave the coveted victory a bitter taste of defeat. "I will return," Vega said before he took the final blow, before the Shadow whirled him away. "I'll return to you."

But centuries came and faded away, silent. Oh, she looked for him. Yet only silence came for an answer. Vega's frequency seemed to be gone, lost for this world, and the world became darker. Still, she knew, knew as one knows in the middle of winter that a spring shall come, that his soul would find its way back to hers. His love and his promise were the strongest of bounds. And she prayed for the day when Vega would hear her call.

And return he did, although not as Antares' dreams whispered. Tragic was the occasion that had summoned him back, and torturous it was to see him. *Vega, her Vega was there with her...!* And yet he was not. His gaze was the gaze of a stranger, polite but cold. Just like Sirit had said.

Antares closed her eyes. She understood, with frightening clarity, what kept Vega away for so long. As if a locked secret gate had opened for her, she could suddenly see it all – his agony when captured and tormented by the Shadow; still alive, but life leaving him slowly, so slowly, as the cursed flames were burning at his feet, and yet with all strength left in him, Vega kept fighting...even as the flames engulfed him, even as dark poison started flowing through his veins. He did not yield. The pain was trickling down in streams of red, scorching, blinding, and yet the Shadow did not, could not force Vega to bow his head, not once. The final blow came in a shattering blast – the messenger of death Vega wished for – the raging hellish blaze consumed him, burning through, disfiguring his mind. And he was gone.

When he was born again, his scarred soul had lost the memories of who he had been. For many lifetimes since, he tried to find his path, wandering, searching sightlessly, led only by a strange vague longing from within, the feeling that he was meant for something greater, something he could not fully understand. He was not anymore the Great Star Antares knew.

140

"My light and life," Antares's lips moved soundlessly. She had to find a way to heal his scars and bring his consciousness back. She realised now just how hard her task was going be. Antares could already see it – his current mind, the mind of a Minor Star, was quick to mistake the ego for integrity. It clung to its beliefs and limits. It would not listen to the truth, not even put in the plainest of words. What could she do?

For a while, Antares listened to the lapping of waves.

The resonance principle, she thought. Being around, Vega would inevitably take some of her energy in. That power would begin to change him, wake him up, until he could remember. How quickly though? There was no way to tell.

Antares sighed and put the bracelets back on then got up, rubbing pensively at her wrists and temples. The bracelets vexed her. She never had to wear them for this long.

Chapter X

Svada Orini

The Journey Calls

Their path led south, over the verdant fields and tracery of streams carrying their healing waters from the Averea Heights.

Nesteri lingered for half a step and looked back. The long grass bowed and whispered in the wind. Far in a distance, Meldēan beaconed white, a small dot. 'I bet we'll never return there,' a strange thought crossed his mind. 'And if we do, it won't be the same us anymore.'

Noticing Nesteri's gaze, Hagal turned his head too, and a passing melancholy touched his heart. It had been only a few days, yet unexplainably, Meldēan felt like home. Hagal glanced ahead, to where the shadowy vaults of the Aven Forest waited for them.

The road unfolds into the mist
The lands unnamed and tales untold;
The wind and stars will guide our way
And heal the memories of old…

He mused. 'The memories…'

He noticed it now, the long-forgotten feeling. A strange serene emptiness within, where pain used to be. The burning, crippling pain that had been always there since the Fall… it was all gone, vanished away. Hagal took a deep breath – the air, fresh and sweet, tickled his nostrils. *He was free*. Free, for the first time in years.

Hagal slowed down, dazed and silent, as a sudden understanding grew in him. What he first saw as a trial was a gift. He shook his head. 'The choice!' he thought feverishly. 'So that's why she had shown us home. That's why she told us to choose…She healed us. She knew!' Startled by his realisation, Hagal looked at Antares, speechless.

As if answering his thoughts, the Great Star glanced back and favoured him with a smile, warm and brief like a glare of sunshine on the water. In her high-collared dress, silver, jade, and diamond, she looked ethereal and otherworldly like a forest goddess.

"Where are we actually going?" Curiosity got finally the better of Tei.

"To a city called Reh," Antares told him.

"Reh? Sounds an unusual name," Nesteri said. "Does it mean anything?"

"In the language that used to be spoken there it means 'sorrow'," Antares said.

"Ugh," Tei cringed. "That's sort of ominous. Why would they call a city like that?"

"It was not how it was named, only nicknamed."

"Why?"

"Its past," Antares said. "You shall find out when we get there. There is nothing menacing about it, though. Although forsaken, it's beautiful still."

A flock of butterflies fluttered past, white and turquoise, shimmering like airborne gems.

Tei just nodded, feeling lost somewhat, a huge *whatever* painted on his face. The whole idea of going to some ghost town with a dodgy name seemed rather weird. 'Let's hope it will be worth it,' Tei consoled himself in thoughts.

Antares turned to him, amusement in his eyes. "It will be. You can take my word for it." Looking at his abashed grin, the Great Star added: "Thought screening, my friends. It's time to learn this skill, I reckon." The Quarta's ears pricked up, she could tell. "The easiest way," she began, "is using a mantra. With some practice and repetition, you will be able to create a constant background sound and hide your thoughts in it. Using mantras is good for quieting your mind, too."

"What's a mantra?" Tei asked. He picked up a small stone and now was playing with it, tossing it into the air and catching.

"A word, or a phrase you choose for yourself to focus on."

"I actually know about them," Nesteri joined in. "But I could never think of anything I'd resonate with."

"How do you know?" Tei asked, throwing Nesteri a quick sidelong glance.

"The library," Nesteri answered simply. "Way back in our Academy days. I was browsing there once and came across a book called the Path of

Silence, or something similar. The title intrigued me, so I requested it. It wasn't even a book really, more like a pile of crumbling pages… one of those you're not allowed to take home. For a few weeks, I would go there and read. It talked about staying in the Present, and the mantras. It referred to them as 'silence keys'."

Tei sniffed at those words. He was never seen in the library except before exams, and often not even then. He much preferred the practical training, the wind in his face, and the weight of steel in his hand to the dust of old books.

"We too call them the silence keys or *sives clarii*," Antares responded. "A great power can be unlocked by them."

"But how does one find his own?" Nesteri asked. "I did try a few, but nothing felt right."

"How do you choose your weapon? You don't, it chooses you," Antares said. "Finding your clariē is an art, but there are some signposts on your way. Firstly, decide what kind of energy you need, what kind of influence would add to your strength. Then, whether to resort to an existent formula or to create your own. There are pluses and minuses of both. Old mantras hold more power gathered over time, but personal clarii can be more meaningful, and easier to tune into. Having set your goal, keep your mind calm and receptive – and your mantra will soon come to you."

"Is there any sign by which to recognise it?" Hagal instinctively checked the notebook in his inside pocket. As soon as they stop somewhere he would write this down, he thought.

"You will feel it on a deeper level. There is also something else that clarii can help you with…"

"What is that?" Nesteri asked curiously.

"Finding the path to your true Self beyond the noise of your mind."

Hagal nodded, remembering suddenly their talk a few days ago. He still wasn't sure what Antares meant, though. 'The true Self, hm… Something to meditate on later.'

The Aven Forest opened its green arms to welcome the strangers. The wind rang with the music of birdsong.

"Holy Star," Nesteri asked, trying to make his voice more confident than he really felt. "May I ask if there is any clariē that you favour?"

"I tend to work with those that have no words," the Great Star said. "But the one I like the most can be pronounced as Aham Prakasha Dhāman." A strange, numinous beauty resounded in these words as Antares spoke them.

"Aham Prakasha Dhāman," Nesteri repeated slowly after her. "What does it mean?"

"It's a reminder of your true essence, the power of Light that is within you."

Nesteri smiled a bright smile. "I like it. I will try this one." He silently said the mantra a few times to memorise it.

"Psst, Hagal, you're going to write this down, right?" Tei nudged his friend. "Just in case." He opened his fingers and let the stone slip through to the ground.

"You know me well," Hagal smiled with a corner of his lips.

"So," Tei returned to his previous thought, "that place we are going to, is it where the bridge is?"

"The bridge?" Antares glanced at him questioningly.

"Well, yes, that one you told us about earlier, Holy Star," Tei said. "The bridge we need to find to rescue Farien."

Antares looked away. The difference in perception was so deep and glaring it was almost wearisome.

"It was not a physical bridge," she said slowly, "that I spoke about. Your strength is what going to save him. The skills you learn and the awareness you develop. The bridge is your own consciousness that shall connect all levels of your being. When you awaken to who you really are, you will unlock the power you seek. The power that will set you and your friend free… and many, many others. By changing yourself you change the world."

"Alright," Tei sounded determined, "if that's what it takes, that's what shall be done. Please teach us."

"If you be so kind," Hagal added for him.

"You are learning already," Antares replied. "But there is more to discover still. Follow me and you will find your Path."

Tei nodded, considering her words, but soon the usual impatience flashed in his eyes. "Very well. But still," he said pushing a huge fern leaf out of his way, "I don't get it. I'm sorry if I'm going to sound…err…"

"Impertinent," Nesteri suggested with a grin.

"Whatever," Tei screwed his face. "I mean, I'm just curious. That place that we are going to, Rev or something, what's special about it? If it's nothing but a pile of ruins? I don't question your choice, Holy Star," he added quickly and somewhat cheekily, "I'm just trying to understand better."

Antares threw Tei a pensive glance. Be that Kano, or Famaris, or any other Great Star, she could just say the reason as it was. But then a Great Star wouldn't ask.

She thought of a story so many centuries ago, which the city of Reh was a witness to; a life thread severed before its time and an oath unfulfilled. It was Him… and not Him. Unbeknownst to Vega's sleeping soul, the oath sworn back then was still holding him in its fetters. Its power had not faded, not even lifetimes later, although the memory of it had. His tragic death had changed the fate of the kingdom, and dark were the times that followed. Wars scarred and emptied the realm. The capital city of Tvorndaln, once resplendent, turned into an echoing ghost, a wind-cursed shelter for the crows and sand.

Vega's gateway to freedom was through healing his past, all its scattered fragments. He needed to awaken them within himself, way and way back, until he could remember all he was. The old debts had to be paid.

"Well," Antares said. "All cities on Lagu are portals. They exist in their own realities one may step into. Reh may prove more interesting than you think. Wait till we get there. Patience is a virtue, warrior." She smiled at Tei with her luminous eyes.

"I know," Tei said grudgingly. "It's a damn hard one. But fine, I'm intrigued now. How far away is it?"

"Let's see how it goes," Antares said enigmatically. "Focus on the journey for now. Every moment is important in its own right."

"Fine, sure," Tei gave up. 'Light and gods, I wonder if I'll get to understand Her thinking, ever…' he thought, then added out loud: "I look forward to seeing Rev then, wherever it is."

"Reh," Antares corrected.

'Reh…' For some reason, the name felt wrong to Nesteri, so wrong. 'She shouldn't call it that!' a thought sprung into his mind. The sound of it had touched something within him, something deeply hidden and unknown. Surprised, Nesteri grasped the thought hoping to bring out more. He walked in silence, minutes trickling by; yet no matter hard how he tried, the dim silhouettes did not get any clearer. Then suddenly, with a strange shiver, he realised *he knew*. As if an unseen barrier had burst, Nesteri's mind was besieged by images and sounds, forceful, tumultuous, and chaotic like broken puzzle pieces. Some visions were grim and bloody, so dark they made him grit his teeth. Reality quivered and slowly receded, crumbling apart. He was alone, blinded and trapped by the memories, drowning in them, suffocating in them. Nesteri halted in his tracks, gasping for breath.

"Nesteri, you alright?" Hagal's voice came muffled and dull, as if from afar. In a moment he was already there, by Nesteri's side, a hand on his shoulder. "What happened?"

"Hey, little weirdo, what's up?" Tei who walked slightly before them stood next to Hagal only an instant later.

Nesteri didn't answer, frozen in his trance as if someone else had taken his body over. He didn't even feel the touch of Hagal's hand.

"Nesteri!" Hagal shook his shoulder. "Speak to us!"

After what felt like an eternity, Nesteri bit his lower lip and gradually raised his gaze. Hagal flinched, surprised – so alien were the eyes that looked at him. Aloof and cold they were, and shadowed with a weary gloom of superiority Hagal had never seen before. Startled, he took his hand away. "Nesteri, what is going in with you?! What's wrong?"

"Leave him," Antares said. She knew, the only one. "He can't hear you."

Hagal and Tei stepped aside, lost and confounded, shooting anxious glances at Nesteri and then at Antares, and back again.

"What's up with him?" Tei asked in a whisper.

"Memories," Antares answered.

"Memories...?"

"Yes."

She stood before Nesteri, quiet for a moment, then touched his forehead and temples in a quick sweeping motion. Nesteri felt as if a stream of radiant water washed over him, restoring him to life. His senses were returnings slowly. At last he quivered, batted his eyelids, and looked half-conscious around.

He seemed the same as before, and yet something had changed. Brightened by the scattered leafy sunlight, Nesteri's face seemed unexplainably older. A consciousness of a different life, of faraway lands and times was glowing in his gaze, a dim flame. He now remembered what had once bounded him to Creljatrn. He knew the true name of the Forsaken City.

Strange tiredness and weakness shackled him for a reason Nesteri could not name, as if after an exhausting fight. He took a deep breath trying to regain control. A heartbeat later, though, a wave of luminous energy filled him bringing new strength. Healing magic...?

Only then did Nesteri realise Antares was there, so close, her hands still on his shoulders. Nesteri's breath caught in his throat. He looked at the Great Star, and then instantly away, trying hard not to blush, and failing.

'I'm a warrior,' he reminded himself, 'and warriors fight.' Nesteri straightened his shoulders and made himself look at Antares again. Golden fire was smouldering in her eyes. 'Thank you for your help, Holy Star,' Nesteri said in his thoughts. He knew that Antares would hear.

The tangled heart of the forest it was getting darker; the sun struggled to pierce its way through the dome of moss-encrusted boughs. Huge roots, gnarled with age, sprawled on the ground. The sward was soft with fallen leaves.

"Hey, Nesteri, are you good now?" Tei predictably couldn't keep from asking.

"Yes."

"What was that?"

"I don't know."

"Oh come on!"

"I don't know." Nesteri repeated, firmer this time. A shadow of pain broke through his voice. "It seemed like visions from a different time. Some other life."

"What other life?"

Nesteri pressed his lips together. He wanted to be alone right now. He wanted it badly. "You weren't there when Holy Star told us about that," he said after a pause. "This life is apparently only one link out of a chain of many. And the other ones, you simply don't remember...or you're not supposed to. But still, they do exist, deep inside your consciousness somewhere."

"I recall that conversation," Hagal chimed in. "I'm not sure how one can tap into those memories, though."

"If I work it out, I'll tell you," Nesteri replied somewhat darkly. "But believe me, it's no joy."

After a while, the forest opened onto a sun-laved glade. Its middle took a group of trees, runty and white-barked; their curious fruits glimmered gold amongst the foliage.

"Odd but cute," remarked Tei when he noticed.

"Golden apples," Antares said. "The unicorns love them."

"The what love them?"

Antares smiled. "The Aven Forest stretches out for many miles," she said. "Crossing it all by foot would take us quite a while."

"So what shall we do, then?"

"Just wait and see."

Shortly, a light rustle reached their ears — and the shrubs emerged four snow-white horned animals, slender and graceful like hinds. Their hooves cast golden glints on the ground. The Quarta stared at them, bewildered.

"Light and all gods, unicorns! They do actually exist?" Hagal whispered under his breath.

'So that's who watched us then,' Nesteri realised, remembering their first walk. He should be surprised, he thought. Yet he felt nothing but weariness and a strange burning inside. Dull at first, it was gradually growing stronger. That restless flame was puzzling, and somewhat worrying.

One of the unicorns stepped closer to Antares, accepting gracefully an apple she had offered, then gently nuzzled his head into her hands. The Great Star laughed and hugged its neck.

"This is Meerou," she said stroking the unicorn's mane. "He and his friends agreed to take us to the Lake Aëldi. From there, we will have to continue alone — the unicorns never leave the Aven forest."

Meerou nodded, clearly understanding her words. He knelt before the Great Star so she could mount him, and the rest followed in his wake.

The Quarta got on the unicorn backs with ease that revealed both habit and good training. Tei was the first one up. Known for his great riding skills back in Siltarion days, he was now prancing around, grinning from ear to ear.

"What's his name?" Tei asked, patting his unicorn's neck. Riding without any harness felt unusual but the Star soon got used to it.

"Eenotin," Antares replied.

As evening fell, coils of mist slunk their way through the forest; veils of finest gossamery haze, all-enshrouding, they woke a mysterious shimmer amongst the trees.

Quick as an arrow, the small squad raced south through the bracken and sagebrush, following the secret paths to the Lake Aēldi. The whistle of the wind and the thud of hooves ruffled the sleepy peace of ancient woodland.

Darkness had already coloured the lower floor of the woods; mist was imbibing it slowly like blotting paper draws in ink. Here and there, will-o'-the-wisps danced and flickered, teasing the travellers. From the depths of the forest came cries of nocturnal birds, unknown crunching and murmuring, subdued whispers and sighs. 'Hurry, hurry!' rustled the leaves. 'Night is falling.' The trees creaked in the gale; high in their crowns, something hooted and glided down with the soft swish of powerful wings. Water tinkled away in a distance.

The mists lightened up now with a gauzy glow, growing brighter ands brighter. Flocks of radiant birds curiously gathered around, their tails and long feathers in the colours of flame. Some perched on the branches overhead, some flew swirling beside like a fiery cortege. Joy, glitter, and wonder they were, but soon they were all gone.

"Those were phoenixes," Antares said later.

By the first moon, the Stars reached the edge of the forest. Aēldi opened up before them, a cold shine through the lattice of trees. It was time to part ways with the unicorns.

Nesteri dismounted slowly, his limbs aching after a long ride. It had been a while since he was on a horseback, and he had almost forgotten what an enlivening feeling it was. The Star wished he could keep Sentimē for longer. He patted the unicorn's neck. "Farewell, friend."

Tiredness and a hint of melancholy washed over Nesteri as he was about to walk away, the surrounding forest dark as the future ahead. Then suddenly, the unicorn spoke to him. Nesteri froze, astounded. In his mind, he clearly heard a quiet voice. *'Tai de,'* said Sentimē with a cautious sidelong look to make sure that Antares wasn't watching. *'Nesteri ve naryo so. Cai to Ceiveri.'*

The unicorn briefly bowed his head and joined the rest, before anyone could notice. The team lingered for a moment, their horns glistening in the moonlight, then turned away and disappeared, merging into the shadows.

The fire burnt stretching its blazing arms towards the night skies. Logs sizzled and crackled, shooting sparks into the wind. Warm glares brightened the Stars' faces.

Tei was singing a ballad, a fern leaf in his hair rocking to the beat of the music. The young hero of the story was naïve and lost, and his search for the meaning of life led him into all sorts of nonsense.

Hagal threw twigs and cedar cones into the fire, watching the flame take them in its arms with hasty acceptance. Out of the trembling gleams, a vision of Nesteri's eyes swam up at him, uninvited. Hagal shuddered lightly. The look that Nesteri had measured him earlier in the forest was hard to forget. Hagal cast a quick watchful glance to his left.

Nesteri sat there silent, calmly and pensively gazing into the flames, as if the odd change had never come upon him. 'Maybe I shouldn't trouble myself with that,' Hagal mused. 'All in all, he's always been quite a peculiar type. On the other hand, I wonder how remembering one's past lives can be possible...if that's what it really was.'

The ballad came to an end and Tei started singing a new tune. Nesteri winced as he instantly recognised it. It was a song Tei wrote to *her* – the

Star who had nearly caused the Quarta's split. Nesteri narrowed his eyes; music had summoned back memories of those days. 'It's weird how time can change so many things,' he thought.

After Morionwē, their friendship had never been the same. Would it have survived at all if not for the Crystal? Who knows. Perhaps. Or perhaps not. Tei's attitude was a complete let-down, and Nesteri couldn't force himself to feign indifference, much less consent. His very nature and integrity rebelled against it. He saw emotions as the enemies of discipline, and 'love' as nothing but a fancy word for self-indulgence. As sure as the dawn, Nesteri knew that *he* would never let his mind slip like that. His self-control was something he was secretly proud of. Tei's weakness appeared even more irritating in contrast. 'I wonder what came on upon him to bring up that stupid song now?' Nesteri frowned and looked over at Tei.

Tei was strumming an akhenbi, his head lowered so that nobody could see his eyes. It had been years since he had played one, but the strings of the sarod-like lute still felt familiar under his fingers. Tei's voice was mist and haunted shadows.

> You gave me more than I could dream,
> You've taken all I've ever been,
> Before I knew.
> Your touch awakened my heart
> Like sunrise wakes up a new day
> With the brightest dew.
> A fire too radiant to last
> The wind of time has swept away
> And you were gone.
> Wind took the ashes of my soul,
> The moons have waned, the sun has set,
> I stand alone.
> The staircase of the Milky Way
> Had broken into little shards
> But life goes on.
> I'd rather not be in this world
> Than know the darkness of the nights
> Without you.
> No matter where my path will go
> Your name will always be my light,
> Forever true.

The second moon appeared over the horizon. The sky above was boundless and still, and the warm breeze rang with cicadas. The new adventure was exciting, the food delectable and the drink plenty, and so the Stars sang and talked, deep into the night.

"It's all well, but how about getting some sleep?" Hagal suggested finally with a yawn, as tiredness started taking its toll. Staying up until late was not in his usual custom.

"It's the wisest thing you said in a while, Hagal," Tei grinned. "Yes to that." He pulled out the fern leaf and glanced at it pensively, hesitating as if he might throw it into the fire, but then he didn't.

"Night, all!" Tei announced, lying down.

"Till tomorrow!" everyone answered.

Before his eyelids slowly glued together, Nesteri turned his head and quietly looked over at Antares. The Great Star sat lit up by the fire, with a huge white tiger sprawled at her feet. The tiger gazed into the flames, squinting his eyes.

Bright in the first rays of sunshine, the morning mist over the lake was cool and fresh. It woke up the Quarta earlier than usual.

On the sandy shore, they soon noticed Antares's silhouette a few feet away. The Great Star stood looking pensively in the direction of the Caeron Mountains; their distant peaks gilded by the rising sun.

'I feel like I'm running out of *time*,' she thought to herself with a sad smile. 'What a peculiar feeling to have.' Sensing the Quarta's gaze, Antares turned her head. "Morning, warriors."

After the Minor Stars sleepily returned her greeting, she added: "Get ready soon – we have a lot to do today."

Only now did they notice that Antares was wearing a warrior outfit instead of a usual gown. The Great Star looked incredible. Inappropriate as it was, for a moment the Quarta couldn't take their eyes off her nor wipe the silly grins off their faces.

The day certainly promised to be interesting.

The outskirts of the forest were all breeze and sunshine.

"How good are your close combat skills?" Antares asked, stopping suddenly.

"Well," Tei replied, "we used to practice regularly back in the Academy days, then also after the Fall. But not since Farien was gone. It was a bit tricky with an odd number of us–"

"In other words, I guess we've slacked off a bit," chimed in Nesteri. "Why do you ask, Holy Star?"

"It's a proficiency you'll need," Antares told them. "Long distance energy combat is all good, but it can make you too complacent and thus weaken your focus. Your minds and your bodies should be trained in equal measure."

"That's what our teacher used to say," Nesteri smiled.

"Do you suggest a training session, then?" said Tei, beaming from ear to ear. The very thought of a training made him feel excited.

"Your mind-reading is getting better," Antares joked. "Go on, show me what you're worth."

She pointed to her right. A heap of weapons shimmered there on the grass, bristled up with chainsticks, triple staffs, short and long swords of different kinds, and even double-bladed swordstaffs, which Nesteri was particularly pleased to see. Next to them piled up bracers, pauldrons, gauntlets, leather jackets and other guards.

"Choose what you want to start with," Antares said after a warm-up.

"Swords, of course!" Tei exclaimed as he pulled out a typical Siltarionese sword, a broad blade with two smaller at the base. "Feels great to hold one of these again!" He swished it through the air.

Soon, the woodland was filled with the sounds of fighting and the cold music of weapons. Antares' blows came precise, powerful and relentless – soon the Quarta got to see first hand what a formidable enemy she could be.

Attack, thrust, flip, parry, swing out of the line, attack, thrust… repeat. Repeat. And repeat again. They went on for hours with hardly any breathing space, only changing weapons.

But with another swish of Tei's triple staff, Hagal suddenly yelped and staggered, hit – the price for gauging his distance wrong. His pauldron had taken the blow that could otherwise fragment his shoulder, yet even though his left arm felt paralysed.

"Hey, you alright?" Tei lowered his triple staff.

"Yes… I'm good," Hagal answered, catching his breath.

The Great Star looked over at them. "Enough for today." She smiled, watching the Quarta flop and stretch on the grass as soon as they heard her words. "You've done well."

"I'm knackered," Tei breathed out. "But I loved every moment of it."

"We shall continue tomorrow," Antares said. "Hagal, your shoulder?"

"Sore," Hagal admitted, "but I'll live."

"Let me take care of it," Antares said and focused her gaze. The pain vanished.

"Why, thank you, Holy Star," Hagal responded, his lilac eyes wide open with amazement. He touched his shoulder and moved it as if to make sure. It was completely healed. "How extraordinary!"

"If we lived in times of peace," Antares uttered somewhat pensively, "I would devote myself to healing with the greatest joy. I much prefer restoring life than taking it."

"Here, have these," she added, handing over to the Quarta three silver chalices.

"What is it?" Tei asked smelling the dense, garnet-red drink.

"Virapana is what it used to be called. It will help bring your energy back."

Aven Forest was left behind. A tapestry of meadows stretched to the east as far as the eye could see, relieved in the south by the glittering ribbon of the Teréan River. Far beyond reigned the misty silhouettes of the Caeron Mountains. Eternal autumn minted them all gold.

Hagal's attention caught flowers that were numerous here – three blue or golden bells crowning a dark stem. As the Stars moved forward, the flowers' number grew, until they filled all around. Watching the bells trembling in the wind, Hagal suddenly felt ill at ease.

"I have a bizarre feeling that they are 'watching' us," he finally confessed to Antares in a low voice.

"You're right, in a way," the Great Star replied. "They can sense us."

"Who can sense us?" Tei asked, jumping into the conversation as the sniff of a mystery.

"These flowers," Hagal said pointing at the bells.

Tei gave them a suspicious glance. "Is that right? That's weird…"

"What are they called?" Nesteri enquired somewhat nonchalantly.

"Leinirei," Antares said. "Voices of the Past. They have a curious ability. Listen."

The Minor Stars stopped and went quiet, yet they could hear only wind.

"Not with your ears," Antares said. "Listen with your heart. Make your mind still and empty of thoughts, clear like a mirror, and you will hear."

The Quarta closed their eyes and silenced all noise within as they would in meditation. Before long, a swarm of images began to flow and flicker, drawing in – visions of strange worlds, vague echoes, lulled thoughts… *Memory* hovered over the flowers like a trembling mist, rising and falling in waves of softest sighs, until they slowly started forming words, the Quarta heard them: *'Wait…'* the flowers whispered. *'Leinirē taimē okinu. Tunir veisté kē. Grass looks up at the sky with the bright eyes of dew. Listen…embrace the past that is still you. Do you remember? The rock by the waterfall, the swallow amongst the clouds. A shining star on a rainy night…we remember. The days that will never come, the days that will never return. Leinirei…leinirei…'*

The road called for the travellers though, so away they went, measuring the path with pensive steps. For a long while, nobody said a word. The whisper of leinirei had stirred the hearts of the Minor Stars, summoning back the sorrows of times gone, thoughts of their lost homeland and Farien, of the emptiness behind and the uncertainty ahead.

A sudden pang of pain pierced through Tei, sharp like a crack of a whip; the memories of Morionwē came storming back, alive and vivid, as clear as if it was yesterday. 'Light, give me strength…' Tei gritted his teeth. He wished he could forget. And yet he couldn't; the heart of a Star always remains true, even if the mind orders otherwise.

Later, Antares taught them an old ditty about leinirei flowers, Nesteri liked it most:

Derē-Veraimi
Li, o netē,
Renemi lē
Sono, vē taimi.
O-iē emmentē
Reedis mo
Nereino
Leinirei-arintē.

Summer was still upon them, yet its glory was waning slowly. The gusts of wind turned fresh and crisp, and mornings came imbued with the scents of early autumn. Across the river Teréan, a forest glowed gold and crimson red.

"Far beyond," Antares said pointing northeast, "lies the town of Reh, at the foot of the Caeron Mountains."

The steep right bank of the river was almost barren, braved only by a few scarce trees. In the south, dense water mist trembled with rainbows over the Vale of Hundred Waterfalls. The roar of falling water could be heard despite the distance.

Antares told the Quarta that at the time of the three moons, spirits of nature would appear and dance there swirling amongst the waterfalls, joined by the magic birds sīnamrū, who are said to be all-seeing.

'Being all-seeing even for a while would be handy,' Nesteri thought. A ghost of a sardonic smile touched his lips.

He longed for clarity. The stinging feeling that had crept into his mind was troubling and unsettling. Nesteri couldn't understand what was happening. His self-control would never let desires of any kind take root, let alone influence his thoughts. And yet…he realised he craved Antares' presence. It seemed to have awoken something in him that he never even knew nor could understand. Nesteri wanted to be close to her, so close…at the very thought, thin strings of fire run piercing through his body, pulsing at his fingertips. 'What is this?' Trying to suppress the unknown emotion was strangely painful. Nesteri focused and shut it down, regardless. He wouldn't have it any other way.

It was late afternoon when the Stars finally forded the river; Eité Forest greeted them with shade and shimmer. Using the short rest, Hagal pulled out his notebook and returned to his questions.

"Reluctantly, I must admit that I still find it challenging to grasp the concept of source-stars," he said continuing his thought from before. "Could you elucidate, perhaps?"

"Source luminaries would be a better term," Antares replied. "Look," she created a network of shining spheres floating around, "the Universe. All these stars are ports, or gates, to enormous power. Each one is different, although they make up groups that work together, the constellations. If you align your own frequency with a particular source-star, you can become its envoy."

"And channel its power?"

"Precisely. With the entanglement, you wield more force than you could possibly imagine, although it does come at a price."

"What price?" Tei asked curiously.

"As the power of a luminary becomes yours, your life and its life merge together. You become its embodiment, in a way."

The sunlight filtering through the foliage filled all with a quivering glow, serene and otherworldly like a dream. The sweet scent of fallen leaves was spilt in the air.

"How does it work?" Hagal spoke again. He sat on the ground with his legs crossed, thoughtfully playing with a pencil in his hand.

"Through your source luminary you become the ultimate instrument of Light, a formidable weapon–"

"Fancy that!" Tei exclaimed. Nesteri threw him a quick scorning look.

"However," Antares continued, "if for any reason your luminary were to be taken over by the Shadow, that blow would hit you, too." The gleaming spheres around slowly faded and vanished.

Nesteri narrowed his eyes as if contemplating something. "What happens then?" he asked.

"It depends. Some yield and join the enemy, and become Dark Stars. Some choose to let their bodies die so the bounding link can be weakened for a time."

"For a time?" Tei chimed in.

"The war ebbs and flows. All Dark Stars used to be Light once, and all luminaries used to be pure. Sometimes the Shadow succeeds in dimming them, though, so it can use their energy."

"But not forever, right?"

"No, not forever. No amount of dark poison can change the Stars' true nature that is Light. However, a path to recovery can sometimes be long... very long." Antares suddenly got up. "Let's go."

"The Gates of Time and Space have always been a key target for the enemies," she added as they walked. "A while ago, when Sirit's luminary was under attack, dark times were upon us. Do you know why she's called 'The Guardian of the Labyrinth' in your legends? Sirit holds the keys to all different variants of the future. In her absence, this part of the Universe had lost its understanding of the multitude of paths and the points of choice. People started to believe that their future was predetermined and foreordained and that nothing could be done to change it. We have retrieved Alpha Canis Majoris, though. Now Sirius a light star again."

A small tinkling brook cut across their path. On its bed, small pebbles shone like colourful gemstones through the crystal water.

"There is something you should know," Antares said stepping over the stream. "The amount of power you can wield is down to the structure of your mind. The more Light you allow into you, the more powerful you become. Your mind is what limits how strong you can be."

"So if I change the structure of my mind, I could change what I am, correct?" Hagal asked in an affirmative tone. "Perhaps even become a Senior Star, like our teacher was?"

"You can and you should," Antares replied. "Your goal as a warrior is to master yourself and to grow, becoming a more powerful weapon of Light. We are the first line of defence against the Shadow, never forget that. Our responsibility is to guide and protect those who are not yet strong enough to fight for themselves."

"Thank you, Holy Star," Hagal said, deep in thought. Little did he realise that those words were going to shape his future and reverberate in his memory in the years to come.

A pair of lion-like animals run past, chasing each other. Their auburn fur merged into the gold and copper of the foliage. Spotting them in the thicket would be a hard task, if not for their wings.

"The path of a true Ariya warrior," Antares continued, "is to change yourself and your reality in conformity with your will. Your life is a music you're writing yourself, every single moment. It may seem to you that some things happen without a reason, but it is your command that brings them forth out of the multitude of possibilities. The more energy you wield, the more influence you have on the fabric of reality."

"It reminds me of something our teacher used to say," Nesteri said, joining the conversation. "To be free, accept responsibility for your thoughts, your words and your actions."

"Absolutely right," Antares said. "If you don't learn to consciously choose your attitudes, you won't know which ones are truly yours – and may soon become a servant to someone else's Will. For a warrior in spirit, it's the worst kind of enslavement. Your Will is one of your two strongest weapons in your battle with the Shadow. Develop it, master it and strengthen it in every way possible."

"And what is the other one?" Nesteri asked.

"It is Love."

Tei flinched inwardly at the sound of the word; he took a deep breath and lingered for a moment before speaking. "I don't understand what you mean, Holy Star," he finally said with assumed indifference.

"Love is one of the aspects of Light," Antares explained. "This life-giving, healing and creative power is one of the staple differences between our enemies and us. The Shadow comes in many guises and wears many masks, some of them very convincing and misleading. Sometimes it disguises itself as False Light. But if you know what to look for, you will never be fooled. The Shadow knows nothing about Love."

"What should we look for, then?" Nesteri asked.

"Evil can't create anything," Antares said. "It can only copy, defile and distort. You can see that in every sphere of life. Where harmony and beauty have been stifled amongst ugly imitations and cacophonous sounds, where truth and virtue are shamed and ridiculed – that world has been affected by the virus of evil. It is there where us, Stars, are needed most."

"We've been to a place like that," said Hagal. "For a short while thankfully, but it was tough. I imagine it must be quite a challenge for those living there."

"Battlefields are usually dark and dirty places. But hardships are your allies in this fight – they teach you about your strength."

The Stars came out to a small glade; tall trees surrounded it like a leafy cloister. In the falling dusk, the whisper of the wind was soft and soothing. Antares called a halt there.

"Yes to that!" Tei agreed enthusiastically on behalf of all three. The Quarta were weary somewhat from the long miles of marching. "A fire would be great," he added casually.

"Leave it to me," the Great Star said.

Obedient to her will, dry twigs and branches swiftly drew to the centre of the glade. When the last pieces of brushwood had taken their place, the Great Star conjured fire. Noticing the Quarta's admiring gaze, she smiled. "If you think I'm good at this, you should see what *Sirit* does."

That name brought to Nesteri's mind a vision of the gold-haired Star of the Future and the evening they first met at the Meldēan Hall. Then Antares' song rang in his memory again – a mesmerising stream of honeyed notes, shimmering like water. Nesteri looked at the Star of Time. Brightened with the last of sunset glow, she was twining a wreath from the autumn leaves scattered around; laughing and tugging each other, Tei and Hagal were passing them to her. *Golden leaves in her silvery hair...*

Nesteri shuddered as something moved within him, taking over, engulfing, sweeping over him like a wave, gentle yet scorching hot. His head spun lightly. The Star pressed his lips together and took a deep breath, his heart pounding in his chest. 'Damn emotions. Whatever this is, I have to make it stop.'

That night in his dream, Nesteri saw a nature spirit dancing amongst the iridescent mist of waterfalls, and triangles with wings, which guarded a golden goblet at the end of the rainbow.

Chapter XI

Aē Åm Kelumi

Light and Shadows

"To see the truth, you have to first unlearn what you have learnt."

"Enverai taisé mo keté o-iē so. Nori on dē, Ke-Nireis Veri."
Having sensed a stranger's presence, the Quarta instantly woke up. Dew-spangled blades of grass stood silently around, fearful of losing the glittering gifts of dawn. Close to the Stars, the grass was curiously dry, though. It looked like something that Antares would arrange.

The Quarta noticed her a little way off, by a stream amongst the trees. Two warriors accompanied her; an officer and his superior, one could assume. Standing in front of Antares, the commander was tall and sharp in his silver-strewn uniform. The hood of his cloak was down, revealing a face that had seen many storms and many battles. It was hard to tell how old or how young the Star was. His movements were quick and youthful, but his dense black hair was touched with grey. He spoke to Antares softly in a foreign language, from time to time nodding his head.

His officer stood separated by a few hundred feet, frozen in the pose of courtesy – his arm right across his chest, head slightly bowed. His unruly auburn hair was tied back with a dark green string – the colour of time past. The officer's uniform was ash, emerald, and copper, marked with a symbol the Quarta didn't recognise.

Tei rubbed the sleep from his eyes and slowly rose on his elbow, then jerked up to his feet. "What the heck?!" he whispered fiercely to his friends. "Guys, do you see what I see? It's Phatiel, I swear! What is the damn demonoid doing here!?"

"Ai to onē," Antares said to the commander. Neither of them paid any regard to the Quarta, who got up and were now walking slowly towards Phatiel.

At the sound of their steps, the officer lifted his head and they met his eyes – the luminous eyes of a Light Star. He looked at them with serene curiosity.

"Err…Phatiel?!" Tei said, somewhat baffled, but still with a tone of accusation.

"Altais to agini maē, iye…" responded the Star looking mystified.

"What did you say?"

"My name is Altais[7]," he repeated in almost perfect Siltarionese, with only the slightest hint of an accent. "However, some call me Phatiel as well. We've met before? Don't mean to be rude, but I cannot remember. Whom do I have the pleasure of addressing?"

The Quarta exchanges puzzled glances. Something here was not right. Phatiel, it was Phatiel for sure. He did admit it. How come he was a Light Star, though? They would have thought of it to be a trap, if not for his eyes.

After an awkward silence, which felt increasingly more like a staring contest, Tei shrugged and introduced himself. "Tei Dalt, Captain of the Quarta."

"Hagal Trethienn," Hagal followed him.

"Nesteri Astarrien," Nesteri added.

"Altais Riey-Aruna. Pleased to meet you," Phatiel responded, polite but reserved.

"What are you doing here?" Tei didn't try to hide hostility in his voice. The memory of having nearly been killed was still fresh in his mind.

"Our mission is strictly confidential. I am not allowed to reveal any details."

Tei snapped at this answer. "I think you'll have to," he hissed angrily and raised his right hand to attack.

Without a word, Phatiel clicked his fingers. A gleaming energy barrier instantly surrounded him like a wall. "I don't know what your issue is," he said coldly, "but threatening me is pointless."

"What's happening over there?" Antares suddenly interjected.

The Quarta turned around. Two Great Stars looked at them with a disapproving stare.

---

[7] Delta (δ) Draconis, a yellow star in the constellation Draco.

"Tē Loiverai yariné oveti," the commander uttered in an iron voice.

Embarrassed, the Quarta bowed clumsily and withdrew. To their surprise, Phatiel took the energy barrier down and joined them, walking slightly at a distance.

Tei was furiously kicking leaves out of his way. "Told off like little kids!! Like I'm back in the kindergarten! And I tried to do was just to sort that darned demonoid out. What kind of bloody logic is that?"

"I'm actually curious what the other Great Star said," Hagal wondered. "One would assume he told us off."

"He said that we should know how to behave," Nesteri blurted out without thinking.

Hagal and Tei turned to him with a bewildered gaze.

"How do you know?"

"I just do," Nesteri said. "It's just how the words flowed. He's right, though. Ceiveri son meyu," he added unexpectedly. The words felt strangely familiar on his tongue.

Tei lashed forward and his fingers dug into Nesteri's shoulder. "What the heck, Nesteri," he barked out, anger rising within him. "Since when can you speak a language you've never heard before? Or have you? I hate sodding secrets! Where did you learn it? You better explain that. Now."

"Let go of me!" Nesteri grabbed Tei's hand and pushed it away. "I didn't learn it. I just knew the meaning, somehow."

"*He just knew the meaning!*" Tei's voice was thick with mockery. "You expect me to believe that bullshit, seriously? That's as lame as a dead horse."

"I'm telling you the truth."

"Argh, you darn weirdo! You annoy the hell out of me sometimes! Can you at least try and be normal for once? I hate knotting behind my back. Just tell me how you know that language and we'll be done with it."

"Look, Tei," said Nesteri slowly. "I don't have any reason to hide it from you. If I could explain how I understood those words, I would, clear?"

"One of those typical damn excuses of yours. I should've got used by now," Tei gave off a desultory snort. He clenched and then released his fist.

"Just using pure logic," Hagal interjected narrowing his eyes, "how could you say something in a language you *allegedly* don't know?"

Nesteri pressed his lips together. "I–"

"–I think he's being honest with you," Phatiel unexpectedly cut in. His teal eyes gleamed with an ironic expression. "To speak Aē, one has to tune into its frequency. It looks like your friend has managed to do it – simple as."

"What's Aē?" Tei asked brusquely.

"The language of Great Stars," Phatiel answered, pretending not to notice his tone.

"Is that what you spoke to us at first?"

"Yes."

The new acquaintances walked a fair distance away from the Great Stars. Enough, Tei decided and flopped on the grass where he stood. He tried not to show it, but anger was cooling down – Tei could never stay annoyed for too long. The Star gave Phatiel-Altais a long thoughtful stare. "Why didn't you want to talk to us at first?" he asked after a pause.

"I still don't. Violence is hardly a good way of introducing yourself," Phatiel crossed his legs at the ankles.

"What made you joined us, then?" Hagal looked at him puzzled.

"I had to," Phatiel frowned, "since I am a Loiveri as well."

"A Loiveri?" Hagal didn't know the word.

"A Minor Star," Phatiel replied. "Loiveri in Aē."

Nesteri was studying Phatiel as he spoke. The Star surely did resemble the enemy Nesteri knew, and yet everything about him was different. His prowess in parrying Tei's verbal attacks was somewhat impressive, and his effortless command of Siltarionese was even more so. It was worth finding out who he really was, Nesteri thought.

"Ehm, Phatiel," Nesteri said finally, "or should I call you Altais?"

"Whichever pleases you."

"I know we started off in an awkward way. Small wonder you are not disposed to talk. But we fight on the same side, I believe…however unexplainable this is. And those who fight together should stand together."

Nesteri made a pause, then stretched out his hand to Phatiel. "When warriors quarrel, the Shadow wins," he recalled the old proverb.

"What, don't expect me to apologise!" Tei protested huffily. "I'm not bloody going to. He almost killed me!"

"What tried to kill you was a demonoid. It couldn't have been *him*. Look at his eyes!" Nesteri insisted.

"But his face and his name—"

"Antares surely wouldn't let an enemy be here."

"I know, but—"

"Tei, I think Nesteri's actually a got a point," As always, Hagal' was the voice of reason. "I think we must be taking him for someone else. And it's really getting ill-mannered."

Tei threw Phatiel another searching glance. "Argh...fine," he muttered, finally yielding to pervasion, all reluctant and crabbed. "Alright, maybe I was a bit too tetchy."

Phatiel watched the dispute in silence. At the sound of Tei's improvised apology, though, a fleeting smile brightened his face. The Star wanted to play tough, but curiosity got the better of him. He had never seen anyone on Lagu before, except Antares.

"Peace," he said after a pause, stretching his hand to the Quarta. "Do tell me, though, how do you know my name?"

A light gust of wind shook a golden waterfall of leaves.

"What do you mean, how...?" Tei said, confused. "I hate to bring this up, but you and your mates have been a bloody pain for ages! How can you not remember our fights on Thol Easen, Enthuar, Morionwē, and recently – the Blue Planet?"

"Fights?" Phatiel shook his head. "What fights? I've no idea what you're talking about. I haven't even heard about any of those places. And I most certainly have not met you before."

"Right," Tei rubbed his face in what seemed a mixture of awkwardness and perplexity. "That's it. You clearly aren't *him*. Apologies, my bad." This time his voice sounded sincere. He then added, in a tone of explanation, "Honestly, you look a spitting image of someone. I mean, except your Light. Sorry. You must have thought we were some bunch of weirdos."

Phatiel smiled with a quiet irony in his eyes. "Your behaviour did appear very random, true. But it makes sense now. Nothing to worry about. We all make mistakes."

"Thanks," Tei replied.

"Still, who are you? If you don't mind me asking."

"Our team is called Quarta," responded Tei. "Because there are four of... well, now we are only three. We come from Siltarion, as you might have guessed."

"Well, that was pretty obvious from the start. What brings you to Lagu, though? Unless it is a secret."

"No, it's not a secret... as far as I'm aware," Nesteri said. "Antares saved our lives and brought us here, a while ago now, but we still haven't discovered why. Light," he interrupted himself, "just realised how lame this sounds!"

"Didn't She tell you?"

"She did. Sort of. She mentioned something about destiny and such. We couldn't make any sense of it."

"Destiny is a valid enough reason, I suppose. You can trust the wisdom of Ke-Nireis Veri."

"How do you know Her, by the way?" Nesteri asked.

"I wouldn't say that I know Her well," admitted Phatiel. "We've only spoken briefly. She is one of the Principal Generals of the High League – and the commander of my general. I had the pleasure of seeing Her a few times when I accompanied him, just like today. I like being in Her presence, though," Phatiel added with a warm smile. "She's the kindest Star I've met."

"Where are you from, if you don't mind me asking?" Hagal chimed in. "Your Siltarionese is outstanding."

"Thanks! I'm from Estarellié originally, but I love learning languages. It's great fun. I can speak five fluently so far, and another five or six I know just about enough to get by. Nothing to be proud of yet. But I'll get there!" Then, as if he suddenly remembered, Phatiel quickly arranged his fingers in a gesture of complacency.

"Hah, you're good!" Tei grinned.

"Why Siltarionese, though?" asked Hagal.

"Oh, that was an obvious choice. Siltarion is so scenic. It borders the area I patrol, so I go there any chance I get."

"*Used* to border," Hagal corrected him.

"What do you mean?" Phatiel shook his head. "Why, it's there, safe and sound. I would know if anything happened to it."

"So you've been there recently, you say?"

"Yes."

"How is it poss–" Hagal began.

"Wait!" Nesteri almost exclaimed, his eyes widened with a sudden realisation. "What he's saying means… oh my word… it means that we must be in the time *before* the Fall. We've travelled back in time!"

"Nesteri, you crazy nerd! Time travel is a fantasy," Tei cut him off.

"But there's no other explanation!"

Phatiel looked at the Quarta sharply. "Light, so you're from the future? Are you?! Tell me, are you??!" He stared at them wordless for a moment, bewilderment in his eyes. "Oh my life, I understand now. It's probably because of you–"

"What's because of us?" Tei jumped in.

"That blast of temporal energy not long ago. It seemed like an explosion… so huge it tore through the multiple energy levels," explained Phatiel, his face lit up. "It was surreal. My captain said that it happens when a large object is being moved in time. A side effect of sorts. I didn't know. So it must have been you, then! Oh. My. Life. I'm speechless. You got the Septenary to alter the structure of time!" Phatiel's voice was filled with undisguised wonder. *"Who are you??"*

"Err…just regular warriors," said Tei somewhat baffled by what he had just heard. "We're not anyone special, I think."

"Oh get off! They wouldn't do it for some 'regular warriors', that's nonsense. Oh Light, save us…Do you realise that the Septenary have rewritten the future?? You know what that means?! I would rather–" Phatiel froze suddenly in the middle of the sentence as if trying to hear something.

"Arini, Ke-tosu. I hear you," he uttered under his breath and rose to his feet, suddenly sharp and composed. Then, addressing the Quarta, he said: "Sorry, I do have to go – my duties are calling for me. But my word, what a meeting..! It was great talking to you, Siltarionis Loiverai. May the Light guide you on your way."

"So it *was* Phatiel, after all! Well, if that wasn't weird I don't know what is," Tei shook his head incredulously. "We've just had a friendly chat with our sworn enemy. A random fact of the day."

"With our *future* enemy," Nesteri corrected him.

"That means he will be darkened later," Hagal said pensively. "Maybe we should have warned him?"

"Hey, you can come over!"

Antares waved at them from the other side of the glade. She was on her own now. The Quarta got up; dry leaves rustled under their feet as they walked.

"Time for us to get on our way," said Antares. She seemed quiet and thoughtful.

"Holy Star," begun Tei cautiously. "We're sorry."

"Hm?"

"We apologise for being a nuisance earlier."

"Don't trouble yourself with that," Antares tossed her hair behind her shoulders. "It's alright. You didn't know."

"Also, Phatiel said…"

"I know what he said. Yes, it's true."

"We are in the past?!"

"Yes."

"But why–"

"Look. I could tell you. But right now, you would not understand. Why don't you give yourself a little time till your mind becomes capable of seeing more? You'll find your answer then."

It was clear that Antares was not in the mood for questions. The Quarta respectfully went silent. A taciturn journey was a burden, though;

after a while, Hagal and Tei started talking in a low voice, walking slightly behind.

Nesteri remained quiet. Eventually, he turned to Antares but then abandoned his intention, hesitant to speak.

"Yes?" some indefinable, elusive expression glistened in the eyes of the Great Star when she looked at him. It flashed and was gone. "I'm listening."

"Thank you," Nesteri said. "There was indeed something I wanted to ask. Something I thought about for a while... but I could never understand. How does a Star become Dark? Are we not supposed to be warriors of Light, all of us? How is it even possible that someone can turn away from their own essence?"

A shadow flickered across Antares' face. "At the beginning of time, all Stars were Light," she said. "Since the invasion of the Shadow into this realm, however, things have changed. Our part of the Universe turned into a battlefield, and many have fallen in this battle over the millennia that followed."

Tei and Hagal stopped talking and drew closer.

"The Shadow has no creative power; its army is an army of hostages. To keep the battle going, it constantly needs more... and so it captures souls with doubt and pain. But *not* the kind of pain that teaches you and helps you grow. The weapon of the Shadow is the pain that blinds your mind. The kind that makes your consciousness shrink into one point, until all other thoughts and feelings disappear, until despair is all you can perceive. The present moment turns into a prison, locked into the eternity of suffering. It seems as if that dark night of the soul will last forever, and the dawn will never come. The more disempowered one allows himself to feel, the more gates he opens for the Shadow to enter and to take him down. This eternity of pain an illusion," sadness rang in Antares' voice, "it's only an illusion, but to the ensnared consciousness it appears very real. Through the power of despondent thoughts, the Shadow tries to erode the warriors' mental defences and break their Will. If it succeeds, they forget who they are... and are thrown at its mercy."

"Is that what usually happens?" Tei frowned.

"The Shadow has many arms," Antares said. "Its other favourite is fear. Many had been defeated through it. Fear has a much lesser grip on us, though. Verily, many Stars are resistant to it, hence when fighting us, the Shadow tends to resort to doubt and torture instead."

Nesteri narrowed his eyes. "How does one fight off an attack like that?"

"If you stay fully attuned to the Light within you, nothing can bring you down."

"Not even the fiercest attack?"

"Absolutely nothing."

"In that case, how can the Shadow ever succeed in darkening anyone?" asked Nesteri again, puzzled.

"Only with their permission."

"That surely can't be true!" Tei exclaimed. "*Nobody* would submit to the enemy by choice! I'd rather die than become a slave of the Shadow."

"It's not a 'come and get me' kind of permission," explained Antares patiently. "You give your permission when you stop fighting. You are defeated when you start thinking that evil is 'needed' in this world, that 'resistance is pointless', and that 'you can't win'. Those traitor thoughts sap your strength; it is as if you had willingly put your weapon down. After that, the Shadow has an open gate."

"Why those thoughts, though?" Hagal asked.

"Because they take you away from your true essence," said Antares. "The Shadow knows all too well that for as long as you are connected to Light, you are invincible. So it wants you to falter. It wants dark thoughts to grow in your mind, and contaminate it until it turns into your own enemy. That's why mastering your mind is one of the most important arts for the warrior."

Hagal nodded, thoughtful.

"But…what if there is *really* no hope?" asked Tei.

"There's always hope."

They made a stop amongst the magnificent ruins of a castle, partly reclaimed by the green fur of ivy and moss. Through the remains of stained glass in tall windows, sunshine was falling in, scattering into colourful puzzle pieces on the stone floor.

Their training and a lunch were now over, and the Stars were enjoying a blissful moment of repose. They sat on a rug together, silver chalices with virapana by their side. Soft glints danced on the dark ruby surface of the drinks.

Hagal was scribbling something in his notebook, as he got into the habit of doing, while Nesteri was strumming pensively an akhenbi. A sunray flowing through the stained glass tinted his hair emerald green. #Antares sat nearby. She was creating complex energy structures in the air and watched them change, with her eyes half-closed. Nesteri gazed for a while too, wondering what those might be, but didn't ask.

"I have a bizarre feeling," Hagal said softly, lifting his head, "that time is flowing much slower."

"It is," replied Antares unimpassionedly, deep in her thoughts.

"How?!" Hagal asked, surprised that he could still be astonished after all he had witnessed so far. Nesteri stopped strumming and pressed his open palm against the strings to quieten them.

"Because of me," Antares said. The energy structures around her faded away. "The speed of time depends on different factors... And it can be altered, too. You exist in two layers – one is the universal flow of time wherever you are, another one is your own temporal field. You can influence the universal flow with your temporal energy, if focused enough."

"Do you mean one can make time around him flow slower or faster at will?" Nesteri squinted with disbelief.

"Exactly right."

"But...how is it possible?"

"Through the Infinite Domain."

Nesteri rested his head against the akhenbi's neck. The idea of being a master of time felt surreal. "What is the Infinite Domain, Holy Star?"

"In our world," Antares said, "there are two kinds of time, two natural domains – the Finite and the Infinite. The Finite Domain is what you know so well, it's what you're used to, all your todays, and yesterdays, and tomorrows. This kind of time is fixed, it only flows in one direction. But the Infinite one...it's like white light that combines all colours. Every moment there contains the present, past, and future, all in one. There is no division between the rays. Even though you spend most of your lives in the Finite Doman, it is the Infinite where you truly belong. The closer you are to your real essence, the more power over time you have."

A short silence fell after her words, filled with the leafy whispers and the cooing of doves coming from above. 'Time dissolves into the white light... that knows no time. Light is what awakens eternity within!' Nesteri suddenly realised.

"Talking about time," Hagal looked around with a frown, "I wonder where Tei has disappeared off to. It's been a while now."

For an answer, Antares pointed up. On the far side, Tei was climbing, slowly descending the jagged wall.

"I could have guessed," Hagal muttered. "So. Very. Him."

Noticing being watched, Tei started moving faster, in an obvious bet to show off. And show of he did, with smooth lizard-like dexterity using dents, cracks and lumps of stone for support. When less than ten feet separated him from the ground, Tei decided not to bother further. He jumped down, twisting his body in the air, landing on his feet and hands and rolling over his back, then strengthened up.

It was almost flawlessly executed. Almost. Some bad luck, or the lack of practice, or perhaps both, got in the way when they were least needed. 'Damn, my ankle!' Tei realised, as soon as he got up, he must have sprained it. He cursed under his breath, then forced himself to smile and joined his friends pretending that nothing happened.

"The view is incredible up there," he said walking up to them.

"What did you see?" Nesteri asked.

"The forest stretches out for miles. I tried to spot that Reh place but I couldn't find it. The mountains in the east look tremendous, though." Tei smiled lightly, remembering the stunning vista of snowy peaks, the kisses of breeze on his face, and the flocks of white birds in sunlight. "Is that where we are going to?"

"Yes," Antares said. "You shall see the Caeron Mountains before long."

"Right," Nesteri took the hint. He finished his drink and rose to his feet. "Let's go, then."

"Let's go," Hagal echoed him.

Two figures hurled down a dark and muddy road. One, tall and hooded, marched with long confident strides; his iron-shod boots rang a heavy thunder on the cobblestones. A golden emblem – an archer aiming from a double bow – shimmered on his purple cloak, the mark of a Captain of the City Watch.

At a strong gust of wind, the cloak flew open snapping behind the captain's shoulders, and the hilts of two swords gleamed coldly in the uncertain light of the stars. Captain Angford was well prepared. A small dagger, unseen, was hidden at the top of his right boot. Since the moon had vanished, the city streets were far from safe, especially the grimy beggars quarters like this one.

A short humpy figure trotted hurriedly by his side, struggling to keep pace. Cropt, one of the best spies of the Empire, had been in captain's service for two weeks now. His all-rounded speech and sleazy servility vexed Angford, yet he was forced to give Cropt's skills due. The old cad certainly did know his job. He needed merely two weeks to do what others failed to do for months – through his secret channels, Cropt had finally got on the trail of Dio, the enemy of the state, the biggest thief and traitor of the Creljatrn Empire. Soon, they would seize her and regain the Rainbow Tear. The girl would be too stupid to sell it, Angford reckoned.

Only His Brightest Highness and the Venerable Magi Council knew the truth, but Angford, like the common folk, believed in the gem's magical power. If nothing else, one thing was sure – the loss of the giant diamond brought about the dark nights. Three moonless months had passed since the heist.

It was in the most blessed year 853 when Tazerd the Strong had started a revolt beheading the old king, to crown himself in the Red Citadel only a fortnight later. It was then that the amazed people of Tvorndaln first saw a silver oval in the sky. The disc shone brighter than the brightest of the stars, the priests spoke of the heavenly sign for the monarch, and the annual Revelation Day was set to celebrate the beginning of a new era.

The Rainbow Tear appeared soon after, brought by a farmer boy. The poor idiot was mumbling some ridiculous lie about a shooting star that fell onto his field. The thief was jailed and tried, to no avail. The City Watch had been known to open even the most stubborn of mouths, yet the boy kept saying the same story. His body proved to be too frail, and the rascal died before they could get the truth out of him. Much to Angford's annoyance.

The diamond was reported in a due form and requisitioned by the crown at once. The King ordered it to be locked in a secret place and guarded more than all treasures of the Empire. The only man (except His Brightest Highness, of course) who knew about the gem would never speak again. Angford smiled wryly at the memory.

A crooked row of crumbling dwellings slowly emerged before him from the gloom. The captain cringed as the reek of sweat, dirt, mould, and rotten food hit his nose, all at once.

"Lead on," he ordered Cropt.

The spy shuddered like an anxious hound then leapt forward with his sickeningly hasty and slightly limping step, which Angford usually found so irritating. But now the captain didn't care to notice. His thoughts were focused entirely on their chase. In his mind's eye, Angford already saw himself in Major's uniform, blue and white. 'And who's laughing now?' he gloated. 'Angford the oaf, yeah? A moron, yeah? I'll show ya now who's the moron! Ya'll see…ya will all see!'

They stopped before a wretched door barely hanging on two long rusty hinges. Predictably, it was locked. Angford growled angrily. With a kick of his heavy boot, the door went flying in and the two chasers burst inside.

The chamber was empty. On the crooked table, a lonely candle end was burning down. Dirty rugs piled in the corner for a bed. No one there.

At this sight, Cropt erupted with a howl. "I told you! Put guards around the place, I said. Did I? But no, you feared that they could snatch your reward. Your damned greed! And now, what now?! She's gone! For the mother of all sins, she's gone!!"

Boiling with anger, Angford jerked towards the spy – a rapid swish of a cloak blew the candle out. Cropt's plaintive whining and wailing were still ringing in his ears. The captain swung his arm and sent a furious blind blow in the direction of the mewling noises. A muffled moan came out from the darkness – then silence.

"A short rest, perhaps?" Antares finally suggested.

"Agree and agree again," Hagal yawned. "I'm really sleepy for some reason."

"Same here," said Nesteri. "Almost like there's something in the air."

"That's right," Antares nodded. "We are passing near the grotto where the Dreaming Stream takes its source from. Everyone who tastes its water falls asleep."

"For ever," Tei joked in an ominous voice.

"Just for a while," Antares smiled, "but in their dream, they turn into a fish."

"Random." Nesteri raised his eyebrows.

"Why is that?" Hagal asked.

"Because of the shell-grass that grows around," Antares explained. "It's the grass, not the stream that spreads the drowsy spell. You will find that in the grotto, the air is clear and fresh, thanks to some other springs. It's rather interesting there. I'd have a look if I were you."

"Are you not coming with us, Holy Star?" Hagal sounded surprised.

"I'll wait here," Antares said. "Let it be your adventure. When I'm around, all I do is teaching. And all you do is listening. Go have some fun."

Hagal shrugged his shoulders – he didn't mind either way.

"Err, I'll stay," Tei said unexpectedly. Nesteri and Hagal exchanged puzzled looks.

"You'll what?" Nesteri said. "What's up?"

"It doesn't sound like you," added Hagal with distrust. "Is everything alright?"

"All's good. I'm just a bit weary. Need a break."

"There's something *fishy* going on there," Nesteri quipped narrowing his eyes.

"Stop sniffing that grass, Nesteri. The nasty visions will soon go away. There's still hope for you," Tei retorted.

"Tei, you sure you don't want to come?" Hagal asked again, studying Tei's face.

"Yeah, next time. Sorry. I'm...tired. Just tired."

"Hm, fair enough," Hagal gave in, still unsure what to think about it. He never heard Tei complaining about being tired, ever. "Well, see you later, then."

The Stars soon disappeared amongst the trees. The rustle of their footsteps faded slowly, merging into the sound of splashing water.

"Holy Star..." began Tei when they were left on their own.

Antares looked at him. Ironic sparkles danced in her luminous eyes.

"I know why you have stayed," Tei continued, visibly discomfited. "I'm sorry for that nonsense earlier. It won't happen again. I promise I can change!"

Antares sat on the grass showing Tei to do the same. "What do I hear? You want us all to die of boredom?" she teased him.

"No! Why, that would never...Not in your company, anyway," he finished with a cheeky smirk.

Antares smiled back, pensively somewhat. "You're bright and joyful, Loiveri," she said to him. "Don't change that. You are needed in this world, just the way you are."

The breeze ruffled her hair, blowing a strand across her face. Antares combed it back with her fingers. "You'd do with some help, I presume?"

"Yes," Tei admitted willingly, rubbing his right ankle, which had become noticeably sore. "I'd hate to be a burden and delay our trip."

"Very well," Antares said.

Tei's pain vanished in an instant. "Whoa, incredible!" he wiggled his foot. "You probably know this, but Nesteri can do healing, too. Although it takes him much longer. Thank you, Holy Star."

"Don't mention it." Antares looked at Tei as if seeing through to his soul, the look that reminded him of Famaris. "And what about your other wound?" she asked. "The one you're hiding in your heart."

Tei pressed his lips together and looked away. He'd rather not talk about it. "It's still hurting," he said.

"It's hurting because you resist," Antares told him mildly. "It doesn't have to be that way."

"What do you mean?"

"Love only hurts when you mix it with illusion. When your mind is overgrown with expectations of what could and couldn't be, like a wild field with weeds. The gap between the expectation and reality is what causes pain. If you embrace the present moment as it is, nothing can disturb your peace."

"Uhm…I'm not sure I can follow right now. I'll have to meditate on that," Tei said. Yet unexplainably, he did feel better. Something in Antares' words gave him hope. "I appreciate the advice."

He took a deep breath and dreamily looked around. Antares' presence filled him with unusual serenity and bliss. 'I haven't felt like this for years, if ever,' Tei mused. His gaze wandered up towards the sky, clear and lucid, as only the autumn sky can be. A leaf fell down, sun-gilded, swirling by his side. Tei watched it dancing in the air. "I've just remembered a good song," he said, "Do you want to hear?"

Antares conjured an akhenbi for an answer. Tei took it from her hands and struck a few gentle chords. The song known from his childhood tasted of light melancholy, after so long.

> "Autumn came with the sighs of the evening wind,
> And the golden whisper of leaves…"

A small bird, grey-yellow, perched on the branch nearby. The branch swayed and the bird flapped its wings to keep balance.

> "She has painted the world amber and amaranthine –
> The mystery shades of her dreams…"

After a while, Hagal and Nesteri returned. They flopped on the grass next to Tei itching to share what they had seen, all at once, laughing and interrupting one another.

"You should have come with us," Hagal said. "The place was quite remarkable."

They told him about icy stalactites and the glittering walls, and the flat oblong pebbles that shone when the Stars approached, and the blue stones that lit up at their touch.

"What have you done to Nesteri? He looks even more zoned out than what I'm used to," Tei joked.

"It is because," answered Hagal indignantly, "he drank from some unknown spring there! Ignoring all my warnings."

"You don't know what you're missing, Hagal," Nesteri said, grinning.

"I'm missing nothing! Certainly prefer being dry, too."

"What?"

"He tried to push me into the water when I refused to join the lunacy," Hagal explained, unimpressed.

Nesteri sniggered. "That would refresh your senses! How's your backside, by the way? Still sore?"

Tei raised an eyebrow. "His what?"

"He parked his bum on a nest of some small lizardey creatures. By accident, he said. Hah! Apparently, they were endowed with sharp teeth." Nesteri said laughing.

Hagal grimaced at the memory.

"Maybe just as well I didn't go with you." Tei chuckled.

Nesteri's put his hand in his side pocket as if to show something but then changed his mind.

"What's there?" Tei asked, noticing his move.

"Well, if you really want to know…"After a short hesitation, Nesteri pulled out and opened his hand – glowing between his fingers was a green pebble from the grotto.

Trees wrapped in autumn fire rustled above their heads, a fire that doesn't burn only deceives the trusting heart with the promise of warmth. The wind carried leafy flames kindling them underfoot. The forest floor was all dark moss and crimson red.

To his surprise, Hagal spotted a sietri flower, lost amongst the huge trees of the alien world. The Star imagined how at night it must unfurl its petals, a tiny sparkle in the dark, alone, knowing nothing about thousands of them blossoming far away... And when sietri blossom, the meadow turns into a lake reflecting the night sky. Gaze for a while, and your senses are spellbound, and soon you can't tell anymore what it is your hear – the splashing of waves or the rustle of grass, and strange visions are summoned into your mind...

Nesteri suddenly slowed his gait and looked around curiously. "Hey, where are we?" he asked.

"What kind of question is that?" Tei snorted patronisingly. "In the Eité Forest, kid."

"No," Nesteri shook his head. "No. Look! It's a seabed, I think. I mean, it was a seabed once... Oh, wait," he focused again. "Before that, there used to be a city here. An ancient one, older even than Tvorn. Can't you see?"

"Older than what?"

"Tvorn or Tvorndaln, as the place we are going to used to be called in the past. Long before it became known as Reh," Antares explained.

"Alright, but how would *he* know?" Tei snapped. "Argh, he's doing it again!"

"Doing what again?" Antares raised her eyebrows.

"Being freaking annoying, that's what!"

"Indeed," Hagal joined in. "Earlier he spoke to us in some language called Aē."

Their astonished faces made Nesteri chuckle. "Oh come on! I'm sure if you had paid any attention you would notice, too. Why are you making so much fuss about it? Look, I simply–"

Then suddenly, Nesteri met Antares' eyes. Joy, relief, and something else that no words could express, mixed in her gaze. It was as if his whole life came together to a single point, his whole life was just waiting for this moment. Nesteri would give anything in the world to see that gaze again. Disarmed and mesmerised, the Star forgot completely what he was about to say.

CHAPTER XII

TRESAI ODEMENUIS
FACETS OF REALITY

*"Hazaron saal nargis apni benoori pe roti hai.
Bari mushkil se hota hai chaman mein didahwar paida."* [8]
~*Allama Iqbaal*

"I want to know what's going on here," Tei said gruffly. "I think an explanation would be good." He and Hagal stood studying Nesteri, their arms crossed.

"What explanation? That I looked around when you didn't?"

"I can't see anything but the forest, you git. Your stupid showing off starts getting on my nerve. As do your lame excuses."

"Talking about lame – I think that's something *you* excel in."

"No chance I'll never master it as much as you have done."

"Oh, stop it!" Hagal cringed. "For Doregi's sake. I feel like I'm back in the kindergarten." He looked at Antares and added, "My sincere apologies for these two. They get like this sometimes. It used to be much worse."

"Err... sorry!" a somewhat bashful yet cheeky smile emerged on Tei's face. "We're usually good... ish."

"Vigilant, alert and ready," added Nesteri with a grin, joining by Tei's side. Now they both stood before her, heads slightly bowed, uncertain how Antares would react, and what they should do.

Antares smiled. "Good," she said. "Keep it that way, warriors."

---

[8] "For a thousand years, the eye-shaped narcissus flower has been lamenting its sightlessness. Someone with real eyes is rarely born in the garden."

Hagal shot at them disapproving glance. "I'm curious, though, what is that place Nesteri spoke about? Where is it?" he asked the Great Star.

"It's here," Antares responded. "All around you."

Hagal looked at the trees, then the yellow leaves under his feet. "I see no oceans and no ancient cities," he said.

"If you only focus on what you expect to see, you'll never notice anything else," Antares told him. "Your beliefs and attention filter your reality. But if you keep your mind alert and still, you will learn so much more."

"What are we actually talking about?" Tei joined.

"On Lagu, like elsewhere in the Universe, there are different layers of existence, for which space is constant and time is variable."

"Urgh, I wish I hadn't asked."

"Imagine a book with many pages," said Antares. "Space is the binding, and the pages are the times that the place has existed through. As you make your way through the book, you only see the page you're at."

"That's right."

"Yet all the earlier pages are still there," Antares continued. "And if you wish, you can go back, and discover what the place was like years, centuries, millennia ago... though the further back you go, the more energy you need."

"So that means that the past is always there, it's still alive, even in the present?" Nesteri asked.

"Yes. The energy of time, like other forms of energy, can neither be created nor destroyed."

"But what about the future?" Hagal wondered. "Can we see the pages that lie ahead?"

"It's possible," Antares said. "To navigate through the labyrinth of the future requires certain mastery, however."

Hagal pulled his notebook out and scribbled something hastily, as he walked.

"Well then," Tei said, direct as always, "I want to see those 'other pages', too." His eyes swept the forest, brass and copper-red, glittering in the sunshine. "Can I see them?"

"Of course." Antares smiled a magician's smile.

Tei could not tell if Antares did something, and what it was she did. But the Eité Forest disappeared. The Stars stood surrounded by an incredible garden. The rows of trees and scented shrubs studded the web of curved pathways around them. Small winged creatures buzzed in and out of the strange pipe-like blossom.

After the rain, the air was fresh and tranquil. Water twinkled in little puddles, and wet leaves shook off drops of glitter in the wind. But the path! Hagal breathed out a sigh of wonder – the slabs were made of gold, or so it seemed. As he looked closer, the chaotic pattern of cracks and dents came together as curious etchings, partially lost to the ravages of time. The pictures shimmered in the sun, whispered, crooned, warbled and called to him – but in vain. He didn't understand the tongue.

"Holy Star, what does this mean?" he asked, pointing down. The slab he stood on was marked with a cascade of streams flowing from one source.

"Freedom," replied Antares. "There are three hundred and sixty of these, times two. Just choose one each."

She jumped onto a different slab; engraved on it were triangles with wings. Nesteri thought he'd seen them before…but where? He looked again and his eyes opened wide – suddenly he remembered. 'I saw those in my dream! A weird coincidence.'

Tei walked forward and stopped. An enigmatic picture of a flag turning into an eagle was his choice. Hagal picked an image of a crystal gazer. Nesteri hesitated. He was drawn to the mysterious vision from his dream, but that would mean to stand next to Antares. His heart speeded up its beat. 'You're an Astarrien,' Nesteri reminded himself, 'Astarriens step back for no one. Do as your truth tells you.' He finally took a step and stood by Antares' side, his face cool and decisive, betraying nothing of the tumult he felt.

The Quarta waited, looking at each other and at the Great Star, curious what's next. The path under their feet yielded the honeyed gleam of molten sun.

Antares watched them in silence. "Your choices are the threads the fabric of your life is woven with," she said.

And in that moment, they could see. Not one path and not two, but hundreds upon hundreds stretched out before them, and every slab was a gateway. An opportunity. A seed of what might or might not be.

Then the visions came. Their future swam at them, rough sketches, maybies, whats and whys. Hagal saw books and scrolls, a hut amongst the mountains, and a young Star braving a long and rocky path looking for him. From afar, a storm was looming, drawing in, but the skies were still bright above the valley...

Tei's vision was fire and battles, and the cold vastness of space torn with explosions of light. He saw the eyes of those who would fight by his side, those who he would lead. Then a face...had he seen it before? A piercing gaze, a scar on the left temple, and the jet-black hair traced with silver. For a moment, Tei felt like he knew who it was. Or somehow ought to have known...

Nesteri looked up. His path rose in spirals, high and higher, but where to, he could not tell. The world became a blur. A figure of Light, a sword and a chalice shone in his mind again, flashbacks of that strange dream he had on the Blue Planet; too close, too far, dazzling, unsettling. 'Cai to Ceiveri,' said the unicorn. What did that mean? Did it matter that Antares stood on the same slab? He felt somewhat light-headed from her presence.

Nesteri closed then slowly opened his eyes. The maze around was alive with shimmer, as clear as if it belonged in this reality – and yet it did not. It trembled, throbbed, whirled in a dizzying rhythm, constantly readjusting; new rays of chances flared from every point of choice, new paths were splitting and merging together. Nothing felt true anymore. 'Light, *what is this?*! I must be going mad...' Nesteri looked to his right at Antares, still and peaceful, amongst the wild phantasmagoria of gleam. Her serenity had calmed his mind.

"Who built this?" Nesteri whispered.

"Priests of the temple where the main path leads to," Antares answered. "They were adherents of freedom of choice." Her voice cast the visions away. The frenzied dance of realities had stopped. The garden was quiet again – just the thin lapping of leaves – and the golden path was only one.

"They were?" Hagal asked. His everyday tone of voice made Nesteri wonder if Hagal saw the shimmering labyrinth as well. Something told Nesteri that he didn't.

"They are long gone," Antares said.

"What happened?" Tei was inquisitive as always.

"One of the choices had led them astray," came an enigmatic answer. "Millennia grassed their footprints since."

'Reality is just a reflection, a multitude of reflections. Stop and watch, with your mind quiet, and you'll recognise your true power over it,' Hagal would write in his notebook later. *'Attention, focus and willpower are the true weapons of the warrior's mind. Seek mastery in all three. Beware of the habits and attitudes that go unnoticed.'*

Led by Antares, the Quarta followed with curious steps. On both sides of the path, the shrubs sighed, the trees rustled and the silver spheres trembled anxiously on their long stems amongst the grass. The breeze carried exotic fragrances.

More oddities were there in quite a number, resembling large shells growing upside down, bright blue. Their edges were spangled with glassy drops. Tei touched one lightly – it gave in, soft and warm. At his touch, the shell squirmed repugnantly, and its surface rippled with hundreds of cracks, plopping hastily like spasmodic mouths.

"Damn!!" the Star jerked his hand back. "What the heck is this?!" he asked, his lips twisted in disgust. "Excuse my language."

"Tfoxtexs."

"Forget the name," Tei muttered, examining his hand. "I hope it wasn't poisonous or something…what even was it? A plant, an animal?"

"It's a bit of both," Antares smiled at the look on Tei's face. "They're quite harmless."

Tei shook his hand, disgust still bubbling in him. 'Think before you act,' he remembered the words his teacher used to say. Tei sighed. More often than not, he failed to heed them.

Hagal walked looking down, fascinated. Unknown cities, fantastic beasts and mysterious scenes were passing before his eyes in a kaleidoscopic flow. A window curtain turning into a cornucopia. A butterfly with a third wing on its left side. A man with a globe on his head. What did these mean? What kind of choice did they point to? Hagal shuddered at the creepy vision of a three-headed figure stretching out its right hand. The Star jumped over that slab.

At the end of the golden path, they saw a forsaken temple. Echoes of forgotten ceremonies and years of dead, stifling hush reigned within its walls. Pallid shafts of sunlight fell in through the cracks in the roof like thin quivering feathers. A pensive glow brushed on the enigmatic murals and metal ornaments, and scattered across the floor thin polished rods, strangely untarnished by time. The rest of the large hall was drenched in shadows.

Silence sealed it all. It watchful presence shrouded the intruders, binding them to keep quiet. The Quarta trod softly, following Antares' steps. Under their feet, old rugs crumbled to dust.

Deep inside where no light reached, an altar crowned a set of steps; twinned tiers of polished pillars locked it in a semicircle. Long crystals came out of the podium, marked with a faint gleam.

'You are more than you think you are...'

Soundlessly, Antares walked over and went down by the altar. Soundlessly, she started picking up from the floor the unknown glossy rods. The Quarta watched, mystified, not daring to say a word. With a soft click, the rods slid into some clefts invisible in the dark, and the crystals suddenly came to life. Their light was green and coral, dim at first, but flaring up as quickly as a bird flies from an open cage.

And surely, the ghosts had soon arrived. Just as they would have done millennia ago, craving the light, enthralled by the light, drinking the light in. Yes, they were there. Antares glanced over at Nesteri, at his amazed eyes. He could see them as well. The Great Star stepped towards Hagal and Tei and briefly touched their temples. Quickened by her presence – too inebriating, too close – they held their breaths and froze to attention.

'...you are...'

Their vision expanded in an instant, sudden and startling as if a blindfold had fallen off. Now they too could see. Around the altar, a crush of eidolons was gathering, wispy and colourless, ethereal like the wind. Hoods covered the ashen faces.

'What are they?' Tei thought, but for once hesitated to ask aloud.

Meanwhile, the swarm was growing in size, as if compelled to the crystals by some force beyond its will. The Stars stood motionless as the foggy stream surged and swirled around. The ghosts stayed away though, always at a distance, and none of them stepped close.

'Around us, there's a whole world we cannot see. A world we know nothing about! It feels like I lived all my life with my eyes shut,' Hagal frowned.

'You're more than you think you are…' A strange voice sounded in Nesteri's head, coming as if out of nowhere. The world around quivered and went dark.

'Who are you..?'

'You.'

'I don't understand.'

'Wake up.'

'Who are you??'

'Wake up, before it's too late.'

'Too late for what?'

'Open your eyes!'

The Star obeyed, but what he saw was nothing like he could expect. The shrine, the glimmering altar and his taciturn friends – all were there, all was right, except the perspective. Nesteri stood slightly above, and opposite them, it seemed – he could clearly see in the flickering glow of the crystals. Antares smiled with the corner of her lips and raised her gaze. The strange smouldering fire stirred up in Nesteri again when their eyes met. The Great Star looked at him without a hint of surprise. As if she knew.

Tei and Hagal were further behind, glancing around, unaware. And he was there too, Nesteri realised, there, to Antares' left, his face lifeless and blank. *His* face..? Shock washed over him like an icy wave. 'Have I died??' He shuddered, stunned, back in his body, struggling for breath. The place felt dizzy and surreal. It wasn't death, whatever came after him. What was it…?

Breathe, he said to himself.

Breathe calmly and deeply. Nobody needs to know.

Nesteri secretly pressed a point under his left thumb, praying to remain still. A few long moments passed, chimed out by the heavy rumble of his heartbeat, echoing in his temples.

Breathe.

The cold spell of shock was slowly receding from him. His vision became clearer, or maybe the shadows inside the temple became lighter.

Nesteri could see tripod braziers, and banners, and metal symbols on the walls. He didn't notice them before. Two narrow doors framed the altar on both sides.

His mind was now cool and sharp, and strangely quiet. "Light be my guide," Nesteri lips moved soundlessly. A hazy glow of the crystals reflected in his eyes. "Show me my path. Whatever happens, I will not step back."

After a while, Hagal and Tei's usual vision returned. The misty creatures had faded from sight, although their presence was obvious still. But the altar had changed, shimmering with a wet gleam, as if splashed with water. The rods began to melt, trickling down in glittering drops.

Seeing that, Antares turned around and headed towards the door without saying a word. The Quarta followed her. They felt they shouldn't stay there, not for a moment longer.

Daylight, white and dazzling, greeted them outside. The garden seemed different from before, but what had changed, the Quarta could not tell.

"Holy Star…" Tei began, his voice soft and pensive, unusually for him. "What was that?"

"A long time ago a kingdom stood here," said Antares. "But greed swept its glory away. Three brothers fought for the crown, craving power more than the good of their country. Villages burnt and towns lay in ruins over the years. Finally, of the three brothers there remained only two. Equally powerful and equally dangerous, they had clashed time and time again, but neither could win."

"So they perished in war?" Hagal asked.

"It wasn't the weapons but the secret arts that destroyed them. One of the brothers ordered his priests to create an artefact, a likeness of which had never been seen before. It would sap the life force of his enemies and give it to his own army. And according to his will, it was done. His brother was defeated, but those who used the artefact became its slaves. They needed its energy to live. When the enemies were no more, the energy withered, the hope vanished, and they turned into ghosts."

"Then what we saw was…"

"Just a vision, no more. Every place keeps reflections of its past."

Hagal suddenly understood.

"They have never left their time, haven't they?"

A scene from the era bygone troubled his mind. A land, beautiful once, torn by hatred and greed. The days of laughter, dreams and promises, all gone. Long lost are the kings and their armies, he thought, and where they once stood now it's just grass and whispers. All for the scattered rods on the dark temple's floor. How was it worth it? Hagal sighed and said nothing more.

A deep crag lay across their path. Down below, a shallow brook was hurrying its waters, the trees barely reaching it with their gnarled roots. Far to the right, a crumbling wooden bridge was making promises it doubtfully could keep.

'I wonder if we ever get out of this forest,' thought Tei somewhat wearily, looking down. The place was way too peaceful, and his soul craved danger and adventures. 'Or we'll grow old and die before it ends…'

A fleeting smirk touched Antares' lips. "Don't worry, you shall be out of here way sooner than that," she said reassuringly.

"Damn! Not again. I totally forgot!" Tei cringed. "I forgot to screen my thoughts. Bloody forgetfulness!"

"Don't swear," Antares narrowed her eyes.

Something in her voice made Tei shrivel inwardly. He never heard that tone of voice from her before. "I'm sorry," he hastily apologised.

"Our teacher would tell us off every time whenever he heard any swearing," Nesteri remarked casually. "He was very adamant about it, for some reason. Not that Tei would listen, of course."

"Oh shut up," Tei pushed him with an elbow, then realised he just confirmed Nesteri's words. "Oops."

"Well, to me, it's just distasteful," Hagal chimed in.

"I couldn't understand it then and I still can't understand it now," said Tei with a petulant shrug. "It's *just words*! Chatter doesn't amount to much, does it?"

"Never underestimate the power of the spoken word," Antares replied. Confirming Tei's worst anticipations, she turned towards the rotten bridge. "The energy projected through your voice is mightier than you think. The stronger you become, the more formidable the effect it can have. It's not unusual for swear words to work akin a deleterious spell."

"A what, excuse me?"

"Deleterious means harmful," Hagal told him. "It's really good to know," he added. "I understand now why swearing never felt right to me. I wish I teacher explained that. I wonder why he didn't."

"I would assume he didn't want to tease your curiosity and encourage unreasonable behaviours in your younger years," Antares said with a smile.

"Yeah, I can see that," grinned Tei. "I totally can see."

The bridge was now before them, dark and creaky. Antares joined two fingers of her right hand and drew a symbol in the air above. The symbol flashed green and dissipated, its particles slowly falling down and melting into the wood.

"What was it?" Nesteri asked.

"A Rune of Power. You too shall learn about them. Before long."

They stepped onto the bridge. Now it felt strangely solid and as safe as if made of stone, even though nothing in its appearance had changed.

"Hear me," the Great Star continued. "Your voice is a music that touches the fibre of the Universe…a distant echo of the song of Creation itself. Its magic wakes the Elements and transforms reality. Be mindful when you speak. Words that you say remain imprinted in the field of Force forever. They can both harm and heal."

On the opposite side, the ground was rising gently, folding up into a hill. A double stone circle crowned its top, the smaller monoliths surrounding the larger ones inside. Thick moss yielded under the Stars' feet, swallowing the sound of footsteps.

"Wait," said Antares. "Let me show you something."

She looked up. The sky had swiftly darkened with a storm of clouds summoned by her will. Antares' sleeves snapped soaring in the wind, flapping like wings, dazzlingly white against the ashy stones. "Your task is to make the sky clear again," she said, "using the power of your voice."

"Please teach us how," Nesteri asked her. He suddenly remembered the Academy. The Masters there were said to wield the weather. Their teacher certainly could. Nesteri never thought he would be lucky to ever learn that skill himself.

"What do you know about the mindgates, warriors?"

"Not much," Tei admitted. "Only that they exist. Our training was only focused on one, the Feorn Point below the navel. The one we use for fighting."

"Mindgates are the energy points of the body," Nesteri added. "As Tei said, we didn't have a chance to learn much about them before the Fall, but I did find a book–"

"Nerd!" Tei snorted.

"–and it was an interesting read. Even though the manuscript was written in an old style, quite tiresome to follow."

Antares nodded briefly. "That is right. Your mind is an energy structure, which is connected to the outer world through multiple points of contact, or gates. Of these, 7 are of the most use to you right now. They are positioned alongside your spine, all the way up to the crown of your head. Learning to use the Gates consciously is a path to self-mastery and a key to great personal power."

"Perfect," Tei's eyes sparkled eagerly. "What are we waiting for, then? Let's do it!"

Antares favoured him with a light smile. "Each Gate works on its own frequency, which we perceive as rainbow colours–"

"What if I don't perceive?" Tei asked.

"You will, with time," Antares told him patiently. "These are more subtle energies than those you're used to. The first one, at the base of the spine, is red. Its power is to connect you with the level of the matter, health, vitality and stamina. It's blocked by fear and the feeling of not belonging."

Hagal sat down leaning his back against a rock, and pulled his notebook out. "I don't mean to be rude," he said. "Just need to write this down. What is the meaning of 'blocked'?"

"It means that there is not much energy flowing through that point. And if that happens, you lose the freedom of self-expression in that sphere. Shall the Root be affected, one becomes easily fatigued, the sleep cycle often goes out of balance, too. The level of vitality is low and tends to stay low. The Heart Gate, which is green in colour, when blocked creates a struggle to feel love, to express one's feelings and to connect with others. The weak Brow Gate, dark blue, divests one's of ability to concentrate, to comprehend complex patterns and to remember."

Antares went on explaining the mindgates system as a whole, pausing to let the Quarta discover the gates one by one, and answering their questions. It was late afternoon by the time they finished.

"Let's try it out now?" Tei suggested restively.

"We certainly shall," Antares responded. "Close your eyes." She paused. "Now, turn your attention to the energy within, and focus on each mindgate in turn, moving upwards. Let me know when you're ready."

The Quarta nodded their heads, and Antares continued, "Direct your attention on the Orange and Yellow Gates, then draw their energy up to your throat. Now, set your intention on clearing the clouds…and sing it out."

Hagal cringed. Singing in front of others was something he would much like to eschew.

Antares glanced at him. "Tei, would you care to go first?"

"Absolutely!"

"And you, Hagal, can use the voice of command instead if you prefer."

"What is the voice of command?" Nesteri asked.

"Another way of channelling the energy of voice. It's mostly used in mind control, although it's good for other purposes, too. Remember to keep breathing down your diaphragm…that's right."

"So, shall I start?" Tei said with hardly concealed impatience.

"Go ahead."

Tei stepped forward and sang a few lines.

"You need to see the result very clearly," Antares corrected him as she noticed that the Star soon got distracted. "Create a picture of the sunny sky, feel the warmth of the sun on your skin…that's right. Keep the picture before your mind's eye, sharp and clear."

Adhering to Antares' directions, Tei tried again. To his bewilderment, the clouds started to slowly dissipate.

Whoa, amazing!!" Tei gasped out, excited like a child. "It feels like magic! Does this only work on Lagu?"

"In works everywhere," Antares said with a smile.

The Great Star brought the clouds back. "Now, you two."

"Well..." Hagal ran his fingers through his hair, somewhat nervously. He was frantically trying to come up with some words to say.

Seeing his indecision, Nesteri stepped forward.

"I'll go first," he said considerately.

The evening was drawing close; in the fading daylight, the wind was caressing the leaves of the Eité forest, whispering its otherworldly lullabies. At a distance, Nesteri spotted a tall gate, shimmering white among the trees. It looked almost ethereal in the deepening shadows; for a moment, he wasn't sure if the vision was real.

"Holy Star," he called Antares. "I think I saw something over there."

"Oh, the gate? It's the entrance to the Golden Tower," the Great Star said. "We shall shelter there for the night."

As the Stars approached, the big old lantern above the gate suddenly flared up. Curious copper shadows danced on the white walls, bringing to life an enigmatic script that covered them like so many auriferous butterflies. Beyond, the Quarta's eyes descried the golden flicker of the Tower. The maze of shrubs around it was tall and swathed in twilight.

In Antares' hands swiftly appeared a diamond-shaped lozenge made of brass. The bright light shining through the filigree on its sides illuminated the path ahead. Antares took her hands away and the lozenge floated in the air above the Stars' heads.

"Note this well," she said as they were crossing through the gate. "The Golden Tower is what you always seek."

"I wish I knew what that means," Tei responded, puzzled.

"The Golden Tower is the awareness of Self. To reach it is one of the main quests of the warrior. Finding your way through the labyrinth of thoughts, desires, and delusions, you finally arrive at the understanding of who you truly are. Whenever you're lost and looking for answers, meditate on finding your way back to your Golden Tower, the awareness within you."

As the first pale stars sprang out in the gloaming, the wind subsided, yielding to the soft reign of the night. Dry gravel scrunched under the Stars' feet as they walked.

"The snares and lies of the Shadow can deceive your mind but never your true consciousness," Antares continued. "To win your battles, you need to awaken and strengthen it, and to embrace it fully, lessening the grip of the ego, letting the ego go. Through the power of awareness, you can turn your mind into a powerful weapon."

"How does one go about it?" asked Nesteri.

"Meditate on your true essence that is Light, and make it a habit to keep your mind still during the day. Silence the mental chatter. The inner understanding will then come to you."

A flock of tiny luminescent birds fluttered by, their long tail feathers floating in the breeze.

"The power of your awareness grounds you in the now – the only time where you can make a difference, where all your battles happen. The warrior lives and acts in the Present. Train your mind to adopt the *state of flow* – fluid and flexible, free from the regrets of the past and the fears of the future, ready to rise to the challenges as they come. The Shadow is rigid in its ways; fluidity and speed are your advantages against it."

"But what about the past and the future, still?" Hagal mused.

"What about them?"

"I wonder if there is a way of employing their energy, too."

"Imagine it as a triangle," Antares said, stopping for a moment. "The Past and the Future are at its base, like this..." The Great Star drew a *glowing line* in the air, connecting all three points. "...and the Present is where both lines converge. The energy of the future bestows the ability to analyse and learn, to think strategically and to make choices. It empowers your intellect and your conscious mind. You need it as a compass to navigate you through the sea of life. The energy of the past is revealed in intuition, memory, instincts and feelings – the realm of the subconscious. It is where you find the roots of your integrity, as well as your ability to heal and love. And for the perfect balance, you need all three."

Nesteri looked at Antares as she spoke, her face painted softly by the filigree of light and shadow. 'She is so beautiful...' he mused, suddenly dreamy, suddenly drawn closer with some compelling force. Nesteri shuddered and snapped back to reality, ashamed and puzzled, frightened by what was happening to him, hoping with all he had that nobody had noticed.

The triangle slowly faded in the air, as the Stars continued on their way. Hagal and Tei kept asking questions. Nesteri listened to them, half-absent. He slowed his gait unnoticeably, more and more, until he separated from the rest. Only a few yards, but the voices were coming fainter, muffled by the leafy walls.

"It's been always something I strived towards, albeit not consciously..."

"...and what if..."

"That is the essence, I suppose..."

"Still, if I were to... wouldn't it be wise..."

They didn't notice him lingering behind or maybe pretended not to notice. Antares must have seen for sure, Nesteri thought. He didn't care. He needed to be alone, even just for a moment.

Nesteri was angry with himself. His own mind, and his discipline he had always been so proud of, showed him unimaginable disobedience. It was more than disconcerting. It was worrying. The strange spellbinding feeling was dragging him in, deeper and deeper, and he was drowning. Many times, Nesteri caught himself daydreaming. He tried to push those thoughts away, but they returned, always. And yet Nesteri was determined. Nothing could break his will. *I'll never give into this. Never.'*

The foot of the Tower bulged like a gigantic tree, with its roots sinking into the ground. Rising towards the starry sky, polished walls were crowned with crenellations.

Antares drew a symbol in the air and the outline of a door appeared before them, as if shining its way through the stone. Soon, they could see it clearly: a shimmering crystal, with secret sigils carved upon both wings. Antares touched its middle; streaks of light run through the carvings from her fingers.

The door opened, revealing an armed, hooded figure in a dark green cloak. Without a word, the figure barred their way.

"Aimayo-e," Antares greeted the apparition and drew another rune. Still in silence, the phantom had accepted it into itself, then bowed and disappeared.

"What was it?" Tei asked in a whisper.

"The Keeper," Antares told him. "He wards off those who are not ready."

"Was he...alive?"

"Not in the way you would know, but yes. He exists in a time vector that is different from ours."

"But he looked like a ghost!"

"Not all those who share this world with you have physical bodies."

The inside of the Tower was filled with a flickering glow, coming as if out of nowhere. A grand spiralling staircase of pale stone opened to them from the entrance. Up and up they went, until Antares opened a heavy door – and the Quarta saw a columned hall with a string of windows. The hall was dark, lined by the slanted stripes of moonshine falling in. At the further end, beds appeared to be waiting for them, a surprise more than welcome. Despite the breaks and the plentiful virapana drinks, all three were dog-tired.

"Have some rest," Antares said. The golden tracing on her dress glistened as she turned to walk away. "I shall see you in the morning."

Nesteri tried to sleep, but thoughts were swirling in his head too fast, and his suspicions were all too unsettling. Finally, he opened his eyes.

He noticed Hagal's bare-chested silhouette nearby, bathed in cold moonshine. His friend was diligently scribbling something in his notebook. Nesteri turned over to his side. "Light, how come are you not knackered?"

"I am," Hagal responded without lifting his head. "Wanted to jot down some points from today though, while still fresh in my memory. About the power of voice, especially."

"Fair enough." Nesteri sat up on his bed and stretched his right hand out, palm up. A small ball of energy floated above it and dwindled. Nesteri created another one, but it didn't last much longer. He sighed. "I wish I knew how to make them stable."

"What for?" Hagal asked, still writing.

"For healing," Nesteri replied simply. "And I would like to learn those Runes of Power, too, fingers crossed."

A large nocturnal bird passed by the windows, obscuring the moonlight.

"Ah yes, I'm rather curious about those, in fact. Do you think Antares—"

"Will you two shut up?" Tei's voice cut in, sleepy and gruff.

A cheeky glint flashed in Nesteri's eyes. He thought of what Antares taught them earlier. It was too good an opportunity to waste it.

In a split second, he brought energy up to his throat and into his Brow Gate, then out with his voice. *"You don't want to sleep,"* he pronounced slowly, talking to Tei in a tone of a peremptory command. *"Get up!"*

To his own and Hagal's sheer bewilderment, Tei did get up at once. He battered his eyelids, puzzled at first, but soon it dawned on him. "Argh, don't you ever dare using those tricks on me!" he growled. "Trying to be funny, yeah? You asked for this, you git. Just you wait." Tei narrowed his eyes.

Sauntering towards Nesteri, he said in the voice of command: *"Your will is mine. You want to obey me. You want to kiss my... hand."*

He was already close when watching the scene Hagal chuckled. Tel lost his focus and sniggered, and Nesteri with him. The momentum was lost.

"I wonder if we could bring something into existence just like that," Hagal mused out loud. "What if the myths about spells are more than myths?"

"What if? A swell idea!" Tei clasped his hands excitedly, forgetting all about being tired. "Let's do it!"

He walked a couple of yards away and sang a stanza from one of his best-loved songs. The sound of his voice washed through the hall like a wave, but nothing happened.

"What were you trying to do?" Nesteri asked.

"I wanted to light up the hall using energy. Rats, I know what I did wrong. I've forgotten about the higher mindgates. Let me go again."

Tei focused. His voice sounded different this time – it echoed with unusual for him, almost metallic overtones. Both Hagal and Nesteri could swear that for a short while they could see a faint glow enveloping him.

"Impressive!" commented Hagal.

Tei gave a theatrical bow. He seemed pleased.

"That was quite something." Nesteri appreciatively shook his head. "Let me have a go."

He lightly jumped off from his bed and swapped places with Tei. Instead of singing, though, Nesteri chose the voice of command. "Let there be Light!" he said in Siltarionese.

"Andue neria Thil….neria Thil…" a vague echo rolled through the hall.

Nesteri made another attempt, and then another, but in vain. "Maybe I just don't have the skill," he shrugged in the end, somewhat downcast. "Or need to practice more."

"Why don't you sing instead?" Tei suggested.

"I guess I could."

Nesteri crooned a line in a half-hearted manner, but then straightened up and forced himself to fully concentrate on his task. As soon as that, the columns behind him quivered and appeared blurry, as if seen through hot air. Nesteri didn't notice. "What an idiot!" he sighed. "I've just realised I've forgotten all about the lower mindgates now."

"Let's try together," Tei walked up and stood next to Nesteri.

"Which one?" Nesteri glanced at him.

"Well, since we're playing with magic here, why not 'Totally Spellbound'?" Tei's lips stretched into a smirk.

"The one we wrote on the Blue Planet? I remember it. Sure."

Their voices rose and melted into one. A little tempest, moderate at first, it swelled, unfolding, building up with every breath. Entranced, the Stars kept singing, and the sound surged, thickening with force. *Enough, enough,* cried something deep inside their hearts, but they couldn't stop, not now. The power they unleashed billowed and broke free, erupting in a blast. Fierce and unrelenting like a windstorm, it swept over the hall and far beyond, startlingly formidable, drenching, mesmerising.

The world quivered dizzily. The pillars and the walls trembled, wisps of smoke, all of a sudden no more substantial than a mirage. The Quarta froze, trapped by the spell they had accidentally cast, all three fettered where they stood. Tei cursed in thoughts. He tried to move, to jolt, to free himself – in vain.

"Hagal?" he called, relieved greatly that his ability to speak did not defy him.

"I'm here," Hagal's voice came from his right, calm and sarcastic. "Congrats, you have unlocked a whole new level of ridiculous. Well done."

"Hey, how could we know that *this* would happen?!" Tei protested huffily.

"Hagal, you look totally spellbound!" quipped Nesteri who faced in his direction.

"Shut up. Trust me, you look just as stupid as I do."

"I wonder how long we're stuck for," Nesteri made another hopeless bid to move.

Tei thought for a moment. "Maybe if we sing again, then–"

"No way I'm doing it again! It could just make it worse." Nesteri suddenly imagined the humiliation when Antares returned in the morning to find them in this absurd state. 'Just like a bunch of kids.' He cringed.

"Alright, what other bright ideas do you have, genius?"

"I don't have any," Nesteri was forced to admit after a pause. "Maybe it will fade out? By itself. Somehow."

"A very constructive plan," Hagal's tone was bitter with mockery. "Remarkable."

"Well, why don't *you* think of something?" Nesteri snapped at him.

"Me? It was you and Tei who got us into trouble, you fix it."

"I wish I knew how! Argh, fine. Give me some time."

The words felt dry and empty on Nesteri's lips as he spoke. He didn't know how to break spells. Up until now, he didn't even know that spells were real. 'That's it. There's nothing you can do. You're gone for,' a quiet voice in his head said. The sight of beds, so close and yet unreachable, brought tiredness back. He sighed.

For a longer while, Nesteri stared blankly at the shaft of moonlight, which was gradually slinking closer as time passed by. Clouds of shackling energy leisurely swirled around. They showed no signs of fading. An awful sense of helplessness crept in, cold and sleazy like a toad. 'This is ridiculous. We can't stand here all night! Caught like stupid rabbits in a snare,' something rebelled inside him, stirring up his pride. 'You're an Astarrien, star-born,' he reminded himself firmly. 'Keep fighting. There must be a way. There must be.'

Nesteri looked through the window. Far beyond, dark trees rustled, sprinkled with silver. His gaze returned again to the cold streams of moonshine. Where their pale fingers touched the energy haze, it came to life in cascades of tiny sparkles, trembling akin the particles of dust in the light.

"Light..." Nesteri's lips moved soundlessly. "That's it, Light!" he added out loud, as a sudden understanding flashed through his mind.

"What's that? You said something?" Tei mumbled languidly, startled from his drowse.

"Yes! I've realised... The Aē language...Aē means Light!"

"Congrats on your linguistic findings," Tei responded sardonically. "It's what we need right now. Just when I hoped you came up with something useful for once."

"You don't understand. The words they say...must be *the words of power!*"

"They?"

"The Great Stars."

"What do you imply?" Hagal chimed in.

"Hagal, I would expect you to know about it," Nesteri said to him.

"It rings the bell. But I still don't follow what you mean."

"The words," repeated Nesteri excitedly. "The power to shape reality! You're with me?"

"Not really, no."

"I'm getting tired with that babble," Tei said. "Words this, words that... Try to get some sleep better."

"Wait, I'll show you."

"Show us what?"

"Just wait."

Nesteri closed his eyes. Unexplainably, it felt as if he had always known. It felt like coming home. Led by a sudden impulse, he drew in energy then pronounced slowly, calling every sound into existence:

"*Aē annava!*" The deep commanding voice didn't seem to belong to him.

Hagal and Tei flinched, astounded. The words darted through them like the streaks of lightning, forcing a shiver down their spines. A flash of white light flooded all, engulfing them, dazzling. The spell was blasted, broken in an instant.

Tei flexed his hands incredulously and rubbed his face trying to gather thoughts. Hagal froze as he was, his eyes wide open.

"What was that?! What did you... freakin' weirdo, what did you do??" Tei gasped.

"I said, 'Let there be Light', in Aē," Nesteri explained simply. He sounded like his usual self again.

"How did you know??"

"I didn't. It was just an idea. I thought it might work."

"I still don't understand how come you speak that language," Hagal frowned. He and Tei exchanged glances.

"I *can't* speak it. Sometimes words just come to me, I told you. Intuition, I guess."

"Intuition, heh?" Tei didn't care to even pretend he believed it. "I wish you would admit you were learning it in secret all this time. Liar."

"I'm not!"

"Don't waste your breath, Tei," Hagal said. "He's not going to tell you."

Nesteri bit his lower lip and said nothing. In the bright circle of moonlight, his shadow darkened slim and tall, a single clock hand. For a few moments, Nesteri lingered there pensively looking down; his ashy hair and the silver on his uniform reflected a soft gleam. Growing in him was a peculiar sense of loneliness. There was no place where he belonged and no soul who could truly understand him.

CHAPTER XIII

VAYĀRITĒ DOVA

WINGED COMPANY

A narrow path led them by the stream to a green plateau, opening to a breathtaking vista of the Caeron Mountains. The snow-clad colossi rose proud towards the sky, cold and majestic in the light of the new day. Large blocks of granite framed the plateau on the right, breaking the stream into a tinkle of small waterfalls.

"Holy Star, are we far from that town yet?" asked Tei.

Antares pointed down. Beyond the torn rim of the forest, a river rushed its way across the expanse of rocky land. Pale coils of mist swirled over the plain, still drowsing in the shadow of the mountains. "That is where Tvorndaln stood in ancient times," Antares said. The morning glow gently touched her hair and charmed it with shimmer. Roseate tones painted the shoulders of her high collared white dress.

Nesteri forced himself to look away. He fixed his gaze on the foot of the mountains as if it was the most fascinating thing he had ever seen.

"A few hours from now," the Great Star added.

Tei sighed with suppressed impatience. "Can't we just get there straight away? Erm, I mean, please. By some magic or something?" His right hand opened and clenched unwittingly into a fist. "We've been walking for miles and miles, and I all I could think about was why we're wasting time and keep Farien waiting. Surely there must be a quicker way? We could get some horses if there are any, or maybe hop on the back of dragons or whatever..."

Hagal chuckled. "Since when are you confident riding dragons?"

"I can ride anything!" Tei declared smugly.

"Braggart."

"There must be dragons here, I saw one in the picture."

"What picture?" Nesteri asked him.

"The one in the library…oops! Erm, well, you probably know about it already," Tei glanced at Antares and then away, awkward about his slip of the tongue. "When we first ended up here and we were looking for Nesteri, we walked in there, by accident. Apologies. I bet you know, though."

"I do," Antares responded mildly. "Don't worry yourself about it."

"So," Tei stubbornly carried on, "I'm not sure how big real dragons are, I've never seen one, but maybe we could fly them if they can carry the weight? The one in the picture seemed huge. Is it possible to ask them to take us there?"

"It's not about what is possible," Antares told him, "but what is reasonable. The real journey is never about reaching a point on the map. The goal you seek is not without but within… and the discovery of self takes time. It is no good to arrive at your destination before you're ready."

"I'm ready!" Tei exclaimed. "I've never been more damn ready! Argh, sorry. An awful habit. I'll get rid of it, I swear."

Nesteri shot him a disapproving glance. "If the real journey is within," he said to Antares thoughtfully, "then it wouldn't even matter where we go, would it?"

"It would matter," Antares replied. "What you see and experience touches the inner strings of the soul. Those chords must come in a certain order to help you learn…and wake up. Learning with no structure and no thought would serve you less."

"Wake up?" Nesteri's lifted his eyebrow. His green eyes flashed with curiosity. "In what sense? I am awake right now."

"No," said Antares softly. "No. You're asleep, locked in a dream of your mind. You don't know who you are. None of you do."

"I hate to admit I don't even know what we are talking about," Tei frowned, "but whatever it is, why does it matter?"

"For as long as you're asleep, you can't help your friend," Antares explained.

"How do we wake up, then?" A strange note flickered in Nesteri's voice.

"Through learning and then practising what you've learnt."

"Sounds like being back at the Academy," Tei pulled a face. "Is there any other way?"

"The other ways can prove rather lethal, I wouldn't recommend them."

Hagal stood silent, listening. He couldn't help but admire Antares' patience. 'You can trust the wisdom of Ke-Nireis Veri,' he suddenly recalled Phatiel's words. "I wonder what that means…" Hagal mumbled under his breath, but Antares heard. The Great Star turned to him. "Ke is a polite form of address," she said. "Nireis Veri means 'Star of the Past' in Aē. Good memory indeed."

"Why thank you," Hagal sounded flattered. He playfully bowed his head.

"Competing with Nesteri?" Tei jeered. "Argh, enough! I'm not having you both driving me nuts. That's it! I'll learn it, too," he added heatedly. "How to say 'hi'?"

"Aimayo-e," Antares said. "It really means 'good to see you', rather close to 'welcome'. The most common greeting."

Nesteri nodded. "It was what you said to us in Meldēan when we met. The very first word."

"Yes."

"Aimayo-e," repeated Tei slowly. "Noted." He studied the long and steep descent – a tangled mess of brushwood, moss and stones, held together by the tree roots. "I always dreamt of breaking my neck," he quipped. "And it looks like today is the day."

Nesteri chuckled. "Be careful what you wish for."

"So what's the plan?" Tei turned to Antares.

"What do you want to do?" she teased him with a smile and a look from under the lowered eyelashes, just like Kano would.

"Fly dragons!"

"Very well. Go ahead and summon one. They live in the Caeron Mountains."

"I can't!"

"Why not?"

"I don't know how to do it."

"I see. Has that ever stopped you in the past, Tei?"

"Err, no." The question forced a smirk on Tei's face. "Not once."

Hagal gazed at the mountains. In the clearing air, he now noticed a dark moving dot. And then another one. "But if a dragon comes, won't it try to kill us?" he asked.

"Not unless you give it a reason. Like most Older Ones, dragons will respect you if you treat them with respect. A power recognises another power."

"Let's do it, then!" Tei's eyes lit up at the promise of an adventure.

"Caeron Mountains must be some 50 miles away if I'm not wrong," said Nesteri squinting his eyes to see. "Will they still hear us?"

"Focused mental energy knows no distance," Antares replied. "All you need to do is to imagine yourself being in the mountains, standing there. Look at the dragons as they fly above, then pick one. Greet it well, and send it a strong impulse of your request, and an image of the place where we are now. I would suggest choosing a white one for this task. They have a better temper."

"So the dragons are in the mountains everywhere?"

"They tend to nest around Khadavesnidarra – a mountain ridge laced with crevices and caves. Slightly off to the north," Antares said.

"Alright, leave it to me," Tei declared cockily as he sat down into his meditation pose. "Give me a sec."

Predictably, it was longer than a second. Some half an hour later Tei opened his eyes. "No luck," he said. "I couldn't get them to respond. Must be doing something wrong."

"What mindgate were you using?" asked Nesteri.

"Argh, I forgot again. Which one should I use?"

All three looked questioningly at Antares.

"What do you think?" she said.

"The Third Eye?" Nesteri supposed.

"Correct." Antares nodded. "It would be easier if you both help Tei, by the way."

"Yes, ma'am!" Nesteri and Hagal sprang to attention with cheeky smiles, then sat on either side of Tei's and focused together.

For a moment, Antares pensively watched them meditating. A light breeze was gently ruffling Nesteri's hair.

The sound of giant wings made the Quarta jump and gape with their heads up. High above, a large majestic creature was gliding down, circling over the glade.

It finally landed with a heavy thud, the giant claws furrowing the ground. The grass around shivered and bent in waves. The dragon uttered a short screech, then fixed its gaze on the Stars. It looked nothing like what they expected. Slender and gracious, it seemed almost ethereal despite its size. The sunshine gleamed and glittered on its wings and body, each of the thousands of scales yielding a nacreous shine. Its eyes were blue, and bright like a drop of summer rain.

"Light and all gods!" Tei breathed out in awe. "So this is what a dragon looks like!"

"Her name is Críe," said Antares reading dragon's thoughts. "And she is curious about what we are doing here. She came around to find out. Restless like all teenagers!" the Great Star smiled.

"She is a teenager?" Nesteri asked incredulously.

"She's very young, so yes, one could say so."

Críe turned to the sound of Nesteri's voice and nuzzled at the Star's shoulder, knocking him off his feet. Dragons don't laugh, but Nesteri could swear he saw a snigger in her eyes. He got up, brushing the grass from his uniform.

"Could you tell Críe we need to get to the valley down below?" Tei said to Antares. "We would like to ride on her back."

"Please," added Hagal for him.

The young dragoness made herself comfortable amongst the rocks, wrapping her tail around. She shook her head as if understanding Tei's words.

"Críe says it's a terrible idea," Antares translated again. "Even if you did manage to climb up on her back somehow, you wouldn't last there a minute. The force of wind would push you off as soon as she took to the air. And with the four of us around her neck, it could upset her balance when flying."

"Ah, sure," Tei rubbed his forehead. "Makes sense. I didn't think that one through."

"How untypical for you," Nesteri teased him.

"Shut up."

Crie yawned, showing rows of sharp pointy teeth, and put her head flat on the ground. Antares reached up and rubbed the dragoness neck, just behind the little horns. Crie's eyes narrowed into sleepy slits. She whistled out a high-pitch sound akin a chirp, got her claws half out and then back in again.

"We need to work out some plan," Tei feverishly tried to come up with a solution quickly enough to save his face. "We need something…"

"A basket," Antares said.

"Hm?"

"Crie reckons she could carry us down in a basket."

"She reckons?"

"Well, she's never done it before but she believes it should work fine."

Tei unwittingly wrinkled his nose. In his mind, he fancied riding a dragon just like he would ride a horse – proudly upright, reins in his hands, wind in his hair. Being carried in a basket didn't at all seem that heroic. "Uhm… sure… yeah, a great idea," he said hesitantly, forcing himself to accept the inevitable. All in all, it was better than walking on foot all the way down.

Nesteri thought he could see a twinkle of a smile in Crie's eyes again. 'I wonder what she really thinks…' he mused.

'Yes, I do think you're funny, little ones,' a quiet voice in his head suddenly said. 'Crie?'

'At your service,' the playful insolence in her tone was slightly disconcerting.

'Erm. Please accept our heartfelt thanks for offering your help.'

'It's quite alright. The most amusing way to start a day indeed.'

Meanwhile, Antares had created a light woven cabin made from wooden splints, lined with silks and cushions in the manner of Siltarionese travelling palanquins. The memory cast a ghost of a smile on Hagal's lips.

"Hold tight," the Great Star said as they all got in.

Crie rose to her feet with a leisurely stretch, walked to the edge of the cliff and jumped off. Her wings spread out with the sound of hoisted sails, dazzlingly bright in the sun. The dragoness flew away. A moment later she returned, a glimmering spark growing rapidly in size, and the wind swished and whirled around. The cabin creaked as Crie caught it in her claws.

They went up with a sharp jolt, then down and up again. Holding tight was indeed a timely warning. The cabin rocked like a piece of brushwood on the waves, and more than once the Quarta fell upon each other in a pile, tried to regain their feet and fell back down again, laughing.

"I suspect dragons may remain an uncommon means of travel for a while," Nesteri joked pushing Hagal's hand from his face.

"Why no, I think it was a brilliant idea," Hagal joined in as he tried to pull his legs from under Tei. "We all know that Tei's well-considered plans never backfire."

"Never," laughed Tei rolling to the side to let Hagal free.

Nesteri shot a quick glance at Antares. The Great Star watched their messing about with warm amusement, still as if she was merely a vision. 'Is She really here with us?' Nesteri suddenly questioned his perception. 'Maybe all this is a dream. Maybe if–' The moment of distraction cost him another landing on the floor. Nesteri dodged and caught Tei's fist flying towards his ear. 'The times I'm grateful for my training,' he smirked to himself.

Antares looked up and mentally asked Crie to fly slower. It certainly did help; the cabin regained some stability at last. The dishevelled Quarta got back to their seats, finally able to catch the view outside.

The first flight in their lives, it felt like magic. They rode the breeze, trees whispering beneath, the mountains getting closer. The Quarta looked around with their eyes wide-open, surprise giving way to the long-forgotten childish joy. The feeling of freedom was inebriating.

The view brought to Nesteri's mind a memory of their apartment in Meguro, so high up in the sky. He thought of Farien but soon banished those thoughts.

A grassy plain was now before them, cleft by a river coiling its way around a hill. At its foot, the river slowed its pace swelling into a lake. The restless flow of clouds above troubled its surface with the play of light and shadow.

Crie circled over the hill and with a chirping whoopee went gliding down, cutting through the air. Close to the ground, she opened her claws letting the cabin go. The Quarta held their breaths anticipating the hard crash and a tumble that would follow. They could hear the dragoness landing nearby.

The moments dragged by, long and silent, each chimed out by the dull heartbeat in the temples. Another second…then another…

"Alright, fine, I admit it!" Tei exclaimed suddenly. "It was a retarded idea. I'm sorry! No more dragon flights! We should've walked. I'm sorry."

"Well, that wouldn't be quite as exciting though, would it?" replied Antares with perfect equanimity. Just as she spoke those words, the cabin touched the ground, as softly as a falling leaf. Antares opened the door. The Quarta gaped at her, then outside, then back at Antares again.

"We have…landed?" Tei asked, surprised.

"Indeed."

"But how come we didn't–"

"Reality adjustment. I've used… you would call it magic."

"Light and all gods, incredible!!" Tei said stumped and staggered.

"It's extraordinary," Hagal echoed him. "Just when I thought nothing would surprise me here anymore."

The Stars walked outside. Behind them, the cabin slowly vanished out of sight.

"Why don't you use those powers all the time?" Nesteri asked. "I would be tempted to. It would make life *so much easier.*"

Antares glanced at him. "Because of the cost," she replied after a pause. "Some kinds of magic attract too much attention."

Crie joined them trotting lively, with a look on her face that could pass for a grin. 'How was it? How was it?' the dragoness spoke to Antares, but Nesteri realised he could hear her as well. 'All good? I hope you enjoyed it!'

"Yes, we did," Nesteri responded instinctively. "We're grateful for your kind help."

Antares glanced at him. "We all had good fun," she said. "Thank you for your time."

'Ah, not at all,' Crie responded, flattered. 'It was my pleasure. Good luck with your travels.' Antares translated for her.

"Hey, you were great, massive thanks!" Tei said momentarily forgetting all the setbacks. "Flying for the first time felt terrific!"

'Liar, you were scared,' Crie laughed but Tei couldn't hear her thoughts.

"Thank you again," repeated Antares. "May your days be blessed with wisdom, and your wings with strength," she added a traditional dragon greeting.

Críe gracefully bent her neck. "Dali-e," the dragoness pronounced carefully, the only word she knew.

A broad paved road led up the hill, its top crowned with a ring of ruins resembling city walls. Their shattered reflections danced on the waves below.

The Stars stopped in front of the gate.

"Here we are," Antares said. "Welcome to Tvorndaln."

"There's not that much left of it, really," Tei remarked doubtfully, looking at the scattered stones.

"Patience," Antares smiled.

She raised her right hand. Suddenly, as if a world were gradually returning to the eyes woken from a deep sleep, the silhouettes of towers, houses, and roofs began to shimmer hazily into existence. Wispy and translucent at first, with every minute they grew clearer. Soon, the entire city showed before the Stars, gleaming in the sun with hundreds of its windows, arches, spires, and fountains. It was so real... and yet as ephemeral as a cobweb, its splendour no more than a fleeting dream. Empty were all the streets and houses of bleached stone.

The Quarta crossed the gate with mixed feelings. The city greeted them with silence and the distant chirruping of birds. Grass and small yellow-brown flowers forced their way through the cracks in the road. "Losn evedth," Antares said pointing at them. "'Kiss-of-autumn'."

"Why is there no one here?" Hagal asked in a low voice.

"The city has been dead for thousands of years," Antares told him.

'It's been dead...' In Nesteri's eyes flashed a drifting memory of the time so long ago, of Tvorndaln thriving and alive with song and chatter, with children's laughter and with merchants' yelling. At noon, the bells would strike thrice on the highest tower, a peal so skilful that it made all stop and listen. The bells toll was heard one more in the evening – the City Watch heralding another day of peace.

Then suddenly, Nesteri heard it. A quiet cry, echoing through the labyrinth of time. A sound that wasn't there, but in his mind the Star could hear it, as clearly as if it were real. Alone and lost, a child was crying hopelessly for help. 'You are needed there,' a voiceless voice said.

Nesteri shuddered. 'Who are you?'

'You.'

'I don't understand.'

'I know. But right now, it doesn't matter.'

'What do you want from me? Leave me alone!'

The voice laughed.

'Hear me,' it said. 'You remember your oath, do you not?'

'I do.'

'Good. Now it's your chance to put things right. Just tune yourself into the frequency of transition, like this...'

You're needed there. It sounded more than an order. It sounded like a call of duty. Nesteri felt he had no choice but to heed it, and he did. One moment he was there and the next he took a step back, almost soundlessly, and was gone.

END OF BOOK ONE

THE GUARDIANS